# CITY MAID

'Let's get our little mare saddled up, then,' Emily declared at length.

Eleanor was guided upright by the two women and led into one of the stalls. There were saddles and all kinds of riding gear there, but even when she saw them what had been said meant nothing to her.

'Down.' Mrs Hampton ordered.

Eleanor began to turn to ask her mistress what she meant, or planned to do, but at a sharp slap on her bottom she decided she was in no position to argue. She quickly got down on her hands and knees and waited nervously as Emily selected some leather straps and a halter from the pile then walked behind her. Suddenly Eleanor realised that they meant to use the harness on her, and she almost rose to protest. Being spanked and serving her mistress with her fingers and tongue was one thing, but this was depravity on an altogether different scale.

# CITY MAID

*Amelia Evangeline*

This book is a work of fiction.
In real life, make sure you practise safe, sane and
consensual sex.

First published in 2007 by
Nexus
Thames Wharf Studios
Rainville Road
London W6 9HA

*www.nexus-books.com*

A catalogue record for this book is available from the British
Library

Typeset by TW Typesetting, Plymouth, Devon

Printed in the UK by CPI Bookmarque, Croydon

ISBN 978 0 352 34096 2

# One

*In which the reader learns of the perils of a young lady travelling alone, and of the illicit pleasures to be enjoyed by serving girls beneath the stairs.*

Lying in bed, dressed in only a thin cotton nightdress, Eleanor felt the familiar warmth spreading between her legs. She turned on to her side and tried to ignore the sensation.

Reverend Fendlestock, the parson back in her home village, had made it clear to his congregation that pleasuring oneself was a mortal sin, which made the experience grow all the more hot with sin and shame in her imagination. And yet his condemnation also made it a compelling proposition.

She supposed she must be a wicked young lady and wondered if other girls were similarly tempted. Perhaps Chastity, the innkeeper's daughter with strawblonde hair and delicious pert breasts, felt that same maddening urge to touch herself until she became breathless. Eleanor imagined how that might look, her school-friend lying in bed at night, her sheets dishevelled to expose her body as she dipped an experimental finger inside herself, but she quickly dismissed the thought. Even if it wasn't sinful it was most definitely causing her to grow aroused and she could not risk getting herself in a state, at least not tonight.

1

Since her sister had left home to be wed she had been used to a bed alone, where her fingers could toy and press at herself in delicious ways. Not so here at the Hamptons' London townhouse – now that she had entered service she had no choice but to share her bed with Betty, the tweenie maid. If Betty minded sharing her bed she gave no sign of it, for which Eleanor was very grateful. Betty was a cheerful soul who had welcomed her arrival with a hug and an immediate stream of chatter. In the strange and unfriendly world of London it was a great relief to meet someone who seemed to like her from the first, and while she had not expected to have to share Betty's bed it was comforting to have her so close.

Betty gave a faint sigh and turned on her side, to face the wall. She wriggled a bit, letting their bare legs touch, then pressed her bottom against Eleanor's thigh. After a moment she rolled back to her original position. Eleanor smiled – poor Betty was probably not used to having to share either. Eleanor vowed to sleep and closed her eyes, but it was no use: sleep was the last thing on her mind. She found her thoughts wandering back to the journey from home to London the day before, which felt a lifetime ago already. With her in the carriage had been a young man who had introduced himself as Mr Connor Bishop, a merchant, and an elderly man who had been asleep when she had boarded and remained so most of the way.

It had been a long journey. Many of the roads were bumpy and in places the coachman had climbed down from his mount to guide the horses around holes and ruts. Mr Bishop had tried to engage her in conversation, but his lecherous smile made Eleanor think he might be just the kind of young man the parson had warned her about mixing with in London, so she had kept quiet. She had tried to read the penny dreadful her sister had left at their father's house, but it had proved so full of lurid tales of murder and accidents that she found it unsettling, and so after a short while she folded it and put it aside.

'Off to London, are we?' Mr Bishop had asked, as though he had been waiting for his chance.

'I am, sir, yes,' she had replied, and then, not wishing to seem unduly meek, she had added, 'That is why I am on the London coach.'

He had grunted and taken a sip from his hip flask. With his long black hair and very dark eyes, she had found herself unable to deny that he was quite an attractive young man. Certainly he was far more sophisticated than the men from the village, both in appearance and manner, while his voice carried the hint of an accent she couldn't place.

After their brief exchange, they had sat in silence in the rocking, rattling coach for a while before he spoke again.

'Would you like a sip of this?' he had asked, offering his hip flask.

'I would not, thank you, sir,' she had replied, in a tone of voice of which she was sure the parson would have approved.

Mr Bishop had lapsed back into silence and she had felt a pang of regret, wondering why she was being so cold to him. A drink would certainly help pass the time, and it would hardly be the first occasion she had allowed herself to get a little tipsy.

'Perhaps just a small sip, then,' she had said.

He had looked a little surprised, then smiled and offered the flask. She had poured a measure into the lid in what she hoped was a genteel manner, but her first sip had tasted so awful and seemed to burn so badly that she had nearly spat it back out.

'Oh, that is horrible! What is it? Whiskey?'

3

'It's brandy,' he had replied. 'It's an acquired taste, I'm sure.'

Betty turned in her sleep once more to face Eleanor, and with one leg extended their thighs touched, bringing Eleanor back to the present. She was muttering in her sleep. Eleanor looked over at her and smiled. Betty was a pretty girl, a year or two younger than Eleanor, but with a confidence that the new maid couldn't imagine having. She had large breasts that pressed at her maid's uniform, leaving Eleanor to gaze furtively at the full curves. Now she hardly needed to hide her interest, while Betty's little nightdress allowed Eleanor to see her ample charms more clearly. Eleanor herself was not overly endowed in that respect, her breasts smaller but pert and firm. Betty's, by contrast, were big and capped with large nipples, stiff now and poking against Eleanor's arm. She suddenly felt guilty for looking and reached over to snuff out the candle. Closing her eyes, she tried to sleep but still found it impossible. She felt warm and drowsy, but her mind kept drifting back to Mr Connor Bishop.

They had stopped not far from a little village called Borley Heath, where the coachman had got down and opened the door.

'If you want to stretch your legs now is the time,' he had said, and after stretching extravagantly himself he had fished a paper bag from his pocket and set about devouring a pie.

Eleanor and Mr Bishop had been drinking from his flask for an hour or so, leaving her quite unsteady as she climbed from the coach. She was hugely relieved to be on firm ground once more. The drink sat in her stomach like a ball of lead and she desperately needed to urinate.

'Time to get rid of all that liquid,' Mr Bishop had said, and set off towards the woods at the roadside.

4

Despite her shock at the vulgarity of his remark, Eleanor had found herself in agreement. As soon as his back was turned she had made her way hastily in the opposite direction, heading for the trees and bushes at the roadside. Her need had become extremely urgent, and after a quick glance around she had pulled her drawers wide open and squatted to pee. After a moment spent biting her lip in apprehension of being caught, she had let go with enormous relief as her pee came out in a flood. It had taken a while, and she had held her dress bunched at the waist as she looked around. She had wanted to be finished as quickly as possible, fearing that the coach might continue without her and leave her stranded in the middle of nowhere, but her pee would not stop, and it had seemed as if she would be there all day.

A bird fluttering out of the trees had made her start, and she had turned her head to find Mr Bishop standing behind an old oak, watching her intently.

'Is that better?' he had inquired as she gasped in shock.

'Go away! You dirty man! Be off with you!'

'But I have to answer a call of nature myself,' he had replied. 'The other side of the road is full of nettles and blackthorn. You wouldn't want me to have to take out my little general in the middle of all that, would you?'

His eyes had been firmly fixed on her most private part as he spoke to her, and Eleanor had felt her face turning bright red. Worse yet, she hadn't finished and showed no sign of stopping. Mr Bishop had stood looking at her pale long legs and the spread of auburn hair at her crease. She had pushed her dress down a little lower in the hope of retaining at least some modesty and glared at him.

'You are a vile man! How could you be so horrible? Go away or I'll call the coachman!'

'Do you want him to see too?' he had asked, and laughed. 'It's nothing I've not seen a hundred times before. Here, blot yourself with this.'

He had come out from behind the tree and offered her a piece of old cotton from his pocket. She had been blushing furiously, but, for reasons she couldn't fathom even after the event, she had accepted it, pressed it against her crotch and offered it back to him. He had made a face and so she had thrown it away and quickly pulled down her dress to her ankles.

'I am sorry,' he had said. 'You are a shy one, and it was a mean trick.'

'Leave me alone, or I'll scream and call the coachman. My father warned me there would be men like you on the roads. Highwaymen, robbers, pick-pockets and worse. And you are the worst of them all!'

He had smiled and begun to undo the buttons on his trousers.

'Don't you dare do anything to me!' she had said, scared that he meant to have his way with her.

'You are quite safe,' he had promised her. 'I just need to do the same as you. Don't want that lot sloshing around my guts all the way to London, do I?'

He had reached into his trousers, pulled out his penis and stood before her with it laid on his open palm. She had been unable to help but look. It had been hard and full, its head darker than the shaft, which protruded from the tangle of black hair at its base.

'Mr Bishop!' she had exclaimed. 'Put that awful thing away.'

'Away in you, perhaps?' he had said, grinning. 'I saw you, so it's only fair that I let you see me.'

'I have no interest in seeing such a thing!' she had protested, but she had not moved away.

He had held it between thumb and forefinger, and began to tug at the shaft. She had watched in fascination, never having seen an erect penis in all its glory before. It was a revelation. Beyond a general grasp of the differences between male and female gleaned from animals about the village, she'd had no idea of how a man would look naked, and wondered how any woman could take such a monstrous object inside her. Would it not hurt?

'You like the look of it, don't you?' he had asked.

'Certainly not, it's disgusting. Is it always so big? How on earth do you fit it in your trousers?'

'It's only this way because of what I've seen. I can't pee because of you. When a man sees a pretty little thing like you with her legs apart and her little thatch on show in the bushes, well, it makes it quite impossible.'

'Hurry up and do it, or you'll be left behind by the coach.'

'I doubt that,' he had told her, still standing with it shamelessly held it out. 'I chartered the coach myself this morning. It will wait for me all day if it must.'

'But I have to be in London by six o'clock!' she had protested. 'And we're nearly a half an hour late already! If I'm not at the domestic agency by six they said I'd have to find somewhere else to stay the night and I've hardly a penny to my name!'

'Help me, then. Or we'll be late.'

The thought of what they'd done together had made Eleanor greasy between her thighs, and she had both fingers inside her tight little slit when she realised Betty was awake. She was glad they were in darkness so that she couldn't see the expression on

7

her friend's face, but it was too late for her to pretend she had not been toying with herself.

'Do forgive me, Betty,' she pleaded. 'I couldn't help it. What must you think of me? I would not normally do any such thing, but I needed to so badly.'

'Don't be foolish,' Betty replied. 'Having a little play is about the only thing a girl can do for free in London. You go on and don't mind me.'

Eleanor had already pulled her hand from between her thighs, but at Betty's invitation it stole back, her need too great to be denied. She felt ashamed of what she was doing now and of what she had done in the woods earlier, but the burning heat between her legs wouldn't go away. Betty's invitation was not only hard to refuse, but enticing – Eleanor didn't want to stop. Giving in to the pleasure, she pushed both fingers deep inside herself, enjoying the hot sensation, then drew them back out and pushed them in again. She was wet, slick with her own juices, and she could hear the noises her fingers made going in and out, a sound unmistakable and louder than the clock which ticked at their bedside.

'Deeper,' Betty urged and put her hand over Eleanor's, cupping her cunt and pushing her fingers deeper still.

Eleanor sighed, knowing she was committing a sin greater even than before, but unable to stop herself. She began to wiggle her fingers, loving the silky texture of her flesh and the extra weight of Betty's hand. Her wetness had started to drip out of her and down her bottom cheeks, hot against her anus and her thighs as she bucked against the bed sheets.

'He made me touch it,' she murmured. 'He said I had to or he'd not be able to do it. Oh Betty, please, that feels so nice.'

Betty pulled Eleanor's hand away by the wrist and her fingers came out with a deep sucking noise.

Slipping her own hand between her friend's legs, Betty parted the hair of Eleanor's crease. Her leg was over Eleanor's and she rubbed their skin together, clearly relishing the contact, before taking Eleanor's hand up to her mouth and sucking the fingers, first together and then one at a time. Kneeling up in bed, she pulled her nightdress up and off.

In the pale light from under the kitchen door Eleanor could see Betty's breasts, the big nipples hard, and then she felt her friend mount her. Betty hauled Eleanor's dress up until it was beneath her armpits and her body was bare. Their bellies pressed together, and Eleanor cried out in pleasure and surprise. Betty put a hand over her friend's mouth and began to rub herself against Eleanor's bushy little mound. Eleanor was quivering already, each touch making her back arch and her head roll back.

'Tell me,' Betty demanded. 'Tell me what happened, but quietly.'

Eleanor was so overcome with passion that she could barely speak any more but she began to talk as best she could.

'He said I'd made him excited and if he couldn't go we'd be late,' Eleanor whispered. 'He said I'd have to hold it in my hand.'

Betty cupped Eleanor's breasts in her hands. They were small and firm and she trapped the nipples between her thumb and forefinger, pulling at them so that Eleanor gasped and begged for more. Betty bent down and kissed her, on the cheek at first and then against her lips. Eleanor had no idea what to do; she'd not kissed a girl before, and had barely done it with a boy. She felt Betty's tongue push in and touch hers, and then it came naturally as their tongues slid and pushed against one another. The flavour of Eleanor's sex was on Betty's lips, and the taste of her

9

own juices drove Eleanor to ecstasy, so that her hands soon moved to cup her friend's bottom, squeezing the tight cheeks as their mouths broke apart.

'He had his thing in his hand,' Eleanor confessed, 'twice as thick and hard as a gentleman's walking stick.'

Betty giggled and kissed Eleanor's neck, then licked at the sweat and nipped at her ear lobe.

'Oh Betty, that's so nice!' Eleanor sighed. 'Nobody has ever done that before, it feels so good. He said to come over and hold it, to help him go, but when I did he just began to push it back and forth in my hand. I could feel it throbbing, and it was so hot.'

She moaned, stroking and squeezing at Betty's bottom as she went on.

'He told me to take it firmly in my hand and pull my hand back and then forwards. Each time I did I could feel it growing and pulsing against me. He said to do it faster. The skin was so smooth and soft I didn't want to hurt him, but he said to keep going. He wanted it as fast and hard as I could manage. I could see a drop of wetness at the end, and it ran down my wrist as I lifted his thing up to let me pull on it more easily.'

Betty let herself down on to Eleanor's belly and buried her head in her friend's long hair. She kissed it and licked at Eleanor's neck as their bodies rocked together in the old bed.

Eleanor told Betty everything, and said it without shame. What they were doing now was probably far worse anyway, but she didn't care. She imagined the parson for a moment and, to her shock and mild disgust, she wished he was there to watch them now, perhaps standing with his cane ready to bring it down on Betty's back and buttocks for leading Eleanor astray. She wondered why she would want such a strange thing. It wasn't as though the parson was even a very attractive man. Perhaps she wanted to shock him, to flaunt her lust in front of his disapproval. She doubted he had seen much of it first hand. She rolled Betty off her and climbed on top instead.

'I want to taste you,' Eleanor declared. 'The way you tasted me. Can I? Can I put my fingers in you?'

Betty didn't reply, but just took Eleanor's hand and guided it between her legs. Unlike Eleanor, Betty had barely any hair there at all, just a thin triangle above her slit. It felt coarse and wiry but Eleanor loved the sensation. She touched her friend's lips, which were swollen like hers, but Betty's whole pubic area seemed more rounded, perhaps because Betty was a little chubbier. Her outer lips opened at the slightest touch and Eleanor pressed her fingers against them, delighting in the sensation of feeling the moistness within.

'He said he was getting close, that he would shoot soon,' Eleanor whispered, breathless and distracted by the way Betty had opened her legs wide and raised her knees a little to make herself fully available.

'I could feel something was going to happen, but I didn't know what,' Eleanor continued. 'He was making a face as if I was hurting him, but when I asked if he was in pain he told me to be quiet and keep at it!'

'Cheeky devil!' Betty whispered. 'Touch me here, this bit feels the best.'

Eleanor felt where Betty indicated and her friend at once began to make the most wonderful noises. Encouraged by Betty's sounds, Eleanor began to toy with the little button that seemed to be the key to her friend's whole body. By pressing it to one side she could make Betty writhe and jerk, while gently

11

tugging at it made her swear and beg for more. Eleanor loved the way it made her new friend tremble, and when Betty slipped a hand underneath Eleanor and began to toy with hers she realised why. It felt so good, so good that she believed that anyone who said such things were wrong must never have tried them. How could something so simple feel so good, she wondered, and why should something that felt so good be called a bad thing?

'He took me by the waist,' Eleanor went on, as their hands moved between each other's thighs, 'and turned me roughly around. I thought he was cross because I'd hurt him after all. But he wasn't cross at all, he was mad with wanting me.'

'That is no surprise. I feel the same.'

Betty slid down the bed until her mouth was under Eleanor's wet hole and began to lap at it. Of all the sensations this was the most intense. Eleanor could not help but cry out as her friend's tongue slid from her navel down to the bottom of her opening. Then it was inside her, pushing her lips apart and moving against her clit.

'Go on, tell me,' Betty whispered as she drew back momentarily, her voice muffled and slurred with lust.

'I asked him what he thought he was doing,' Eleanor said, 'but he didn't reply; he just pulled my skirt up, all the way to my middle. I was wet, I thought at first it was from when I'd been squatting in the grass but it wasn't that, it was because I had been touching him and he had been looking at me. The way his hands were, oh, he held me tight there out in the open with my skirt up and then – oh yes, just there, lick it there, that feels so nice. Oh, your tongue is so talented! I love it so much when you push your mouth against my hole like that and lick. I feel so opened up!'

12

Betty had one hand between her own legs and was toying with herself as she licked Eleanor, the expression on her face pained as though she were trying to put the moment off for as long as possible. Eleanor was bucking against Betty's mouth, and the faint scent of ivory soap and the rich smell of her friend's little hole made it almost impossible not to give in to ecstasy.

'He put his hands up over my chemise and inside,' Eleanor sighed. 'He cupped my tits and squeezed them hard. I gasped because he felt so hard behind me, pressed up against my bottom. He reached down and grabbed his thing in his hands and took me by the hair. He pushed it in me, Betty, just forced it into my hole and began doing it. Each stroke made me cry out and he seemed to want it deeper and deeper in me. Each time it went in I felt I was going to break but I didn't, and then he started saying things.'

'What did he say?' Betty whispered.

She had licked Eleanor so much that her friend's crotch was wet all over, her clitoris twitching at each touch.

'He wanted to know if I'd done it before,' Eleanor went on, 'to know if he was the first. I told him I'd never, ever let a man do that. That it hurt a little, that he was too big, but that just seemed to make him more excited. I wanted to tell him to stop, but it was inside me and filling me up and soon I wanted it, then I couldn't imagine it stopping. But he came inside me, a big gush of hot stuff right in my hole. He pulled it out as he came, though. I wanted him to bury it deeper in me but he pulled it out and it ran down the back of my legs and some of it went on my skirt. I felt so strange, so close to something, as I do now.'

'I won't leave you till you're finished,' Betty promised.

'Does a girl do that too? Make all that wetness? Is that normal?' Eleanor whispered.

She arched her back and let Betty work at her with her expert tongue.

'Haven't you ever had it before?' Betty asked. 'Never come like that yourself?'

'I don't think so. I feel close to something now though, Betty, please never stop, please keep going! I don't want to be left like he left me.'

Betty obliged, gripping Eleanor's bottom and pulling her against her mouth as she continued licking and sucking.

'I thought that would be it,' Eleanor went on, her voice thick with pleasure, 'that he'd done with me, but he wasn't. The worst was yet to happen.'

As she spoke Eleanor pictured the woods and recalled the shame of being caught with her dress up and a stranger's bare cock behind her, spurting over her bottom and down her legs. He had told her that he'd done it inside her, that it might give her a baby if she didn't clean herself up quickly. She'd been terrified, and she supposed she had not really been thinking, too afraid that at any moment the carriage might take off without them, charter or not. He had fucked her, or so she supposed, like the girls in the village talked about sometimes. She knew where babies came from and she was terrified that he might be right, that she'd have a child in her at just nineteen years of age from a stranger on a coach. He had told her what to do.

'I had to clean him first,' she told Betty. 'He made me clean him with my mouth, all of it. It tasted salty and thick and I had to do it with my tongue, put it all in my mouth and suck it dry. That was what he told me I had to do, so I did it. Then he put his thing away and said I had to clean myself up next. I could hear the coachman calling for us, shouting to hurry up and what were we playing at? Oh Betty, I was so afraid I'd have to walk to London or go home to my father's house in such a mess!'

'Poor thing!' Betty murmured between long, slow laps at her friend's sex. 'Men are beasts. What did he tell you to do?'

'He dragged me through the bushes to a little stream. He said to clean myself up and told me to take off my clothes. I was more ashamed of that than what he'd done in me, but I had no choice. I took off my travelling dress and then my underwear and stockings and he took them from me and put them in a pile on a rock. I stood there with my hands over my breasts and privates and he told me not to be so stupid, to get on with washing and to make sure I washed inside well. I did it, stark naked in front of a stranger and out in the open on show. He stood watching me and while he did he had his hand in his pocket and he was squeezing his thing, enjoying every moment. Then he told me to get dressed and we went back to the coach. Oh Betty, your tongue feels so good, please push it deeper! When we got back the coachman was almost purple with anger, said he'd have to push the horses as fast as they could go or we'd be late and he'd have his wages docked and no mistake. I got back in and felt so tired I drifted off to sleep. When I woke up Mr Bishop was gone. The coachman said he'd got off already, and wasn't even going to London, which was a relief.'

'Sh now,' Betty said. 'You're with me now. Forget all about it, relax and close your eyes. I'm going to show you the finest thing that a poor person can have, better than caviar or fine wines what all them nobs like!'

Betty sucked Eleanor's clitoris into her mouth and softly ran it between her lips. She pulled gently at it and Eleanor gave a cry of pleasure and surprise as though something suddenly made sense to her. It was as though her whole body was tied to that part of herself and Betty was guiding her like a kite, letting her soar into some strange new part of the sky she'd never seen before. She felt as though she was about to leave her own body, to drift out of it as the sensations washed over her, and then it happened.

Eleanor had her first orgasm, her first real one. It pulsed through her body like a wave and made her back arch and her bottom rise, her thighs tremble and her legs go weak. She fell forwards and grabbed hold of the rail at the top of the bed. She clutched it with all her remaining strength and pushed herself firmly down on Betty's face, grinding herself against her friend like a rutting animal. She bucked and she pushed and she swore, and her first orgasm was followed by a second wave, so powerful that she couldn't even hold on to the bed rail, but lay slumped across it while Betty sucked and swallowed every last drop from her trembling quim.

# Two

*In which a young servant's mind is sharply focused by the
attentions of a cruel ladies' maid, and a chance conversation
ignites a wicked passion.*

Eleanor woke up with a start. The door to their tiny
room was open and Betty was already half dressed.
She had never heard such a commotion and for a
moment she wondered if the house was on fire.

'Wake up, sleepy,' Betty said. 'It's nearly half past
six!'

Eleanor would have given anything to just roll over
and fall asleep again. She felt warm and tired and
satiated and in no mood to get up, but being in
service she knew she had no choice. Sliding from her
bed, she got dressed and joined the others in the
kitchen for her first breakfast as a maid in the house.
She had met the cook the previous evening, but today
the woman was fully engrossed in her work and
barely spoke.

'Sit next to me,' Betty prompted, and Eleanor took
a place beside her friend at the cramped servants'
table in the centre of the kitchen.

They ate well, better than many in the sprawling
city would see all day. There were eggs and toast,
with half a kipper each, and then to work. Eleanor
was surprised and a little hurt that Betty didn't

mention the previous evening. But it didn't seem as important as trying to make a good impression on her first day. She was very nervous and her uniform wasn't helping. For one thing the starched black dress seemed scandalously short, far shorter than anything she'd seen back home in her village. Betty's was the same, though, and Eleanor decided things must be a little different in London, which the parson had been at pains to condemn as a sink of depravity. A good part of her legs was on show and, had she had any to speak of, a fair bit of cleavage too. Betty's far more generous breasts seemed in constant danger of spilling free.

Neither Betty nor Eleanor were considered important enough to serve Mrs Hampton breakfast. This honour was reserved for Amelia, the ladies' maid. Amelia was French and had stood at Mrs Hampton's side during Eleanor's interview. Eleanor found she already disliked Amelia, who had a habit of tutting and looking down her nose at the other servants.

Once breakfast was over, Betty and Eleanor were sent upstairs to begin the task of gathering the washing. Mrs Hampton's bedchamber was more impressive than anything Eleanor had ever seen before. The room was large and looked out on the street below. Tall ferns in brass pots stood on tables at either side of the bed, which was a magnificent four-poster made of solid mahogany. As soon as Betty had bustled away with her washing basket Eleanor sat on the edge of the bed and marvelled at how soft and luxurious the silk sheets felt. She lay back for a moment and closed her eyes, wishing it were her bed and imagining how wonderful it must be to wake up here each morning. The clock ticked solemnly on the wall. She thought to herself that if it were her room, her house, she would never get up at this hour. She would laze in bed all day without a care for what anybody thought.

Such is life that when you cannot, must not, sleep, those are the moments when sleep becomes a luxurious thing impossible to resist. Almost without thinking about it Eleanor closed her eyes again and quickly settled into the sleep of the very tired. It was almost without choice – the exhaustion took over and she was lost. She began to dream that she and Betty were naked on the bed, toying with one another, with Betty on top, kissing her and stroking her hair. It was a delicious dream, recreating a simple pleasure that she longed to experience again and again.

'Betty, not so roughly!' she murmured. Betty was still kissing her but she had become too forceful, pulling at Eleanor's hair. She squirmed uncomfortably in her sleep as Betty tugged. It was a strange feeling, but not entirely unexciting. Then she felt a sharper tug and woke with a start. Amelia was towering over her, one hand holding Eleanor's hair and the other planted on her own hip. She had a face like thunder.

'Oh, Amelia!' Eleanor said. 'I'm so sorry. I just sat down for a moment.'

'Get up, girl!' Amelia ordered. 'What do you think you're doing?'

Eleanor found herself dragged from the bed, half by her own volition and half by Amelia, who still had a firm hold of her hair. Only when Eleanor was upright did Amelia let go of her, glaring at her with eyes bright with anger.

'Forgive me,' Eleanor whispered. 'I'm so sorry, it was a long journey, and –'

'I should go downstairs and tell Mrs Hampton what a lazy little sloven she has employed,' Amelia retorted. 'I knew you were trouble when I first saw you.'

'Oh please,' Eleanor begged. 'I didn't mean to!'

Amelia put a hand on Eleanor's shoulder and spun her around so that she was facing the bed again. Eleanor had expected to be marched downstairs and could not for a moment begin to imagine what was to come next.

'Bend over the bed,' Amelia said curtly. 'You must be punished so you never make this mistake again.'

Numb with fear, Eleanor did as she was told, bending across the bed with her trembling hands on the smooth silk sheets. For a moment nothing happened, and yet she didn't dare look around. Amelia had drawn back from her and was taking something from the dressing table. Eleanor could hear it being picked up and patted in Amelia's hand but she could not guess what it might be. She tried to remember what had been on the little table by the door when she had come in but her memory failed her. The mystery was solved a moment later when Amelia tossed the object on to the bed. It was Mrs Hampton's hairbrush, a sturdy wooden one with hard black bristles, tangled among which were a couple of strands of long dark hair from their employer.

Amelia slid her hands under Eleanor's skirt, starting at her knees and working her way swiftly up to her hips. As she did so Eleanor's dress rode up her body, leaving the new maid feeling very vulnerable and squirming in discomfort. Amelia grabbed her hair and yanked it back, so that Eleanor was looking straight ahead.

'You are in enough trouble, madam. Remain still like I said,' Amelia demanded.

Eleanor did as she was told. Amelia's hands were back on her legs, stroking up to her drawers, which were one of only three pairs she had to her name.

They were a little old and slightly threadbare in places but still modest and respectable. Then Amelia neatly folded Eleanor's dress over her back and picked up the hairbrush. Eleanor began to moan with dismay. Her dislike of the elegant but severe-faced Amelia suddenly burned into something much stronger. The ladies' maid was no more than a few years older than Eleanor herself, so who was she to masquerade as the very image of authority?

But the expected beating did not begin. Instead, Amelia's fingers went to the strings of Eleanor's drawers, and she realised she was to have her bottom laid bare, as if revealing her drawers were not humiliation enough. The strings came loose, and with one firm tug Eleanor's underwear was drawn down her legs and on to the floor, leaving her feeling vulnerable and scared.

'Now step out of them,' Amelia said.

Eleanor reluctantly did as she was told, looking down at the bed as she kicked her drawers from her ankles. Her face was bright red and she considered pulling her dress down a bit to cover her round little bottom, but she knew that doing so would only prolong the torment of embarrassment, so she stood still.

'Place your legs apart,' Amelia commanded.

Eleanor didn't want to; it was bad enough that her bottom was so fully on show without having to display her sex too. But Amelia didn't sound as though she could be dissuaded from whatever was to come, and so Eleanor gingerly opened her legs a little.

'Wider!' Amelia snapped and slapped Eleanor across her bottom with her hand by way of encouragement.

Eleanor gave a little cry and closed her eyes. She could imagine just how she looked from behind and the satisfied chuckle of her tormentor told her that Amelia was getting far more from her task than simple satisfaction in a job well done.

Hadn't Amelia taken a special interest in her from the moment she arrived for her interview? But her scrutiny had been anything but flattering or approving. Amelia didn't like her. It was obvious; Eleanor could tell by the girl's wicked eyes. She was a jealous haughty bitch, possessive of her mistress's attention, and a little auburn-haired beauty like Eleanor must have been the last thing Amelia wanted in the house, she realised. Betty was far too common to attract Mrs Hampton's attention in any serious way and the cook was overly rounded for Mrs Hampton's taste, but a wisp of a girl with a slender body and big doe eyes might well suit their employer, Eleanor surmised with a dawning realisation that was not altogether unpleasant.

Amelia stood back to look at Eleanor for a moment as if wondering what Mrs Hampton might think when she came to view Eleanor in all her glory, as she so surely would, and soon.

'What pretty long legs you have,' Amelia said scornfully. 'Get up on your tiptoes.'

Eleanor did as she was told, which would make her feel even more precarious and exposed, as Amelia knew from her own experience. She ran both hands down the back of Eleanor's legs. They were pretty, not as finely muscled and curvaceous as her own, but still a fine sight. While she was blessed with a large round bottom, Eleanor was a little slimmer, with firm, higher cheeks. Amelia had a feeling that her mistress would enjoy putting her hand on them very much, would love to slap and scold Eleanor as she was about to do herself.

Eleanor's vagina was, of course, fully displayed to her as well. That was part of the reason for her choice of punishment – so she could see it and play with it as her mistress did with Amelia's when she was in this same position. Eleanor had a bush of auburn hair and her lips were pink and prominent through the hair. Amelia traced a finger over her sex and Eleanor jerked as though she were about to stand up.

'Keep your hands down on the bed, you little trollop!' Amelia said through clenched teeth. Eleanor hung her head in shame, unable to escape the intimate examination about to be inflicted on her.

Amelia spread Eleanor's lips open with two fingers, then bent down to take a closer look. The hot little opening looked so unused, so fresh, that Amelia felt a tight little ball of jealousy in her stomach. She let go and stood up, to grab Eleanor's hair in one hand as she brought the other sharply down across the pert buttocks.

Eleanor cried out, her voice strangled by shock and anguish, but Amelia had barely begun. She picked up the hairbrush and ran it over the small of Eleanor's back, the handle down. As soon as the wood touched her, Eleanor's legs trembled with nervous anticipation. The girl clearly wanted it to be over so she could cover herself up again, but also dreaded the pain that was about to come. Amelia knew how she felt and smiled.

Then she whacked one cheek of Eleanor's bottom with the hairbrush – once, twice and a third time. Each stroke landed on the smooth flesh with a resounding slap and made her victim wince, and she landed five strokes in all before she switched to the other cheek and began slapping that one as hard as she could.

\* \* \*

23

Eleanor's legs shook as she bent before her tormentor, waiting for it to be over. She felt deeply ashamed and prayed that Amelia might have mercy on her, but if there was any mercy in the ladies' maid then none was shown. Instead she began to spank Eleanor's legs, first beneath her bottom and then down her thighs until her blows were reaching below the knee and smarting off her calves.

You are a bad, lazy little girl,' Amelia snapped. 'What are you?'

'A bad, lazy little girl.'

'Who sleeps on her mistress's bed as though she owns the house,' Amelia sneered. 'How long do you think you'll keep your position here if you cannot even collect some washing without falling asleep?'

'I am so sorry,' Eleanor managed, close to tears. 'Please don't tell Mrs Hampton. I will never fall asleep on duty again!'

'Up!' Amelia commanded, as though calling a dog.

Eleanor did as she was told, thankful to be less exposed. She stood up and Amelia tugged her dress back down over her aching bottom. Eleanor reached down for her drawers, but Amelia grabbed her wrist and pulled her so close that Eleanor was forced to look into Amelia's pretty flushed face and those dark eyes still full of anger.

'Did I say you could pick those up?' she demanded.

'No, miss!' Eleanor replied quickly. 'Sorry, Amelia.'

Amelia's blonde hair, so elegantly set this morning, had become dishevelled, with a few strands hanging down against her face and making her look a little wild. She let go of Eleanor's wrist and took her by the chin instead, turning her face from side to side and staring at her as if she had discovered an interesting new species of insect.

'I am the ladies' maid,' she said firmly. 'My name is Amelia but to you, I am the ladies' maid. That is what you call me, do you understand?'

'Yes, miss! Yes, ladies' maid,' Eleanor said quickly.

'I will not say anything this time,' Amelia promised, 'but next time you slack or break any house rules I will take you and beat your tight little bottom until you can't sit down for a week. Is that understood?'

Eleanor understood quite clearly. Disobedience in this house wasn't like at home. In her father's house being lazy or disobedient earned her a telling-off, and a mild one at that. In this house, though, you were apt to be forced to bend over and have your clothing disarranged for a physical punishment. Eleanor was very glad indeed that the hairbrush had been replaced on the table and that Amelia, for now at least, was finished with her.

'Please may I have my underwear back on now?' she asked timidly.

'No,' Amelia said. 'As punishment I shall keep these for the day; you may come and collect them when your duties are done.'

At first Eleanor thought she had misunderstood but it seemed she had not. Amelia was intending to leave her without drawers for the rest of the day.

'But you can't!' she protested.

'As you appear to think it is bedtime whenever you want,' Amelia said, 'then you can go about dressed for bed, with no undergarments, until you learn to behave. Now be about your work or I'll take you downstairs and see what the mistress has to say about lazy girls sleeping on her bed!'

Eleanor was out of the room as fast as a hare, with the bundle of washing in her basket, and she didn't look round once. She knew Amelia was laughing at her, enjoying her discomfort, and she couldn't bear to see her tormentor's face for a moment longer. After hurrying downstairs, she carefully placed the washing on the floor with the other laundry piles. But any movement reminded her of how much her bottom ached and how rough her dress felt against the tender flesh, making her want to inspect the damage. So she ducked into her room while the cook sorted the clothes, and looked at herself in the little mirror. Her hair was in wild disorder and she tidied it, then turned to one side and drew up her dress to look at her bare bottom. There were red marks in the shape of the hairbrush embossed all over her soft cheeks. Just to see them was to feel the pain all over again.

She had no time to reflect on what had happened, though: she had plenty more jobs to do and so, with her nakedness under her dress making her blush, she set back to work.

And it was lunch-time before she and Betty were together again, to eat a quick lunch of bread and cheese in the little servants' parlour under the stairs. She was reluctant to tell her new friend what had happened. For one thing she didn't want Betty to think she was lazy, and telling the story would mean explaining the reason for the punishment. She also found the idea of telling Betty about the exact nature of her punishment and the rude inspection by the ladies' maid just too humiliating. As it turned out, Betty guessed.

'Get your botty whacked, did you?' she asked, and gave Eleanor a sympathetic wink.

'How did you know?' Eleanor asked blushing furiously.

'Well, for one thing you're eating standing up,' Betty said. 'And for another, when you bent down to pick up the washing I saw right up your dress!'

Eleanor covered her face with her hands.

'Don't worry, Amelia is a cruel one. She does that to all the new girls. Show 'em that she's in charge and all. She's jealous, see.'

'Of who? Me?' Eleanor asked. She couldn't imagine such a thing.

'Yes, you, silly.'

'But I could never be a ladies' maid, I don't even know what they do!' Eleanor protested and Betty laughed.

'She's not worried you'll take her place cleaning out the grate, you silly thing. I mean she's afraid you'll become Mrs Hampton's favourite.'

'Oh, I see. I doubt that,' Eleanor said, feeling her sore bottom.

'You might. She likes them slim and girlish like you are,' Betty told her. 'I ain't the only girl who enjoys the feel of another one.'

'You're making fun of me,' Eleanor protested. 'I don't believe you.'

'You don't know about her,' Betty said, and Eleanor had to admit she knew nothing about the woman to whom she now effectively belonged.

So Betty told her.

Mrs Hampton had married at a young age, and as was the custom she had married a man befitting her social class who offered her the stability and lifestyle to which she was accustomed. This wasn't to say there was no element of attraction in the union, at least at first. She had done her best to please him and to be a good wife but Mr Hampton was not an easy man. For one thing he was seldom to be found at home, and instead he divided his time between his three true loves: watching horse-racing, drinking at his club and adventuring in exotic places. The horse-racing was something Mrs Hampton could participate in a little; she would stand by his side as he cheered on one horse or another, but she found it intensely dull. The sight of horses galloping around a track did nothing for her, and so when he began to stop inviting her she was somewhat relieved. The gentlemen's club was a closed world to her, of course, and though she sometimes smelt perfume on his collar she never asked what went on there.

As for the adventuring in far-off places, he was often gone for weeks at a time, and once he had vanished into the jungles of the Amazon for a year and a half. She had begun to get lonely and felt rejected and angry, which she took out on the staff, growing increasingly harsh and abrupt with them until the butler left her service and Mr Hampton's faithful valet opted to join his master and face the dangers of jungle life rather than stay behind with her. It was only when Mr Hampton returned from one especially long visit to Africa that Mrs Hampton discovered his other hobby.

'What was that?' Eleanor asked.

Betty was evidently pleased to be the centre of attention and kept her waiting while she sipped her warm milk and finished off the last of her crusts.

'Photography,' she said finally.

'Photography? What's so wrong with that? That's not unusual for a gentleman, is it?'

'He wasn't just taking pictures of the scenery,' Betty said, grinning at her friend. 'He was more interested in the native women.'

'What about them?' Eleanor asked.

'They walk around naked, all day long. Mr Hampton was busy taking as many pictures as he could. He had trunks full of them.'

'Naked! All day long?' Eleanor exclaimed.

'All day,' Betty confirmed.

'That's preposterous and I don't believe it,' Eleanor said. She had little education and knew roughly where Africa was, but no more than that.

'It's true!' Betty said. 'I seen 'em. See, Mr Hampton came back from one trip half crazy with some jungle disease. The doctor was in and out of the house every day checking on him and though they hired the best money could buy he couldn't cure him. A month later Mr Hampton was dead.'

Eleanor had wondered where the man of the house was but she hadn't thought it her place to ask. She studied her friend's face for signs that she was lying, but it seemed she wasn't.

'I don't know much about that kind of thing,' Betty said, 'but if you ask me, it fell off.'

For a moment Eleanor looked blankly at her friend, and then, realising what Betty meant, she burst into laughter and nearly choked on her glass of milk.

'Betty, you are awful! Are you saying he was putting his thing in those women?'

'Oh yes!' Betty replied in the tone of someone blessed with a piece of dark and terrible gossip. 'Dozens of 'em.'

'Do they really walk around naked?' Eleanor asked.

'As the day they were born. If you ask me he liked them big and round and with bare titties and their bushes on show. Bet he couldn't resist. They said it was a snakebite, of course. Well, they would, wouldn't they? More like someone bit *his* snake.'

Eleanor couldn't stop giggling. It was a terrible thing to make fun about, and she was sure the parson back home would have said it was evil to joke about a man doing such wicked things. And yet Betty with

29

her cockney accent and cheeky face made everything seem as if it could be part of an ongoing joke.

'I can't imagine that if I were a native girl I'd let anyone take my photograph naked. I wouldn't be naked, that's for sure,' Eleanor said primly.

'Oh, you would, because to you it would be normal,' Betty told her. 'You'd not think anything of all them men looking at you, or your friends seeing you naked all day long.'

'Oh my!' Eleanor exclaimed.

'If you don't believe me I'll show you the pictures,' Betty promised. 'They're tucked up in the attic.'

'I'd like to see,' Eleanor said. 'When?'

'When Amelia is out,' Betty promised. 'She sleeps right next door to them, and I bet she's had a leaf through them too, the dirty bitch.'

Eleanor began to giggle again but the arrival of the cook, brandishing a spoon and her face red from the heat of the stove, killed the moment. She sent them scuttling off back to work and Eleanor found herself with nothing to do all afternoon but polish silverware in the kitchen and think.

At first she thought about Amelia, who it seemed was not just Mrs Hampton's maid but a little more than that. She began to think of poor Mrs Hampton too, widowed at less than forty years of age by a man she barely knew. She thought of the rough bottom spanking Amelia had delivered with the hairbrush and the way her drawers had been confiscated. Her bottom still felt sore and she felt acutely naked under her serving girl's dress. Most of all, though, as she polished the silverware, she thought about Mr Hampton's photographic expeditions.

She began to fantasise, and in her fantasy she was living in a hut in a village baked by the sun and bordered by thick jungle. Her fantasy was heavily

30

based upon a newspaper cover she had once seen. It had shown an English explorer standing on the cusp of a small hill in a jungle looking down on a ruined city surrounded by huts.

The paper, a dreadful and sensationalist publication, had asked, 'Is this Atlantis?' It had turned out the answer to this question was a resounding no, but that hadn't stopped them from using it as a headline.

She had left the largest piece of silverware til last – a giant bowl, not much smaller than the tin bath she was used to at home. She wondered what on earth it was used for. It was so heavy she had to go and ask the cook to help her lift it on to the table. When she was alone again she began scrubbing it and let her mind drift back to her fantasy.

In it she was in her hut, busy polishing the tribal statues, when she was called out by the chief. Standing in the clearing were a small group of white men, men from England, including Mr Hampton, who in her imagination was being played by Mr Connor Bishop, the scourge of travelling girls. He was accompanied on his travels by the parson from back home, the Reverend Fendlestock, who stood at the head of a small train of bag carriers, two of whom were struggling under the weight of a large camera.

'That one,' Mr Hampton was saying as he pointed in her direction.

The chief summoned her over and as she nervously approached she saw the chief accepting a chest full of bright bronze plates, beads and other curiosities. She was being sold, she realised, transferred from village property to the hands of Mr Hampton and his entourage of young explorers.

They took pictures of her, and although her alter ego didn't understand why, she herself knew that they were marvelling at her bare body, particularly her breasts. All of them were aroused, and she could see the hardness underneath their white trousers, pressing out and making little tents in the fabric. They wanted her, they all wanted her and they meant to have her. They photographed her naked and turned her from side to side so that they could get all the best angles. They were gentle when she obeyed, rougher when she protested. They lifted her up by her arms and legs and spread her legs so they could take pictures of her bush.

At length Mr Hampton, overcome with lust, thrust his fingers inside her. She cried out and struggled but the men held her firmly and Mr Hampton stroked her until she was wet and ready for him. They laid her on the ground and he took out his penis. She cried out to the tribe to save her but they wouldn't. Instead they stood in a circle while the drums beat out their infernal rhythm, and began to dance as he climbed on top of her. He meant to have her there and then, right in front of everybody, all the people she had grown up with, all the men who had looked at her with lust, all the women who had envied her, all of them would see how she looked when she was taken.

She was still struggling, making it hard for him to penetrate her, and the chief, keen not to lose his precious gifts, ordered that she should be staked out on the ground. Thick wooden posts were hammered into the sun-baked earth and thick vine ropes looped around her wrists and ankles. The explorer was pleased; she could wriggle but she could not escape. He thrust himself into her, pushing it all the way inside and grabbing and squeezing her breasts as he did so. The dancing became more and more frenzied as he fucked her, his bare bottom going up and down in time to the music. Around her danced the tribe, the men with their exposed cocks hard and the nipples of the women firm and erect. Mr Hampton was banging at her with determined strokes and running his hands down her sides. He came in her, not as Connor Bishop had done, but actually fully inside her. She came too, as she had done with Betty but this time while filled with a length of cock. Yet still she struggled at her bonds in a vain attempt to escape, but since it was her fantasy and she had no intention of missing out they held firm.

Mr Hampton had pulled himself off her now, leaving her soaked little snatch in a disgraceful state. The results of her orgasm and his were mixed together, seeping from her rudely taken body while she lay helpless. The men of the village, normally constrained by strict rules and ruled over by the tyrant of a chief, could resist no longer. Some fought savagely to be the next to have her whilst other, younger men, who knew their place, simply masturbated over her helpless body. She could feel their hot white liquid splashing her neck and face, pouring over her breasts and wetting the hands of the next in line to climb on her and take her. She didn't want to be saved, wanted no hero to turn up and cut her free. Instead she surrendered herself to the wild orgy, letting them rut and fuck her until the whole tribe had taken her.

The visitors photographed her shamefully despoiled body as she was taken. Cocks were forced into her opening, big black cocks that made Connor Bishop's look positively tiny. When the whole village had taken her the chief ordered that she should be cut from her bonds and brought before him. Her pussy ached from all the different men, all the different shapes and sizes of cock which had been in her, but the jungle drums beat on. In her wild fantasy the chief laid her flat on an altar that stood outside the witchdoctor's hut. Bright torches were being swayed in time to the drums, for the daylight was fading fast. She was pushed on to her front and the chief came forwards. His hard little dick was swollen with desire and nearly dripping with excitement.

'No more!' she begged, but the chief was not going to forego his turn.

Robbed of being the first to take her, he instead went for the only hole that his faithful tribe had not intruded upon. He parted her bottom cheeks and stood behind her while she sprawled helplessly on the altar. The drums took up a maddening beat and flashes from the photographers lit the clearing. He was about to do something very wicked to her, to demean her as never before.

'You, girl!' Amelia snapped and Eleanor got such a fright she nearly screamed.

'Oh, I'm nearly finished,' she said hastily, blushing scarlet as she whipped her hand from between her legs.

Amelia, evidently oblivious to the maid's arousal, tossed Eleanor's drawers on to the kitchen floor and told her to finish the silver then be off to bed. It was nine o'clock already and tomorrow would be a busy day.

Eleanor sighed with relief that Amelia had not seen fit to punish her the way she had before. If she had she would have found a deeply shameful patch of wetness between her victim's legs, and if she'd seen Eleanor's juice-slick fingers she'd have been left in no doubt as to the new maid's activities.

With the last item polished to a gleam, Eleanor gratefully went to her little bed and crawled in next to Betty. Betty was dozing when she got in but Eleanor had worked herself up into such a state that she would not take no for an answer. She was naked herself already and pulled Betty's nightdress off before her friend could protest. In moments Eleanor was kneeling above Betty with her wet sex lips brushing against Betty's mouth.

'Taste me, Betty,' Eleanor begged. 'Lick me and taste me. I'm so out of sorts tonight.'

Betty willingly obliged.

# Three

*Wherein we learn of the shocking behaviour of the servants
when not properly watched over, and the equally shocking
actions of their betters.*

Eleanor doubted she would ever get used to waking
up so early but the presence of Betty, warm and
sleepy next to her, was always a great comfort. They
dressed and washed their faces together and talked
conspiratorially over breakfast. The cook was busy
preparing Mrs Hampton's breakfast as they began
their day's work. Eleanor felt very much at home at
last. Her chores had become less arduous now that
she felt settled in and used to the workings of the
house.

She caught sight of Mrs Hampton leaving at
around ten o'clock; Betty informed her that their
mistress always went out on charitable missions on a
Wednesday. Mrs Hampton visited the poor and the
workhouses, which struck Eleanor as a rather noble
thing to do, even if it was only for the sake of fashion.
Their mistress was by far the most fashionable lady
Eleanor had ever seen, considerably more so than
Mrs Fendlestock, the passably elegant wife of the
parson back in the village. Mrs Hampton was wearing a long flowing dress as raven black as her hair and
a pretty white shawl with a matching parasol to keep

the heat from her pale-white skin. Amelia accompanied her as always and Eleanor was mildly amused and gratified to see that judging by Amelia's expression visiting the poor and the workhouses was the last thing she wanted to be doing.

When Mrs Hampton wasn't home the cook was in charge, but she was cheerful and no slave-driver. A firm believer in taking a breather whenever possible, as soon as their employer had left she had put the kettle on and the three of them sat down to morning tea as though they were ladies of means rather than the girls who served them. It was an unexpected treat and when they were done Betty told the cook that there was the very devil of a mess in the parlour and Mrs Hampton would give them hell if she returned to find ashes on her carpet. The cook waved them away and began work on lunch while Betty and Eleanor headed upstairs and into the hall.

'Ain't no mess really,' Betty confided. 'But Cook doesn't know that and what she don't know won't harm 'er.'

'You are wicked,' Eleanor said, with some awe.

'Come out the front door, quiet, mind. If Cook catches us we'll be in for it.'

'What about the door? We won't be able to get back in!' Eleanor protested.

Betty fished around in her pocket and pulled out a key, which she showed to Eleanor with a wink.

'Stole it last time young master Tom was at the house, I did. He thought he'd lost it but I snitched it in case I ever needed to come and go. Can't go out the tradesmen's entrance, cook watches that like a hawk.'

Eleanor was impressed, knowing she would never have the nerve to do such a thing, and she obediently followed Betty as she unlocked the door and sneaked out. It felt strange going out through the front door but Betty took her arm and they left like regal ladies.

'Who is Tom?' Eleanor asked as they walked down the street.

'Mrs Hampton's son. She's got a daughter too except she's off married. To a sailor, of all things. Can you imagine? Well, I suppose you've not seen her. Little twig of a girl she is and he's as big as an ox. I bet he gives her a right good seeing-to.'

Eleanor giggled and followed Betty down the street until she turned in to a long lane with shops either side.

'Where are we going, Betty?' she asked. 'I don't want to get caught.'

'Me neither!' Betty said. 'But we won't. Cook is busy and too lazy to walk upstairs to check on us. Mrs Hampton will be out for at least two hours and Amelia is with her. We're safe as houses.'

'So where are we going?' Eleanor asked. She was feeling extremely nervous now; people were glancing their way and she felt sure they stood out as errant servants enjoying a morning off when they should be working.

'Here,' Betty said as they arrived outside a butcher's shop. 'Not in the front, though, come round the back.'

'Everyone's looking,' Eleanor said. 'Someone will tell!'

'They's looking because you and I are the finest pair of beauties along this street, that's all. Come on with me.'

Eleanor couldn't help but giggle, because perhaps Betty was right. After all it seemed to be only the delivery boys and the old men standing at their shop doorways who were looking. The women in the street passed them without a second glance. It seemed that to some their uniform was almost a form of invisibility, despite the somewhat abbreviated skirts, and she wondered if Mrs Hampton would even look their way were she to cross along the other side of the street.

As it happened they were soon away from the main road and down an alleyway. The cobblestones were dirty, and above them smut-soiled washing hung from lines stretched between the houses. Everything had a sepia tint of dirt and a glum darkness about it that made Eleanor feel distinctly uncomfortable.

Betty rapped on the back door of the shop and after a moment or two Eleanor was sure that nobody would answer. Then, to her surprise, the door opened and a young man in an ill-fitting suit and apron opened it. He immediately smiled and kissed Betty on the cheek.

'You look great, Bets,' he said. 'Didn't think you'd be coming today.'

'You know how I gets when I don't come all day,' Betty replied, 'but anyhow, my friend here's been seeing to that!'

Eleanor blushed. She had not considered that their illicit late-night romps would ever reach the ears of anyone else, let alone a stranger in a back street.

'Come on in, then, before old man Grundy catches me. Though fine chance of that. Poor old beggar's all but blind these days. You should see the latest set of spectacles he's got, they looks like a pair of posh drinking glasses stuck on his face. Poor old sod.'

Eleanor crept inside with Betty and found that they were in a little room with a bed and a cabinet and not much else. From the door she could hear someone, presumably Mr Grundy himself, talking to a customer.

'Got anything for us?' Betty asked with mock innocence, and the young man laughed.

'Course, Betty, and a little gin too if you wants it?' he replied.

'You're too good to me, Alf Grundy,' Betty said and began to unbutton her dress.

'Betty!' Eleanor exclaimed. 'What are you doing?'

'Paying my bills is what I'm doing,' Betty said a trifle defensively. 'Don't you know how things work?'

'I don't. I mean, I don't know,' Eleanor replied.

'You can have what the nobs throw down from their table or you can have a little extra,' Betty said. Her voice was solemn and serious.

'Meat for a little meat inside you,' the boy explained, and added, 'You might want to earn a bit yourself?'

'Oi!' Betty protested. 'She's here for a drink, not for you.'

'Go on, girls,' he urged. 'Make it the pair of you and I'll give you a bottle of gin, a whole bottle on top of what you normally get. That's not a bad deal!'

Betty gave him a furious stare and stopped unbuttoning her dress.

'Alf Grundy!' she said. 'You are the greediest man in this whole street!'

'I'll do it,' Eleanor said, surprising all of them and not least herself.

'You don't have to,' Betty replied, but seeing the look in Eleanor's eye she smiled and began to unbutton her dress again.

Alf Grundy unbuttoned his shirt in turn, never once taking his eyes off them, and soon had his trousers down and off as well. He discarded his apron and pulled down his underwear. The girls were half naked by that point and Eleanor stopped for a moment to look at him.

He wasn't like Connor Bishop at all, perhaps because of his age. He was slim, slimmer than

40

Eleanor even, and his cock was short and his balls small. He had a little pubic hair but not much, and it was mousy brown. He was lying back on his bed with his erection sticking up, small but undeniably keen. Eleanor shrugged off her dress, amazed at how uninhibited she felt. Having Betty there seemed to make all the difference. She was soon naked and stood next to Betty so the young man could admire them together.

'You pretty things,' he said. 'Now come here and give me a kiss.'

Eleanor and Betty went to him and lay either side of him on his narrow bed with their legs over him so that their wet slits pressed against his thighs. He moaned with pleasure at their warmth and put his arms around them, drawing them close and kissing them both on their necks and cheeks. He kissed Betty for the longest time, gently and eagerly. His little thing was so hard now it left a trail of wetness when it pressed against their flesh. Eleanor took it in her hand and pulled the skin back a bit so she could look at it properly. It was a darling little thing, neat and beautifully smooth. She began to move her hand gently up and down it and Betty reached out and cupped his balls. He closed his eyes and gave a low moan of pleasure as Eleanor bent over him and licked the end. She sucked its tip for a moment and then swallowed him down, enjoying the way it felt against her tongue and lips. His hand slipped between Betty's legs and began to toy with her, first with one finger and then two. When his hand snaked between Eleanor's legs she climbed on to him, her mouth over his cock and her cunt glancing against his lips.

It was a position she liked. She had felt Betty's tongue and now she was ready for his. He didn't keep her waiting very long. Driven on by the sweet smell

41

of her, he plunged his tongue into her hole and tasted that wonderful exotic taste that Betty had been enjoying ever since she'd arrived at the town house. He licked inside her, neglecting her lips, but she found that strangely exciting, enjoying the touch of his tongue as he tasted parts that had until recently been untouched. Eleanor straddled him with her thighs and pushed down so that his tongue could go as deeply as possible.

Watching, Betty appeared fascinated and seemed to feel no jealousy at seeing Alf enthusiastically licking her friend. As Eleanor sucked at his dick Betty rubbed her friend's bottom and felt where his mouth was, helping to excite them.

Soon Eleanor couldn't stop herself – she was coming and nothing would hold it back. Her juice ran down his cheeks, which made him lick even more furiously, and having her clit stimulated as she came drove Eleanor wild. His tongue seemed to know where to go by instinct, or perhaps by experience, and he obviously loved her taste.

As soon as she had come he spurted his own juices into her mouth, and she drank them down with enthusiasm. It wasn't the nicest taste in the world but on that hot day in the back room of the shop it was the most exciting. Finished, he pulled his softening cock from her mouth and lay back with a satisfied moan.

'Hey you, what about me?' Betty demanded. 'I didn't come here for a peep-show! Hope you've got something left for me?'

'Hmm?' he muttered. 'Oh, I don't know about that.'

'Well, I bloody well do!' Betty said and pushed Eleanor gently off him and climbed on top. Eleanor watched enthralled as she climbed over his limp cock and held her lips open. She began to rub against it and it got a little harder.

'Who's a good boy then?' she asked and Eleanor giggled.

Alf looked surprised and then pleased as his cock rose to the occasion and grew hard against Betty's proffered slit. She didn't let it in her at first, instead teasing him by sliding her crease along its length. When he grabbed at her hips, trying to guide her down, she raised herself higher and told him to be patient – she'd let him in her when she was ready.

Poor Alf didn't know what to do other than lie back and wait while she teased him. When Eleanor kissed him, he tasted his orgasm on her lips and squeezed her small pert breasts in return. But Eleanor wasn't looking at his face, her attention drawn between his legs to his little dick and balls, which were now as tight and straining as they had been before.

'Come on, Mr Greedy!' Betty teased. 'Have you got enough for two or is your eyes bigger than your cock?'

Eleanor giggled at her friend's crudeness and that was too much for Alf. Frustrated beyond his ability to resist by her teasing, he took her firmly by the hips and forced her down on him. His cock sank into her all the way and she gave a little cry of pleasure and surprise. He began to rock her while she sat up on him, guiding her back and forth so that her moist little tunnel moved on his cock, a sensation so fine he was moved to put his head back and begin to curse, although purely with pleasure.

'You are so fucking good, Betty,' he muttered. 'You feel so fucking good. You always do, you little harlot.'

She reached between his legs and grabbed his balls, squeezing them and scratching at them softly with her short little nails. He gave a guttural cry and with a spasm that started at his buttocks and ended at his neck he came inside her. Betty was coming too, riding him hard and holding his balls firmly from behind her bottom. The angle meant she had to twist to one side, which brought her breasts into close proximity to Eleanor's face. Unable to resist, Eleanor leant forwards and took one of her friend's nipples in her mouth. She sucked it, licked it and teased it with her lips while her friend bucked and rode on top of Alf, and as Betty had the second wave of her orgasm she pulled Eleanor closer for a kiss.

The walk home was a little less easy than the walk there. They had dressed hastily afterwards, as the clock showed they had been fucking and talking for nearly an hour. On reaching the house they dashed up the steps, and not a moment too soon. A few minutes later Mrs Hampton returned with a bored Amelia in tow. Looking at the maids' red faces and the sweat on their brows she announced she was pleased to see that they hadn't been slacking just because she wasn't home, and promptly went upstairs to change.

Eleanor and Betty managed to stave off the giggles until Mrs Hampton had reached the turn in the landing and then they fell into each other's arms, laughing like two old friends. The embrace turned to touching and carefree and passionate kissing, leaving Eleanor thrilled she had found such a fine friend in Betty.

Amelia on the other hand was in an irritable mood. She had stamped upstairs behind Mrs Hampton with a face like thunder. The levity of the two junior maids infuriated her, and despite their flushed appearance, she was sure they had been slacking, or worse. She was hot and bothered herself, and felt somehow dirty from association with the poor they had visited that morning. It was also far too warm to be out walking.

She followed Mrs Hampton into her bedroom and closed the door.

'Is something the matter, my dear?' Mrs Hampton asked.

'I don't like that Eleanor girl. She is lazy and sly,' Amelia declared.

'Oh, nonsense, you just don't like her because she is pretty,' Mrs Hampton teased.

Amelia busied herself placing Mrs Hampton's discarded hat in its box so that she would have an excuse to turn her back on her mistress. Mrs Hampton came up behind her and slipped a hand around her middle. Amelia made a show of pulling away for a moment and then relaxed against her lover.

'You're a jealous girl,' Mrs Hampton told her.

'What if I am?' Amelia asked.

'Behave yourself.'

'Or what?'

It was an old game, played many times between them, but they never got bored of it. Amelia pulled free and turned to face Mrs Hampton, put on her most insolent face and poked her tongue out at her mistress.

'Oh, you wicked little madam,' Mrs Hampton said. 'I can see I shall have to teach you some manners.'

She dragged Amelia to the bed by her wrist and told her to strip naked. Amelia did as she was told, taking off first her dress then her combinations, and lastly her stockings. She took those off slowly and teased Mrs Hampton by acting very coy and innocent.

'Little strumpet!' Mrs Hampton said with a smile.

'What if I don't feel like doing any work this afternoon?' Amelia asked. 'What if I am feeling lazy?'

'Then you know what you'll get,' Mrs Hampton replied as she began to undress in turn.

Amelia lay on the bed. It felt good to be naked, the slight breeze from the window blowing across her bare flesh and making her nipples tingle. She knew her curves were enticing, and the whisper of pubic hair on her mound looked golden in the afternoon sunshine. Mrs Hampton was looking at her intently, while struggling with her own clothes to be rid of them as quickly as possible. Amelia rolled on to her front and bent one leg in the air with mock nonchalance. In truth she was very excited, as she hadn't been taken for far too long and she was eager for the attentions of a lover. Yet still she pretended to ignore Mrs Hampton, even as her mistress slipped free of her underwear. Naked, Mrs Hampton came to stand over Amelia.

'Lazy girl,' she said, her breath a little short. She advanced on Amelia and rolled her on to her back.

Amelia lay still, as if she could not be bothered to move. Her legs had fallen slightly open and her generous breasts had parted a little. Mrs Hampton ran her hand between them and then cupped the full mounds. She took Amelia's wrists and held them to the corners of the bed, then did the same with her ankles. Amelia lay motionless and passive, allowing her body to be touched at her mistress's will. Her perfectly rounded breasts were cupped again and she watched as her mistress stroked them and pulled at her nipples.

'Such pretty things,' Mrs Hampton said absently.

'What are you going to do with me?' Amelia asked with mock innocence.

Mrs Hampton picked up her stockings and then

Amelia's as well. She placed them beside her on the bed and leant over her ladies' maid.

'Tie you up and take you,' Mrs Hampton whispered. 'Like the dirty little girl you are.'

Amelia stayed quiet but a wicked smile crept into her eyes.

Mrs Hampton took one of the stockings and used it to tie Amelia's left wrist to the nearest bedpost, then took another stocking for the other wrist. To tie this one she had to lean over Amelia's body, and when she did so she pressed her sex against her maid's shapely hips. Taking the other two stockings, she turned her attention to Amelia's legs. Amelia did not resist, nor did she help, simply lying there limp but looking delectable. Mrs Hampton wasted no time, tying Amelia firmly down so that her legs were wide apart then standing back to admire her work. Amelia was spread-eagled and helpless, but now looked defiant rather than indifferent.

Mrs Hampton climbed on top of her maid and knelt over her middle, then took Amelia by the hair and pulled out her little clips and ties, quickly making a mess of her locks.

'Untidy little madam,' Mrs Hampton whispered.

'Punish me, then,' Amelia retorted, looking Mrs Hampton directly in the eye. 'If you dare.'

'Oh, I dare, you may be sure of that,' Mrs Hampton replied.

She slid down Amelia's body a little until her brush of hair was touching Amelia's, then she began to glide over her maid, using her arms to support herself and staying just high enough to keep the contact light.

Amelia let out a hissing moan then drew in a sharp breath as Mrs Hampton's clitoris brushed her own. It was enough to make her bend her legs and push herself up so that they touched more firmly. Mrs

Hampton used her weight to push Amelia back down on to the bed and began to grind her hips against her maid's helpless body. She put her hands on Amelia's shoulders and traced them down her sides as she rode her maid, then moved her touch to Amelia's breasts, squeezing one and bending down to suck a nipple.

Amelia was tossing her head from side to side now, her passion rising despite herself. She felt Mrs Hampton's hand slide under her, grasping her bottom and pinching it. Mrs Hampton had long nails and each nip made Amelia cry out a little and bring her hips up against her mistress's body. She felt helpless and she loved it, as she had loved it since the first morning her mistress had taken her upstairs and done it to her.

Mrs Hampton began to crawl up the bed and the pressure between Amelia's legs lessened. A flash of disappointment gave way to new excitement as Mrs Hampton knelt over Amelia's face, holding on to the bedposts. Mrs Hampton then let herself slide downwards a little until her dark pubic hair was brushing against Amelia's cheek.

'Lick me,' she commanded.

Amelia was desperate to do it, but Mrs Hampton teased her by keeping herself just out of reach. She craned her neck and put out her little rounded tongue as far as she could, but only managed to brush it against Mrs Hampton's thatch, just below her sex lips, and the more she tried the further her mistress withdrew.

'Let me, please let me,' she cried.

'Oh, perhaps, perhaps if you're good,' Mrs Hampton teased.

'I will be good. You know I'd do anything for you.'

'Do you promise?'

'Of course, Mistress,' Amelia said. 'You are my mistress, and I am your maid, and more. I am your slave. I exist only to serve you and please you, you know that. Let me taste you, please.'

At last Mrs Hampton pressed herself down on Amelia's face and closed her thighs tightly around her maid's head. Amelia gave a muffled moan of pleasure and began to lick hard, the way Mrs Hampton liked it best – hard and firm, no half licks or teasing with the tongue for her. She liked it full against her clitoris and she liked it fast.

Amelia obliged and was gratified, delighted even, to hear her mistress moaning in quick hot gasps. Mrs Hampton liked it inside too, deep inside, probing her hot entrance. Amelia pushed her tongue in, questing and searching as far as she could go while Mrs Hampton held her lips open and angled her hips to help Amelia's tongue burrow into her as deeply as possible.

She came hard, her body bucking and writhing against her maid's face. Amelia had anticipated it, knowing her mistress's body well enough to feel the difference in her taste just before the moment came, even if the trembling in Mrs Hampton's body had not betrayed her crisis already. She sucked now, her tongue drawn back into her mouth, sucked and swallowed, loving the way Mrs Hampton's juices tasted and her curious, desperate sounds of pleasure.

'Don't stop,' Mrs Hampton whispered. 'Take every drop of it, Amelia.'

Amelia could not answer, but pushed her mouth tightly against her mistress's hole, and when the flow became a trickle she pushed her tongue deep inside again to lick, each stroke making Mrs Hampton groan and push down.

Licking another woman was no novelty to Amelia. She had learnt from her friend one night in their bedroom above her parents' café and never forgotten the pleasures. Since then she had slipped her tongue into several women, but none of them had tasted as delicious as Mrs Hampton, nor had any of them been so keen to be satisfied by a tongue alone. Mrs Hampton loved to have her wet little hole toyed with by fingertip too, but preferred her servant's tongue.

Mrs Hampton slid off Amelia, deliberately running her hot swollen lips along her maid's face and neck, over her breasts and then down her belly. Her fine black pubic hair tickled, but it was the heat and the swollen satisfied lips that made Amelia rock and struggle to be free. She wanted more but, as ever, it was not in her power to control what happened.

Mrs Hampton climbed off the bed and stood looking at the naked servant girl for a moment. Amelia was staring desperately up at her, her passion burning in her eyes and clearly visible between her legs too.

Mrs Hampton bent over a little and placed her hands on the girl's thighs. She parted them a little more until Amelia gave a tiny grunt and a moan. Then she looked, very closely. Amelia flushed with shame at the intimate inspection. Yes, she was wet, yes, her clitoris was swollen and standing out like a little pea. What did her mistress expect, after the display she'd just made of herself?

Amelia's embarrassment was mixed with fear that Mrs Hampton might leave her in this state; she had done so before. She had left her tied naked with her wet slit throbbing while her employer had taken a long luxurious bath and then, and only then, returned to make Amelia come. She hoped today would not be such a day; her need was too urgent.

'You need it, don't you?' Mrs Hampton asked.

'Yes, Mistress, please, Mistress,' Amelia replied.

'I know what you need.'

She went to the little table beside her bed and opened the drawer. Inside were letters but she pushed those aside and rooted around more deeply. Amelia watched with wide eyes; she knew what was in that drawer. Mrs Hampton took out a belt first, a strange-looking belt that would have made no sense to anyone not intimately familiar with its purpose. It was made of firm leather and had an additional strap, one designed to run between one's legs. That strap was leather too but the inside was padded with the softest velvet. Mrs Hampton put it around her middle. The extra length of it hung behind her like a flat black tail. Amelia gave a little moan and rolled her head away. Mrs Hampton pulled the 'tail' between her legs and fastened it to the front. She looked as though she were wearing underwear made of leather and studs. Then she fished into the drawer again, and drew out a little wooden box.

'Oh look, Amelia,' she teased, 'what have we here?'

Amelia watched as Mrs Hampton opened the box. Inside were several lengths of rubber, each shaped roughly like a man's penis. There was a range of sizes, from tiny thin slim ones to one that looked like a policeman's truncheon.

'A number three today, I think,' Mrs Hampton declared.

Amelia had initially taken little notice of the numbers her mistress had called out when the item had been first purchased. Now she had learnt that the numbers were highly significant: the higher the number, the greater the size. A three was not too bad, but it was still large.

Mrs Hampton fitted the hard rubber cock to the front of the belt and screwed it into its appointed position. When she had done so she turned around and put her hands on her hips. Its black length stood out, almost completely erect but drooping a little from its heavy weight. Mrs Hampton began to walk towards her and Amelia closed her eyes, biting her lip. Mrs Hampton climbed on top of her and let the thing dangle obscenely between her legs, Amelia unable to resist the temptation to peek. Mrs Hampton took it in one hand and introduced the tip of it to Amelia's lips. Amelia squirmed a little, trying to wriggle up the bed, but there was no escape.

'Is this what you dream of in your little servant's bed?' Mrs Hampton demanded.

'No, I dream only of you!' Amelia protested.

'Oh? Never cock, thick hard cock entering that little tight spot?' Mrs Hampton teased.

Amelia was about to answer when Mrs Hampton rubbed the dildo against her. She moaned and tried to close her legs a little. It was impossible, of course: her legs were tied widely open and nothing would stop the inevitable penetration to come.

Mrs Hampton forced it inside her, at first just the tip and then the shaft too, in one long, slow push. It filled Amelia to the hilt, pushing her lips wide apart and making her gasp with mixed arousal and pain.

Mrs Hampton took Amelia's head and forced her to look at the rubber cock, wide and thick and filling her deeply. Then she began to rock back, drawing it slightly out before ramming it back in, hard, over and over again.

Amelia's head fell back against the pillow and she began to swear quietly in French. Each stroke felt like a battering ram, forcing itself inside her before drawing back to prepare for a fresh assault. It was perfectly smooth, its sides wet with her juices, and as Amelia grew used to the girth it began to move easily in and out. Mrs Hampton started to fuck Amelia harder and faster still, so that the velvet rubbed against her own crotch and the ingenious little bud of rubber on the underside pushed against her clitoris. Each stroke drew her closer and closer to a deep hard orgasm, until at last she came for the second time, leaving Amelia in a state of ecstatic frustration until at last a merciful finger was applied to her clitoris.

# Four

*Wherein the reader is introduced to the lustful young master of the house and is presented with more evidence of debauchery amongst the serving staff below stairs.*

Tom Hampton arrived home late at night with Mr Coleman the butler at his side. The butler had the look of a man who has been pushed to the very limits of his patience, and with good reason. The moment he had arrived at Tom's boarding school he had been regaled with tales of depravity and disobedience by Tom's headmaster.

Tom arrived home just in time to bid his mother goodnight and then departed to bed. Mrs Hampton sat quietly while Mr Coleman told her of maids who had been groped, of wild drinking in the dorm rooms and of classes missed.

But sleep was the very last thing on Tom's mind that night. He had the vigour and restlessness of an eighteen-year-old man and while he might have had no choice about returning home for the summer he intended to make the most of it.

Waiting until the house had fallen quiet, he checked his pocket watch. It was nearly 10 p.m. and on a Thursday he knew what that meant, if his memory of the house's rituals served him correctly. He quietly went to his closet and opened the doors.

Reaching within, he moved aside the riding boots and folded piles of coats and tossed them on the floor, then felt around for the loose panel and pulled it away carefully. He had come across the crawl space purely by accident while playing in his room as a young boy. It was only years later that the potential of this secret part of the house had become apparent.

He looked into the dark tunnel behind the square hole in the wall and reached in, brushing aside the cobwebs and dust. It was a brick tunnel that had once been the main chimney. The soot still clung to the walls and was thick in the air, even though the fireplace hadn't been used in perhaps twenty years. Tom wriggled along the passageway and carefully climbed down the shaft, using the rough brickwork as a ladder. He had made the journey so many times he needed no light, while the thought of what lay at the end of his descent spurred him on so that the soot and cobwebs he had to push through were barely noticed.

After five or so minutes of crawling he was at basement level, where the chimney had once been connected to a huge fireplace. The fireplace had long since been bricked up but a small grate in the wall gave him a fine view of the kitchen under the stairs. He had, many years ago, dragged a packing crate down here and it was on that he now stood. He grinned at the sight that lay before him, a voyeur's paradise.

The iron bath was nearly full, the cook adding one more kettleful of water to it before she dipped her hand in to test the temperature. Tom licked his lips; Thursday was always bath night and the finest night of the week as far as he was concerned. The cook, by order of seniority in the world beneath the stairs, was first to use the bath. Mr Coleman had long since been banished to his room and the girls were giggling and chatting. Tom watched longingly as the cook began to disrobe. She took off her apron then unbuttoned her dress at the back, to let it fall down her ample body before picking it up and putting it on a chair. As she bent over Tom grinned at the sight of her large bottom. He had always been fascinated by it, so full and round. She slipped off her white under-dress and put that on the chair in turn.

Underneath she was bare, and as far as he knew she never wore drawers in the summer, which he found strangely exciting. Although he seldom had any cause to talk to her he made sure he exploited any opportunity that arose. The thought of her bare pussy underneath her uniform drove him into such a state he'd often have to go and play with himself if he chanced to see her about her work.

She turned around and he took a long look at her naked body as she dipped a toe into the bath. She was a large lady, busty and a little red-faced, with long hair now tied up in an untidy bun. Her breasts were magnificent, huge and round, and they swung pleasingly as she bent over a little to get into the bath. They were pendulous and utterly hypnotic; he loved the way they swayed, and wondered how those mighty breasts would feel in his hands, or pressed against him. She eased herself into the bath and lay back, sighing as the hot water covered her to the waist, then reached back and let her hair fall out from the bun.

The cook began to soap her body with a flannel and then rinsed it, washing the soap away. Tom undid his trousers and took his hard penis in his hand. He had missed this so very much. At the boarding school he could pay a woman to do things for him – his friends knew lots of loose women – but for them not to know they were being observed was far more of a thrill for him. He watched as she parted her ample thighs and began to wash her most intimate parts, with Tom willing her to stand up.

She did, rising like a goddess from the sea, her bright pink skin covered in tiny bubbles of soap and slick with water. Totally unaware that just feet away the young master of the house was stroking his cock, she turned around and ran the flannel over her crotch and then over her bottom. She knelt for a moment and splashed herself with water, then rose and stood with her back to him, washing under her arms.

Tom was delighted with his view of the cook, and her proud rump in particular was always a joy to see, but he was more interested in discovering what secrets the new girl had to offer. Mr Coleman had been unable to tell him anything about her as he had not seen her himself, and only knew that a new maid had joined the staff. As a consequence Tom had spent the entire return journey fantasising about what kind of girl she'd be. Would she be pretty or plain, tall and thin or short and chubby, dark-haired or light-haired?

He didn't have to wait long to find out. The beautifully rounded cook got out of the tub and wrapped a towel around her middle. He was delighted to see that she didn't bother to cover her breasts and instead left those bare. She had one foot up on the tub and was drying between her toes, giving Tom an exciting view of her crotch, to which his eyes stayed fixed until his attention was distracted by the arrival of Betty and what he presumed must be the new serving girl. He knew her name but nothing else; now he was about to get to know a lot more about her, and the anticipation made his penis throb with excitement.

Eleanor slipped off her uniform and Betty began to unbutton her dress in turn. They talked as they undressed, and Tom began to play with himself. First he gently stroked himself and then, overtaken with excitement, he began to pull hard. He had to be quiet, though; he was so close to them that a sudden noise might make them look up and see his eyes peering down at them.

He craned forwards, keen to see every detail as Eleanor shrugged off her chemise and drawers and put them in a basket by the tub. She was lovely and slim; her body was girlish but she was definitely a woman. If proof were needed it could be seen between her legs, with the auburn blaze of colour showing against her pale-white skin. Her titties were smaller than he had hoped for – he preferred them large and rounded – but she was by no means flat-chested. Her small breasts were still fine little swells and her nipples a delightful pink, a colour only to be found on the blondest or most redheaded of girls.

Tom watched as the girls climbed into the tub together, the water slopping out a little as they eased themselves in. Both girls were facing him, Betty sitting in front of Eleanor as the new maid washed her back. The cook slipped off her towel and began to dry her breasts. Tom had never ceased to be fascinated by girls washing, they seemed to have so many little rituals. Now she was lifting each breast to dry the skin underneath, and the careless, mundane way she went about it excited him nearly to the point of orgasm. He held off, though, reluctantly letting go and allowing his hard cock to stand there on its own.

He peered intently through the grate as Eleanor's hands slid around her friend's front and over her ample breasts. She lifted them and squeezed them, touching and teasing at her nipples in a loving way. Tom was amazed. Eleanor was blatantly feeling Betty up and the cook sat nearby without even glancing over. Tom wished he could walk downstairs and strip off and join them. That would be the finest of treats, to be in that bath too, having his cock and balls felt by them both and putting his hands between their legs, feeling them till they lay back and surrendered to him.

Betty he had seen before, many times, and yet her chubby tits always fascinated him. Once, a few years ago, he had taken her. He had pressed himself on her and she had given in. He had longed to do so again but his absence and her subsequent caution around him had prevented him having the opportunity. Now, watching her being felt up by the new girl, he felt intensely aroused and could not help but let his hand fall between his legs again. His trousers had slid down to his ankles and his prick stood bolt upright in excitement, the tip an even angrier red than before. He began to play with it again, and as he did so Eleanor slipped her hand between Betty's legs while the cook sang something from the music hall, apparently heedless to what Eleanor was doing.

Judging by Betty's open mouth and closed eyes she herself was only too aware. Her legs, which had been tucked up nearly to her chin, now moved and she placed them on the rim of the bath. Eleanor's hand was making little bubbles and Tom could hear the splashing even from his position.

'The dirty little madam,' he whispered to himself. 'She's putting her finger in there.'

And so she was – not just one finger, but two. He got a good look as Betty rose a little in the water. Her face was pink, either with embarrassment or more likely with excitement and the heat of the bath.

Eleanor increased the speed of her hand, stroking fast and deep with her fingers while still washing her friend's back. Betty pushed back against her friend and reached an arm around to Eleanor's own sex. She began to finger Eleanor in turn and Tom could see the moment her fingers touched Eleanor's clitoris by the change in the new maid's expression. Now she was pressed hard against Betty, her breasts against her friend's back and her hand working twice as fast. The cook was still oblivious, evidently thinking nothing of two girls having a bath together. She stood up and stretched and for a moment Tom was unable to decide where to look, wishing fervently that he had two sets of eyes.

The cook won his undivided attention for a moment. Her extravagant stretch was like that of a woman displaying herself to a new lover without hesitation or shame, with her arched back pushing her huge breasts up higher as her legs parted a little. Tom gazed eagerly between her legs, fascinated by the little brush of hair. He had learnt, through experimentation and observation, that a woman's eyebrows are a good indicator as to the colour of her pubic hair. A girl might have long straw-coloured hair, like the cook's, but if her eyebrows were dark then so would her pubic hair prove. This fascinated and enthralled him, and he felt that he was in on a secret unknown to most men. It gave him the power to imagine almost any girl he should see naked and exposed to him.

It was ironic that many of the young ladies he met were impressed by the fact that rather than talking to their breasts he seemed instead to look them straight in the eye. If they had known he had been trying to judge the colour of their pubic hair, so that he could imagine them naked later on and tug himself to orgasm, no doubt they would have found him far less charming.

Eleanor and Betty soon neared the point of orgasm and so did he. Then the door opened and both girls gave a little jump of surprise. In his imagination Tom thought about himself wandering in there as if by accident, apologising and saying that he had not realised it was bath night. No, that lie would never work. There would be questions and ultimately he would probably be sent back to the school, where only the most unwanted young men spent the summer. He didn't want that. London was far more exciting, and besides, he didn't care to be under the headmaster's watchful eye all summer.

Tom had thought the new arrival might be Mr Coleman, come to get an eyeful of the girls, but he realised, when he gave it a moment's consideration, that the butler would no more do that than dance naked on the rooftop. It was Amelia, looking hot and bothered and, it seemed, in a foul mood.

'Are you girls still in that bath?' she demanded. 'How long does it take you two to clean yourselves up? Hurry up and be off to bed.'

'Are you waiting to use it?' Eleanor asked.

'Certainly not!' Amelia snapped. 'I don't bathe with the common servants. A girl of my standing uses the family bathroom, and I wouldn't share my water with you two little brats.'

'Yes, do hurry up,' the cook added. 'Mr Coleman will be wanting his bath soon and the water will be stone cold.'

Tom thought Mr Coleman was a lucky devil for even this meagre treat. He would willingly have swapped the comforts of the upstairs bathroom for a quick dip in that water. From his hiding place he could smell the suds, so feminine and laced with the

61

strangely exotic scent of cheap coal-tar soap. As strait-laced as Mr Coleman was, it seemed unlikely that he didn't secretly love being in that bath so soon after it had been vacated by two attractive young things. Why else would he take his bath last instead of first, as was his right by seniority? It was only because he was a man that he wasn't allowed to use the family bathroom. Such a thing would be wrong, especially with Mrs Hampton being without a husband.

'I'm going to go and tell him you're nearly finished,' the cook announced, and began to get her night clothes ready. 'Out, you two, and get off to bed, Betty. I want to speak with Eleanor.'

Tom watched, fascinated, still stroking his erection. Betty got out of the bath, towelled herself off all over quickly and went to the bedroom.

Eleanor got out of the bath with more reluctance. She didn't feel comfortable being naked in front of Amelia, whose cruel eyes seemed to be calculating her every fault, appraising every inch. She got up quickly and wrapped a towel around her middle.

'Have I done something wrong, Am – I mean ladies' maid?' she asked.

'You do everything wrong,' Amelia said. 'Dry yourself off quickly, now; you don't want Mr Coleman to come in and see you, do you? Or perhaps you would like that? Some girls have no shame.'

Eleanor was aghast at the idea and quickly dried herself, doing her best to keep the towel covering as much of her as possible while she did it. When she had finished she reached for her nightdress, which was airing on the back of a chair, but Amelia snatched it from her.

'We have high standards in this house,' she said,

'and I doubt very much you will be here long, tatty little country girl that you are.'

Eleanor felt ashamed and covered her breasts and crotch with her hands. She was desperate not to cry but she could feel it coming on. Amelia knew just how to cut through her defences and strike where she felt most vulnerable. She was a simple country girl, she knew that. Before she had come to London she had never seen poverty and power so closely side by side. She had never guessed that women like Amelia would really rule the roost, nor that her employer would have a maid who serviced her sexually.

'Please, miss, I don't mean to offend,' she whimpered.

'But you do!' Amelia said sharply. 'Look at you!'

She took Eleanor's wrists and lifted them in the air so she could look at the maid naked. Eleanor began to sob a little and felt the shame burning at her cheeks.

'What do you call this?' she demanded, pointing between Eleanor's thighs.

'Oh miss, I don't – I don't know,' Eleanor moaned.

'You don't know the word for it, or do you pretend not to know what it is?' Amelia demanded.

'It's my crotch, my – my ha'penny,' Eleanor moaned.

'You dirty little country girls,' Amelia snapped. 'You come up to London with your dirty, hairy bodies and spread diseases and lice and all manner of things. You should be ashamed. Don't you know about keeping yourself tidy?'

'Miss, I don't,' Eleanor sobbed. 'I didn't mean to do anything wrong.'

'It is expected that you keep yourself clean, at least,' Amelia said, then dragged Eleanor by the arm out of the kitchen and into the large pantry.

\* \* \*

Luckily for Tom the door was left wide open and with a little repositioning he could see and hear what was going on perfectly. He suspected Mr Coleman could hear everything too, and he wondered how ashamed Eleanor must feel knowing her private parts were being so openly discussed. Perhaps Mr Coleman would ask the cook what was wrong with Eleanor – but would she tell him?

'Hair,' Amelia said sharply, 'is to be kept short. That goes for the hair on your head and the hair between your legs!'

'Oh miss, I am sorry; I didn't realise,' Eleanor sobbed. 'Please don't send me away.'

In the back of her mind she knew that Amelia would do no such thing – *could* probably do no such thing. Yet she felt powerless to resist when she was told to sit on the pantry table and lie back. Amelia fished a straight razor from her apron and Eleanor tried to sit up.

'Lie back, you little urchin,' Amelia commanded. 'You don't want me to have an accident, do you?'

Eleanor very much didn't, and she lay down frozen in fear. She put her hands over her budding young breasts in an attempt at some modesty, and Amelia, for once, did not scold her for it. The ladies' maid made a great show of cleaning the razor and stropping it before she set to work.

'Legs wide,' she commanded.

Amelia's face was mere inches from Eleanor's open legs as she set to work. She touched and spread the pouted sex lips, pushing them one way and then the other as she carefully began to scrape away the hair. Eleanor could feel her precious curls coming off at the kiss of the ice-cold razor-blade, falling between her legs and tickling her bottom too. She felt the ladies' maid's fingers as they explored her, opening and touching her. She moaned but was told to be silent, and so she lay still, sniffing back the tears as her most private place was efficiently shaved bare. It was not a pleasant experience; in truth at that moment she hated Amelia even more than when the ladies' maid had spanked her. There was something erotic about it, though, something about the clean and fresh feeling when it was done that made her wonder how it would feel to be licked or fucked while so bare.

At last it was done, and Amelia took a little washing bowl, splashing cold soapy water over Eleanor's crotch, then stepped back to admire her work.

'Much better,' she announced.

'I will keep myself clean,' Eleanor promised, unable to look at her tormentor's face.

'You will or I shall do it for you,' Amelia announced. 'Now let's see what you think of it.'

Amelia took a little pocket mirror out and placed it below Eleanor's newly shaved lips. At first Eleanor didn't want to see, but at Amelia's insistent commands she sat up a little and looked down. Her slit was now bare. There was not a single hair to cover her, nor any hiding from the fact that Amelia had completely exposed her, more completely than during any of her other humiliations. Amelia had turned her into an object. That was how she felt – she had been turned into something that Amelia liked on the faintest pretext of cleanliness.

She was made to look, to put her own hand down there and touch herself. It felt wonderful, and if this was meant to be a punishment then the punishment was over. The sensation of touching her own bare lips made her shiver, which Amelia evidently took to be proof of shame. This seemed to please her greatly and she told Eleanor to get up and go to bed, lest she take the carpet-beater to her for letting her pubic hair get so unkempt in the first place. Eleanor needed no more encouragement and was off in a frantic patter of bare feet.

Amelia waited for a moment and then, after giving a look towards Mr Coleman's door, sat on the table herself. She lay back against the little wooden table and Tom watched with fascination as the ladies' maid pulled her drawers open to get at her sex. The shaving had left her in an excited state, that much was clear. In moments she had her knees bent and was fingering herself enthusiastically. Her pubic hair was very short and dark, like her eyebrows, Tom noted with delight. She was rubbing her whole slit with two fingers, letting them run inside herself and then drawing them out quickly and thrusting them back in. While she did this her thumb moved in lazy circles around her clit.

'You dirty girl,' she whispered, just loud enough for Tom to hear. 'You bad little madam, making me so hot and wet. Now lick me, lick me hard.'

For a moment Tom had no idea who Amelia was speaking to, until it dawned on him that she was imagining Eleanor still there. He wondered if she knew how willingly Eleanor had touched Betty and whether or not, if he told her, he might get to witness Amelia's little fantasy turn to reality.

Amelia raised her legs until her feet were up in the air and rubbed herself firmly. She seemed especially responsive to Tom, her squeals coming faster and faster and making Tom rub himself harder, matching her stroke for stroke. When she came she jerked violently and Tom was quite amazed to see that rather than getting a little wetter she squirted a little jet of fluid on to the table.

Finished, she sighed, closed her underwear and got up from the table. Seeming a little unsteady on her feet, she hesitated for a moment, but on hearing Mr Coleman's door open she quickly grabbed her underwear, ran out of the pantry and dashed through the kitchen before vanishing upstairs.

Tom gave a little sigh and came with a final jerk on his cock. His spunk splashed on to the wall leaving a new mark on top of all the others he had produced down there over the years.

Mr Coleman came into the room whistling, with his towel over his shoulder. He was only 35 but his service to Mrs Hampton and his previous employer had made him look prematurely old. His hair was flecked with white and he needed small spectacles to read. He was still a good-looking man, though – not that Tom had any sexual interest in him. This was his cue to leave, but he lingered for a moment out of pure curiosity.

Mr Coleman undressed slowly, glancing at the girls' door as if expecting them to burst out at any moment. He seemed a little ill at ease but the house had fallen quiet and, satisfied that he would not be interrupted, he took off his shirt and undid the collar, then discarded his little black tie and undid his trousers. Tom resolved that he should go to bed but the sound of a door opening made him stop for a moment. He hoped the girls were going to walk in on the butler, which would surely be worth a good spanking, something Tom would have enjoyed seeing. He knew that Amelia and sometimes Mrs Hampton herself took hands or hairbrushes to the girls' backsides when they were disobedient, but he had yet to see such a glorious event for himself.

He was slightly surprised to see the cook come from her room, creeping in on tiptoes.

'All clear?' she asked in hushed tones.

'Aye, it seems it is,' the butler replied. 'I've missed you so, my love.'

'And I you!' she replied and kissed his cheek.

'Why must you be away so long? You said only a day at most,' the cook asked, turning her back on him and folding her arms.

'Oh, don't take on so,' he said. 'You know how it is, Master Wet-End was causing trouble at school. It was all that I could do to stop the headmaster expelling him there and then, and then imagine the trouble we'd be in with that little snot here all the time.'

Tom couldn't believe his ears. He had a good mind to shout that he could rightly hear every word and that no servant should talk about their betters in that way. Luckily he thought about it for a moment and realised that nothing that was said below stairs was likely to be a match for being dragged upstairs, having been caught spying. He cursed Mr Coleman under his breath and decided that he would make life difficult for the butler at every opportunity.

As it was, thoughts of spiteful revenge were quickly forgotten as the cook pressed herself to Mr Coleman and passionately kissed him.

'Oh, I miss you so when you are gone,' she whispered. 'You know how I love you, and how I love the way you love me.'

Mr Coleman smiled and slipped his trousers off. It seemed his prick loved quite a lot about the cook too, judging by the way it stood ready for her. She reached gently down and squeezed it, then used it to draw him closer as she kissed him on the neck. He pressed against her, kissing her face and then sliding the dressing-gown from her ample body. She did not protest, nor did she seem to mind as he lifted her nightgown, giving Tom a perfect view of her body from the side. Mr Coleman was a lucky devil, no doubt about it. Tom cursed under his breath. The sly old sod was clearly having an affair with the cook right under everyone's noses.

He watched as Mr Coleman gently caressed the cook's breasts and stroked her backside. She was eager for him and her chest heaved with every deep breath she took. The butler gave a last look towards the girls' bedroom and then turned the cook around. He bent her over the little side table, and it looked funny to see such a large lady so precariously balanced, but evidently this was the way she wanted it. She gripped the table and opened her legs and he guided himself into her, then began to gently slide in and out of her moist slit before banging away at her at a furious pace, with his hand over her mouth to stifle her cries of pleasure.

He fucked her hard, eventually letting go of her mouth and holding her by her wide hips. For a while he pounded his cock in and out while holding her like that, the table wobbling as though it might crack at any moment.

'Oh, you are rough, Mr Coleman,' she gasped.

'Just as you like it!' Mr Coleman whispered back triumphantly, and with that they came together.

Once they were done, Mr Coleman took a long bath. The cook knelt next to him with her head on his chest while they sang a music-hall piece full of melancholy and woe for lovers separated from each other. When he had finished bathing they kissed and went their separate ways, back to their single beds.

As for Tom, he found he had to rest a while in his hiding place, for his fit of extravagant onanism had left his arms too weak to climb back up the chimney. When he did finally reach his room he lay awake for hours, touching himself and remembering what he had seen. He also plotted his revenge on Mr Coleman, who he now hated for being the cook's lover as well as for his comments, which struck him as entirely groundless and cruel. But mostly he thought about the cook, bathing and fucking and her gorgeously large breasts bouncing as she was taken enthusiastically from behind.

# Five

*Wherein the reader learns of the lust of the young master, and the scandal of a servant's defiance.*

Eleanor's morning was busy from the moment she awoke. The task of washing the family's clothes seemed to begin again nearly the moment the last batch was finished. Betty was on her knees with the cook, washing clothes in a large wooden bucket, when the bell began to ring. The bell was marked TOM and for a moment Eleanor ignored it.

'Go and see what he wants,' the cook said. 'Come on, hurry up and get upstairs; Mr Coleman is busy and I need Betty with me.'

'I can go, cook,' Betty offered, but the cook insisted that it was time Eleanor got used to running errands for what she called 'them upstairs'.

Eleanor adjusted her uniform so that it was as neat as possible and made her way up the two sets of stairs to the bedrooms. She knocked gingerly on Tom's door and after a moment heard him call her in. Entering cautiously, she found the blinds still drawn and the room gloomy and close. There was a smell of sweat and something musky on top. She dimly registered it as the smell of men's spunk.

'You rang, Master Tom?' she asked.

'You must be the new girl,' he said. 'What's your name? Ellie, is it?'

71

'Eleanor, Master Tom,' she said.

She didn't much like calling him master, not alone with him in that room at least. It seemed too frank an admission of powerlessness.

'I'm hungry,' he said.

She was somewhat relieved to hear that and started for the door, promising to bring him his breakfast.

'Come over here first,' he said.

She walked slowly over towards him. He chuckled and told her to come close, and that he would not bite her. When she was near she saw that he was sprawled extravagantly in bed, bare-chested. His cock was clearly visible under the thin summer sheet.

'Fluff up my pillows, then, there's a good girl,' he said.

Eleanor hesitated. Doing so would mean leaning over him and she didn't much want to do that. She took the corners of his pillow from behind his head and did her best to shake it back into shape. As she did so she was acutely aware of his gaze on her breasts, each movement she made jiggling them right in front of his face. She blushed and quickly withdrew.

'Good, and let some light in too,' he ordered.

She was happy to do so. The room had a dark and wicked feel about it and she was glad to be away from his bedside. She tugged the curtains open and turned to go, hoping that was all he would want, but of course it wasn't. He called her back over and asked her to make the bed.

'Don't you think you should get up first?' she asked.

'Watch your tongue, girl,' he answered her. 'Do as you are told.'

She went over to the bed, hesitated, then took the sheet and started to draw it back, but could go no

72

further than his tummy. He was obviously naked, naked and excited, and he wanted her to see.

'Master Tom!' she protested. 'You are quite indecent under those covers and I shall do no such thing!'

He took her by the wrist and pulled her on to the bed. She struggled a little but he held her firm.

'Don't be shy, now,' he whispered, his breath hot and hard against her ear. 'I've a feeling you know what I want.'

'Stop it!' she exclaimed. 'I will not be used by you.'

'Oh, but you will,' he said. 'That is unless you want it to be known that you and that little trollop Betty are at it every night, and don't deny it, I know.'

Eleanor froze in shock. She had assumed that what she did with Betty at night was a secret, and yet he seemed sure of himself, convinced without question that they were playing together. She couldn't reply for a moment, but that pleased him even more. He watched her face carefully and began to grin.

Still holding her gaze, he rose from the bed, his hard dick swinging between his legs, and stood before her. She felt his hands on her dress, tugging it up, and then he took hold of her bottom. He felt her, pushing his fingers into the rear slit of her drawers to touch her skin. She gave a little moan, surprised to find that she was both afraid and excited. He pushed her down on the bed and stood towering over her, his hard cock pointing out above her face.

He said only one word by way of instruction and that word was 'suck'. Eleanor knelt down, gently took his cock in her mouth and let it rest against her slightly open lips. He took her firmly by the hair and pushed her head down on to his erection. It looked sore, she noticed, and as she slipped her soft tongue unwillingly over it he shivered with delight. She began to suck him and he relaxed his hold on her hair a little. She bobbed her head back and forth slowly, looking up at him and catching his eye as she did so. He looked back down at her in turn, watching her with a satisfied little smile.

'Now my balls,' he said, dragging her head back so that his cock came out of her mouth with a slippery sucking sound.

'I don't know what to do,' she protested.

She should have known he'd tell her. He ordered her to lick underneath his balls, where they were most sensitive, then to roll her tongue over them, which made him shudder again, going almost up on tiptoes with pleasure as her tongue snaked across them. Then he was ready to push his cock in her mouth again, and this time he pumped his hips as she sucked, forcing it deep into her mouth. She tried to protest but she could not speak, and set to work sucking his cock as best she could.

All of a sudden he decided he could wait no longer, pulling his cock from her mouth and grabbing under her dress for her drawers. He yanked them roughly open and pushed her firmly on to her back, then climbed on top of her and held her firmly by the wrists. His hard cock pressed briefly against her thigh and then he was in her and fucking her.

Eleanor gasped and rolled her head as she was entered. It wasn't the first cock that had penetrated her tight hole, but she was so unprepared for it that it hurt, and he cared little for her pleasure, interested only in skewering her with his erection like a butterfly pinned and mounted.

Again and again he drove his cock into her as hard as he could, smiling as she moaned and struggled vainly in his strong hands. When she struggled he banged her wrists down on the bed and forced her hands together above her head.

Above her his face was red and hot, his naked body gleaming with sweat and excitement. His smooth hairless body banged down on her again and again and yet Eleanor felt her abused slit swell and grow wet. She willed herself to reject the feeling, but being taken so roughly was exciting her in ways she wished and yet was unable to ignore

For one his cock was divinely smooth and as rigid as any she had yet experienced, if not more so. And at the thought that she had driven him to this frenzied loss of self-control simply by the way she looked, she felt a fresh wave of arousal juice in her sex.

'You little tease,' he whispered. 'You know I can't resist taking the new girls; what did you expect?'

It seemed the sound of his own voice was enough to tip him over the edge, and he shot his load inside her, making her hips twist and writhe as though rejecting the spunk. She could not, though, and after he had come and his dick had started to soften he continued to pump into her until every last bit of it was out. Only then did he let go of her wrists and kneel up on the bed above her. He looked uncertain now, less fierce and more scared.

'You are a wicked man,' she hissed. 'Like all men, all you think about is your stupid dick and taking whatever you want.'

'How dare you speak to me like –' he began, but her glare made him stop.

Eleanor had always been a quiet, respectful girl, but something had snapped inside her, perhaps because Tom obviously cared nothing for her: he had seen something he wanted and just taken it. She was lying on a young man's bed with her skirt rucked up to her waist and her wet cunt dripping his yield, yet she no longer felt afraid. Her newfound courage came partly from the state of his cock. Rather than being

75

the fearsome monster that he had pointed at her, it was now as small and tucked-up as a mouse sleeping. She reached for it before he could react and cupped it in her hands, balls and all. He gave a little cry of surprise as she squeezed her hand tightly on it, holding him firmly.

'Let go!' he cried out. 'Stop that!'

'Oh, would you like me to?' she asked. 'Is that what you want, Master Tom? You want me to let go of your little friend, do you?'

He reached for her wrist, intent on prying her fingers away, but she increased the pressure on her little sticky bundle just a fraction and his eyes grew larger.

'I'd keep still, Master Tom, if I were you,' she said. 'I'm not much knowing about these things but I think if I gave you a quick squeeze –' she tightened her grip and he gave a yelp '– like this, you might not be fit for doing anything to a maid again so long as you live. What do you think?'

'Stop it, let me go!' he said.

Eleanor released her grip a little and let the tip of his cock rest between her thumb and forefinger. She had never had the opportunity to look at one in this state before, so small and innocent-looking, and she found she rather liked it. But she liked his nervous face a lot more.

'It's so small when it's resting,' she said, and his face flushed.

'Leave me alone, this instant!' he blustered.

'Or what?' she asked. 'You'll tell that after you forced yourself on me I grabbed your little winkle and gave it a tug? Poor Tommy, such a hard life for you, isn't it?'

She knew that she might be going too far, that any moment now he might slap her or force her hands away and then visit a terrible revenge on her. It was also evident that at some point she would have to release his soft tool, and then she would have no defence against his wrath. She wondered what he meant to do. The least she could imagine was that Tom would see that she got fired. He would probably not reveal the details of his humiliation, nor would he need to. She felt sure her life in London and as a servant was about to come to a sudden end, and she found she no longer cared. She would miss Betty, for sure, but anything was better than being this young man's toy whenever he cared to take her.

Using her thumb, she pushed the skin of his penis back. It was slimy with the juices from both his orgasm and her arousal, which was strangely gratifying. It seemed that Tom found the sensation pleasurable too, and he let out a little moan of delight. She quickly squeezed his balls in her palm until his smile vanished again.

'Now then, Master Small Dick,' she mused. 'What am I to do with you?'

'How dare you!' he fumed. 'How dare you, when you're just a maid!'

'Be quiet,' she ordered, 'or I'll give them another squeeze.'

'Yes,' he whimpered.

Eleanor found his scared face rather exciting. His dick wanted to swell up in her hand but was so tightly constrained it was unable to do anything more than throb in her palm. She looked around the room and caught sight of his dressing-gown on the back of a chair by the bed.

'Pass me that gown,' she said. 'No, just the sash will do.'

He hesitated, but she increased the pressure on his balls until he let out a little shriek and whimpered that he would do it. Defeated, he reached over for the dressing-gown carefully, evidently not wanting to put any more strain on his already sore genitals. He pulled the sash from the middle of the gown and handed it to her. It was bright blue, like the gown, and silky smooth. She took it in her free hand and carefully looped it over his cock and balls, while Tom watched, his eyes bulging. He started to protest as she tightened it around his member, but a little gentle pressure made him fall silent again.

Her father had been a sailor for a while, and when she was little he had shown her how to tie knots. It wasn't easy with one hand but her nimble fingers worked around his dick, fixing the sash carefully into place.

'What do you think you're doing?' he protested.

With one tug she pulled the sash tight, and at the same moment let go of his genitals. He immediately made to grab her but suddenly found himself staring down at his own soft dick in shock. The sash had drawn painfully tight, and he found his balls and cock tied up so securely he could do nothing but stare in helpless amazement. When Eleanor gave the sash another tug he came forwards and instinctively dropped down on to his knees, clutching himself.

'Don't try to undo it!' she warned. 'Back home this is how they castrate sheep. They tie a string around their balls until they turn purple and fall off. Stay still or I'll yank this so hard yours will drop off and roll away!'

Tom whimpered and stopped struggling. The look on his face said it all: he clearly couldn't understand how it had come to this, how he had somehow been reduced to begging a servant girl to untie him and not to torture him any more. She tied the other end of the sash around his neck while he knelt on the floor, cupping his sore balls. He tried to look up at her when she had finished but found that raising his neck put painful pressure on his balls, and so he knelt in position and panted instead, looking at the carpet.

'By the time you've got out of that I will be doing my real work, Master Tom,' she said scornfully. 'But I'll not tell, not if you behave yourself from now on. If you are bad, though, I'll be back up with some rope – not a soft sash but some thick coarse rope.'

He gulped at that, his eyes wide.

'And I'll tie your thing up even tighter,' she threatened, 'so tight you won't be able to escape, and when I'm gone you'll have to crawl over to that bell and ring it for Mr Coleman to have him untie you, Tom. Would you like that?'

Tom gave an urgent shake of his head.

'Good,' Eleanor went on. 'Then you be a well-behaved little boy and there'll be no more trouble. Now, what would you like for breakfast? I'll leave a tray outside your room and you can damn well hobble out and get it for yourself.'

Tom gazed at her in amazement. It didn't look as though he had ever been spoken to in that way by a girl before, especially not a serving girl. He opened and closed his mouth but no words came out.

'I'll see what's going in the kitchen,' Eleanor said haughtily. 'You might have to make do with some crusts today, and maybe some cold coffee. Be a good boy, though, and I'll see you get a little of what you fancy. But take too much of what you fancy and you'll be sorry!'

Tom promised to be good, blubbering that he'd never try to take a maid again and begging her to untie him. Eleanor gave him a final glance of contempt and left smartly, slamming the door behind her.

* * *

79

For a moment Tom knelt on the floor in shock, unsure of what to do, then began to untie the knot as carefully as he could, fearing he might suffer the same fate as the sheep if he wasn't careful. When he was free he left the sash hanging around his neck and began to play with himself furiously. His cock felt dull to the touch, numb even. He couldn't stop, though, he had to spurt out the last drops of come as though ridding himself of it would make the feelings of shame and futility go away.

Eleanor was shaking when she took the tray up to Tom's room, and she half expected to find him waiting outside his door, ready perhaps to throw her down the stairs. She had relented and taken him not scraps but the hearty breakfast the cook had prepared. Outside his door she hesitated, and was about to put the tray down and run when she remembered Black Bess.

Black Bess was the dog that belonged to the blacksmith back in the village. It was a horrible dog, a snapping vicious crossbreed that had chased her every day for years when she walked to the baker's. She hated it and it hated her. It was especially troublesome when she had what her father euphemistically called 'her visitor staying'. It was as though it had sensed her weakness and had been especially keen to bother her. On one such occasion it had chased her right through the village and several people had watched without lifting a finger to help; a few had even laughed. She had been so infuriated that she had grabbed a big stone and hurled it at the dog. By pure luck it had caught the beast on the snout, making it howl in shock and pain. It had run off and she had been overcome with relief and a sense of justice.

It was only the next day when she had been sent back to the baker's that she began to feel full of fear again. Black Bess was sleeping in the drowsy heat outside and she had watched the hound from a distance for a moment before walking towards the baker's. As soon as she drew near the dog cocked one ear and got to its feet, already snarling. She had known then that sometimes you either turn and run or you stand your ground, and that the choice can remain with you for a long time. She had marched straight towards the dog, berating it and warning it that if it so much as got up she'd brain it with a rock. The dog had understood and slunk back into the shade, never to bother her again. With this in mind she knocked loudly on Tom's door and after a moment he called for her to come in. He was sitting on his bed with his robe closed to hide his body, but the sash still lay on the floor, and he seemed uncertain as to what to say.

'Here is your breakfast, Master Tom,' Eleanor said cheerfully. 'I do hope you'll enjoy it.'

For the first time in his life Tom Hampton actually thanked a servant and found, much to his surprise, that his breakfast that morning was the finest he had tasted in quite some time.

After lunch was served, the cook came to them and told them to be off.

'Off where, cook?' Eleanor asked.

'Why, anywhere you please!' the cook replied, and laughed. 'It's your afternoon off, girls, go and enjoy it. Get some sunlight, goodness knows you probably both need it. Go on, I've Mr Coleman's socks and shirts to clean and darn and I don't want you two under my feet.'

They skipped happily out of the back door and sat in the mews behind the house on an old crate.

'Socks and shirts, my eye,' Betty said, and grinned.

'What do you think she'll be tending to this afternoon?' Eleanor asked with an impish smirk.

'His root, like as not!' Betty said.

'I'll bet you're right!' Eleanor replied. 'You'd never guess, though, would you?'

She knew something else Betty would never guess: that she'd tied master Tom's cock up firmly with the sash of his own dressing-gown. It was tempting to tell her friend, but it was her secret, and sometimes even best friends had secrets. Besides, she reasoned, Tom had probably learnt his lesson and she'd been cruel enough. She wanted to forget about him, and more to the point she wanted to forget about the reason she'd been driven to such measures. Instead she wanted to enjoy the sunshine, and could think of nobody better to do it with than Betty.

Betty knew all the best places to go, so she made some suggestions and Eleanor considered their options. An afternoon off was not to be squandered.

'We could see Alf again; that was fun,' Eleanor mused.

'Alf is always fun,' Betty agreed. 'I thought his eyes were going to pop out when you started undressing as well. I bet he's got a few little extras waiting for us and all.'

'But we'll get the chance to sneak off there in the week, won't we?' Eleanor asked hopefully.

'Oh yes, we can always go and see Alf in the week,' Betty agreed.

They settled on the park in the end. They needed some fresh air. They went off arm in arm and sang on the way. Nobody gave them a second glance as they sauntered along, save for a grocer's boy who winked, but they ignored him like the grand old ladies they felt they were that afternoon.

The park wasn't far, yet it seemed a world away from the street they had left behind. There were other servants there, mostly young girls with push-chairs and babies, some of whom dozed under their shades while others wailed and cried and gave their guardians a pounding headache.

There were other people too, like the pair of sailors sitting on a bench laughing and joking, an artist with his easel, and a pair of wealthy-looking gentlemen chatting as they strode along. Eleanor and Betty sat down on a bench and began to tell each other silly stories about the people they saw. The sailors had started a mutiny and stolen their ship, the gentlemen walking so sedately were a pair of spies swapping secrets, and the harassed-looking young girl with the pram was selling bottles of warm beer out of it. They talked about life in service and how glad they were to have each other; they gossiped and joked. They barely noticed the two sailors strolling over to them until they were nearly at the girls' sides.

'Afternoon, ladies!' one of the men said cheerfully. 'Care for a drop of this stuff?'

He had a bottle of something tucked in his shirt, which he pulled out and offered to them. Eleanor was struck by the memory of Mr Bishop in the carriage.

'No, thank you,' she said firmly.

'Oh go on, then, just a drop,' Betty said, and took the bottle.

As it turned out the sailors were actually friendly and a little shy. Both of them were merchant seamen and they told the girls how they had sailed from Bristol to India and back again, with barely a night off the ship. They told their tales of strange ports and native people, of spices and cricket on the beach. Both were handsome men, tanned and fit. They were a little older than the girls but seemed somehow younger, less experienced in the ways of the world. Eleanor supposed that might have been due to being stuck on a ship half their lives.

Eleanor had grudgingly taken a sip of the drink offered and then, as it was her afternoon off, relented and drunk deeply from the bottle as the four of them sat laughing and joking.

After a while one of them put his arm tentatively around Betty's shoulder. She smiled at him and snuggled closer. The other man, a rather handsome dark-haired chap, smiled at Eleanor and then nervously looked at the ground.

'What's the matter?' Eleanor asked. 'Are you shy?'

He blushed a deep crimson and swallowed.

'You can put your arm around me if you like,' she offered. 'You can pretend I'm your sweetheart.'

So he did. And they cuddled up close and he told her stories, and after a while Betty got up and led her new friend away by the hand. She promised to be back soon and Eleanor watched her go up the path then vanish around a bend.

'She'll be fine,' Eleanor's man promised. 'He's a real gentleman, a decent sort.'

'I'm sure she will,' Eleanor agreed. 'Betty is no shrinking violet; it's him I'm worried about.'

That made him laugh and Eleanor joined in, feeling utterly at peace as the sun began to sink a little in the sky.

'And are you a gentleman too?' Eleanor asked. 'Only I've only met rough men, men who take and force.'

He looked at her with such surprise on his face that she knew at once he was a gentleman, in the true sense of the word. A proper gentle man.

'How long have you been on that ship?' she asked.

'Too long,' he moaned, then smiled.

'I'll give you something to think about on those long lonely nights at sea,' she whispered, then took his hand and led him towards the bushes.

She had not planned on anything happening, but she found herself wanting him. More than that she wanted to erase the memory of Tom's rough hands on her. He was gentle, timid and nervous. She remembered feeling the same way not so long ago, and would have liked to guide him away from such uncomfortable humility with gentle hands and the softest of mouths, but her passion was rising and the thought of doing it there, out in the open with just a small stand of trees between her and the walkers in the park, was exciting her. It made her realise just how much she had changed, and so quickly, since that journey by carriage to London. But she was glad she had changed – she wanted to know more about the world and the secret passions of people. It was terrible knowing so little all the time and being prey to such excruciating ignorance and diffidence.

Leaning against a tree, she raised the hem of her skirt until he could see the lace fringe of her drawers.

Immediately he smiled and his eyes grew wider.

'Take a good look, my pretty sailor boy,' she whispered. 'You'll be a long time at sea, so you put this picture of me in your mind like a favourite photograph of your sweetheart and I'll be sailing with you too, near or far.'

'I will, I am,' he whispered back.

She drew her skirt up until her drawers showed fully, then she slipped her hand inside them and gave a theatrical little sigh. He licked his lips and swallowed hard. She could see his cock pressing against his white uniform trousers now, and she beckoned him over. He came to her shyly, not sure if he dared, it seemed. She put her arms around his neck and kissed him gently and then more passionately. He didn't seem to know where to put his hands, so she showed him. She put them on her hips and pushed against him and then slipped her hand in his trousers. He gave a delighted, soft moan as she squeezed his rod and began to pull it towards her.

'I want you,' he whispered.

'Then you can have me,' Eleanor told him.

He slipped her underwear wide and then pulled down his trousers and opened his own undergarment, releasing his cock. Eleanor looked nervously around; from the path they looked like lovers embracing and kissing but their legs were bare and his cock, his magnificent cock, which had known nothing but his own hand, was about to be put inside her.

A couple of serving girls on their own day off passed and giggled, but once he was inside her he could not stop. The girls walked past once, then came back again. They peeked over the bushes and stood watching with shocked faces.

'They're looking at us!' he whispered as he pumped himself into her.

'Let them look, I bet they're just jealous,' Eleanor whispered back.

His bottom was firm and muscled, and when she wrapped her legs around it he lifted her as though she were light as a feather and held her against the tree – not in a rough way, but in a gentle supporting way that made her feel wanted but not forced. He came hard in her and it felt wonderful. She arched her back against the rough bark of the tree and came too, taking his virginity and forever sealing her face in his mind.

When Eleanor and her sailor came out of the bushes, straightening garments and nervously peering about, the girls flushed, pulling their hands from between each other's legs, then clapped and giggled before hurrying off.

Eleanor watched them bustle away and knew that if they were anything like her they'd have the memory in their minds forever, especially at night.

Betty came bounding down the path with her friend in tow; his uniform had leaves and a twig stuck to it. Eleanor giggled and pressed against her lover. He held her and kissed her.

'What have you two been up to?' Betty asked.

'Nothing at all,' Eleanor's sailor said for both of them, but Betty smirked and obviously knew it was a lie.

'Oh my! Look at the time!' Betty said suddenly, pointing at the clock tower in the middle of the park.

'We have to go!' Eleanor said. 'Sorry, we really do have to. You won't forget me, will you?'

'Never, not in a hundred years,' he promised.

'Then I wish you a safe voyage,' Eleanor said, and kissed him on the cheek.

With their brief farewells exchanged, Eleanor and Betty ran home as fast as they could, glancing behind them as they went to see the two sailors waving.

It was only much later, when they were discussing their encounter in great detail, that Eleanor realised she'd not even thought to ask the young man's name.

# Six

*In which the reader will be scandalised by the revelations*
*pertaining to love between two women, and the debauchery*
*of a gentlemen's establishment in the town of London.*

Eleanor heard the tinkling bell and had a horrible feeling that it meant Tom had mustered his strength and was ready to try to take her again. She was somewhat relieved to see that it was in fact Mrs Hampton calling, so she smoothed down her dress and hurried upstairs to the drawing-room. Mrs Hampton was sitting in her high-backed chair with a little table next to her. On it was a pad of paper, an inkwell and a pen.

'You rang, Mistress?' Eleanor said meekly.

'Where is Amelia?' Mrs Hampton asked. 'I was expecting Amelia.'

'Oh!' Eleanor replied. 'I think it is her morning off, Mrs Hampton.'

Mrs Hampton nodded. 'So it is, how foolish of me. I quite forgot I'd given her the morning off. Well, you shall have to help me. I'm not feeling at all well.'

'I'm so sorry to hear that,' Eleanor replied. 'Is there anything I can do for you, Mistress?'

Mrs Hampton told Eleanor that she was entirely out of sorts. She felt faint and needed a rest or she would collapse there and then. Eleanor quickly went to her and helped her up. She did look pale, very pale, in fact.

'Shall I take you to your room?' she asked.

'Well, I hardly think sleeping on the drawing-room floor is fitting, is it?' Mrs Hampton snapped.

'Oh no, Mistress, of course not,' Eleanor replied quickly.

Eleanor took Mrs Hampton up to her room, the one with the lovely pea-green ferns and four-poster bed. She glanced at the bed and felt a blush rising to her cheeks; she had not forgotten falling asleep on it, nor the penalty she had paid that day. In fact her bottom had only just begun to stop feeling tender.

'Help me out of these clothes,' Mrs Hampton demanded.

Eleanor went to her mistress and, from behind, began to undo her long flowing dress. It was a heavy thing, and Eleanor couldn't imagine being trapped in such a huge garment. She undid the ties and loosened it, and Mrs Hampton gave a little sigh of pleasure as Eleanor opened it at her back.

'Is that better, Mistress?' she asked.

'A great deal better, thank you,' Mrs Hampton declared. 'I feel like a woman in an iron maiden sometimes.'

Eleanor had no idea what an iron maiden might be, but guessed it wasn't anything comfortable. She pulled the dress down over Mrs Hampton's arms and then knelt behind her and pulled the central part from the hem upwards, until it was off. Mrs Hampton stood in front of Eleanor in her corset and under-wear, so slim and yet so womanly that Eleanor found herself staring for a moment before she remembered her manners and carefully hung the dress up. Mrs Hampton was wearing stockings, beautiful silk ones that fastened with ribbon at the knees. Eleanor didn't know what to do next, and it seemed impolite to carry on without instructions.

'Undo this corset for me, dear,' Mrs Hampton ordered.

The corset was a work of art, so beautiful that Eleanor thought it a shame that it had to be hidden away under a dress all day. It was made of red silk edged with lace, and both pushed her mistress's breasts together and held them up a little. The lace began at the smooth elegant curves under her breasts, and Eleanor felt her hands shaking as she reached for them. Mrs Hampton stood watching her impassively, but smiled as Eleanor reached for the cord and began struggling with the knot.

'You aren't used to doing this, are you?' Mrs Hampton remarked.

'No, Mistress, sorry,' Eleanor blurted out. 'It's very pretty, though. It suits you very much if you don't mind me saying so.'

Mrs Hampton smiled, and the expression made her look like a different person altogether. A little of the spark of youthful fun returned to her face, pushing away the gloom that normally clouded it. Eleanor undid the tie at the front and then hurried around to Mrs Hampton's back and began to unlace the corset. Mrs Hampton was not a large woman, but the corset forced her into a shape that made her seem taller. With the laces loose, Eleanor put her hands around Mrs Hampton's middle and carefully removed the corset. Mrs Hampton had beautiful shoulders, Eleanor noticed, so slender and white and finely boned. In the warm sun that slipped in through the blinds they looked divine.

Eleanor watched as her employer turned around, and again there was that unfamiliar smile. Mrs Hampton was blessed with fine breasts; they were not large but they were firm and high and her nipples were dark and tight. Eleanor couldn't help but look. They were nothing like her own, but they were a mature woman's breasts and gorgeous to look at.

Mrs Hampton caught Eleanor looking and slapped her face, not hard but enough to make Eleanor cry out with shock.

'What are you looking at, girl?' Mrs Hampton demanded. 'Don't stare at me!'

'I'm so sorry. I wasn't, I mean, I was but I didn't mean to!' Eleanor answered.

'Is there something wrong with me? Is that why you're staring at me?' Mrs Hampton asked.

She was the only woman Eleanor could imagine who could possibly remain fearsome and dignified while standing in just her drawers and stockings, to say nothing of the way her naked breasts jiggled as she put her hands on her hips and glared at her maid.

'No, Mistress! I was just thinking. Oh Mistress, I am sorry. If I say any more I'll be in worse trouble. Please forgive me,' Eleanor said in a rush of words.

'I asked you a question, girl!' Mrs Hampton retorted. 'Answer me.'

'They are so perfect,' Eleanor said, blushing hot. 'Begging your pardon, Mistress.'

Mrs Hampton laughed. 'My breasts? Is that what you mean?'

'Yes,' Eleanor said shyly. 'I am sorry. I did not mean to stare.'

Mrs Hampton took Eleanor's hands gently and placed them on her breasts. They felt warm and soft, and Mrs Hampton's nipples grew hard as soon as Eleanor touched her. She looked at Mrs Hampton for a moment in surprise and then, seeing that she was being invited to do so, ran her hands over her mistress's nipples. Mrs Hampton shivered and closed her eyes for a moment.

'Feel them, girl,' she instructed. 'Squeeze them in your hands.'

Eleanor was very nervous, but also curious. She closed her hands over Mrs Hampton's breasts and began to explore them. They were beautifully shaped, so perfectly rounded, and she took a nipple between her forefinger and index finger, rubbing it gently until it grew hard. Eleanor's heart was beating fast.

'Good girl,' Mrs Hampton whispered. 'Now suck them.'

Eleanor was a little shocked, as she had not for one moment expected to be invited to put her mouth to her mistress's nipples, but she did so without hesitation, kissing one stiff bud and taking it between her lips. She looked up and, seeing Mrs Hampton's face awash with pleasure, began to suck, pulling the dark nipple into her mouth and tugging at it with her tongue. Mrs Hampton put her hands on Eleanor's shoulders and drew her closer. Eleanor felt her own nipples harden under her uniform. She licked under Mrs Hampton's nipple and ran her tongue around it, to make her mistress moan with excitement. At length Mrs Hampton drew away, her eyes no longer hard and cruel. Now that she was smiling they seemed warm and sensual.

'Come along, Eleanor,' she said. 'Don't leave me half dressed.'

Eleanor knelt down to unfasten Mrs Hampton's garters, which she took off carefully and put aside. Mrs Hampton's stockings were tight, and stayed up even without the garters, and Eleanor stopped before her mistress, feeling clumsy and not sure what to remove next.

'Slip these off, dear,' Mrs Hampton instructed, taking a pinch of her drawers. 'I think I'll keep my stockings on a little longer.'

Eleanor reached for the beautifully embroidered drawers and undid the buttons with trembling fingers. Mrs Hampton was watching her intently, apparently savouring the anticipation of going bare as her drawers were unfastened. With the buttons open, Eleanor began to ease the drawers down, and as she did so she slid down to her knees so that her mouth was near Mrs Hampton's bush. Her mistress had a beautiful flat stomach and her legs were gorgeous, stunningly complemented by the pale stockings that covered them. Her pubic hair was as raven-black as the hair on her head, if a little bushier, and Eleanor could see the wetness there already.

Eleanor didn't need to be told what to do next; she could sense Mrs Hampton's need, and her own desperate urge to lick overtook her. She let her mouth glide to Mrs Hampton's inner thigh and kissed her there. Mrs Hampton gave a little cry of pleasure and hugged Eleanor to her crotch, prompting Eleanor to kiss her again, with tender, cautious touches against the inner thighs at first, then with more abandon until she was licking and slurping at Mrs Hampton's crotch. The swell of Mrs Hampton's mons was pressed against Eleanor's open, eager young mouth as she licked. The scent of arousal was thick and feminine, and Eleanor found it irresistible. She clung tightly to her mistress as she licked, allowing her tongue to explore every fold and crevice, to tease the swollen lips and flick at the tiny bud between them.

Mrs Hampton was moaning now, holding Eleanor's head firmly in place and spreading her legs wide so that her maid could see where she was wanted. She took a firmer grip of Eleanor's hair and forced her mouth against her most private place. Drunk with passion, Eleanor pushed her tongue as deep as it would go, lapping at her mistress's hole before turning her attention to the tiny bud she knew would give her the ultimate pleasure. As she sucked her mistress's nub hard into her mouth, Mrs Hampton threw back her head and gave a joyful cry, coming under Eleanor's urgent tongue.

Eleanor kept her face where it was, still licking even when her hair had been released, and enjoying not only the feel and taste of her mistress's sex, but the texture of silk stockings in the palms of her hands and the knowledge that she had given her mistress so much pleasure. At last Mrs Hampton took Eleanor's head in her hands again, gently now, drew her up to her feet and began to kiss her, tenderly and deeply.

Their tongues slid into each other's mouths and Eleanor felt as if she were melting. Mrs Hampton led her to the bed and lay down, parting her legs and beckoning to her maid. Eleanor hastily slipped her dress off, then stepped out of her other clothes. She wanted to be naked. She wanted her bare skin against Mrs Hampton's, and she desperately wanted her own body licked and touched.

Mrs Hampton did not disappoint her. She watched Eleanor undress, and while she did so she put one hand between her legs and stroked herself, while squeezing her breasts with her other hand. Eleanor could not look away, so distracted she had trouble taking the last of her clothes off. Mrs Hampton lay naked except for a small string of pearls around her neck and those beautiful pale stockings, which hugged her legs and gave her already wonderful curves extra definition. When Eleanor was naked she went to her mistress, sliding on to the bed next to her and running her hands up Mrs Hampton's legs, from her calves to her thighs. Mrs Hampton reached out for her and drew her closer. She kissed Eleanor's shoulder and neck, then slid a hand down her back, making her tingle and shiver.

'You are so pretty, Eleanor,' Mrs Hampton said. 'Such a pretty thing.'

'And you are wonderful,' Eleanor whispered back.

She thought Mrs Hampton might laugh at her for being so clumsy and inarticulate with lust but her mistress just smiled.

'I want you,' Mrs Hampton told her. 'Come on top of me.'

Eleanor climbed on to her mistress, her knees either side of Mrs Hampton's hips and her legs wide open. She closed her eyes as Mrs Hampton began to trail her hand down her maid's front, beginning at her breasts, squeezing and gently lifting each one, stroking and pinching at her hard nipples, then sliding lower, feeling her slender waist and running her fingers over Eleanor's bottom. Then she ran her hand over Eleanor's hips, her elegant nails tickling her maid's sensitive skin as they went, moving ever lower towards the maid's shaved crotch. Eleanor could feel the proximity of her mistress's fingers, maddeningly close yet not touching her where she ached for attention. She wanted to thrust herself down, but her legs were as far apart as they could go, and Mrs Hampton had opened hers a little so that the maid could not move as she wished. Instead of touching her, Mrs Hampton leant forwards, kissed Eleanor on the mouth and sucked the maid's tongue between her lips, teasing its underside with the tip of her own.

'Touch me, Mistress, please!' Eleanor begged.

Mrs Hampton continued to tease her with a little kiss on the lips, and then pulled back, her eyes darting between Eleanor's legs before she began to kiss her again.

'Please don't tease me!' Eleanor pleaded. 'I need you. I need your hand down there.'

At last Mrs Hampton's index finger touched Eleanor's spread slit and found her labia, which made Eleanor's head drop and her legs shake. The slight pressure was enough to make her try to grind her hips down on the finger, but for every small movement she made Mrs Hampton moved her hand slightly away, until Eleanor was panting and moaning with frustration.

'Please, please touch me,' she begged, shocked at how desperate she sounded.

'As you wish,' Mrs Hampton responded, and slid her finger against Eleanor's clitoris.

Eleanor gave a little gasp, swore under her breath, then gave a long delighted moan as Mrs Hampton began to rub her sex, stroking it firmly and moving her finger in little circles, first clockwise and then anti-clockwise. Each change of direction made Eleanor jerk a little and she bit her lip to stop herself screaming with pleasure. Her bare pussy felt so wet, she could feel her juice running down Mrs Hampton's finger. But she didn't care, not one bit.

Mrs Hampton withdrew her finger for a moment and slipped it into her own mouth, sucking Eleanor's wetness from its length. Eleanor gave a groan of disappointment as the finger was removed, but it was quickly replaced by her mistress's entire hand, which now pressed firmly to her sex. Again Mrs Hampton began to rub, clearly enjoying the sensation of her young maid's shaved flesh and helpless pleasure.

In just moments Eleanor found her muscles twitching and her bottom tightening at each stroke of her mistress's hand. She began to orgasm, and as she did so Mrs Hampton held her hand firmly in place so that Eleanor could rock against it and control her own pleasure. It was a thrilling feeling, the stillness of Mrs Hampton's hand encouraging her to rock more fiercely, to force the orgasm out of herself, and it felt wonderful, coursing through her body and making her heart beat like a drum. The last few moments were the most intense of all, and she threw back her head and let the cry that had been so long pent-up inside her come free.

Mrs Hampton let Eleanor finish her orgasm, then pushed a finger deep inside her, penetrating her so suddenly that Eleanor gave a little gasp and then another muted cry of pleasure. Her mistress's finger went deeper than she had thought possible, seeming to probe and enter places Eleanor herself had never touched. For a moment it felt as though it would go all the way through her. She lay still, her legs trembling as Mrs Hampton felt inside her, and then, to her shock, she found Mrs Hampton touching her in a place that was even more intense than her clitoris.

Overcome by the sensation of having her mistress's finger so deep inside her, Eleanor found she could no longer rock or move at all. She was transfixed by the pleasurable sensation and soon felt a second orgasm coming. This time it originated somewhere deep within her. She made an inarticulate grunt and began to orgasm hard, so hard that her legs shook and she found herself kneeling up in ecstasy, which gave Mrs Hampton the angle to stroke inside her as deeply as she could. Eleanor was no longer able to control herself, coming so hard the wetness streaked down her thighs.

When the orgasm finally came to a wonderful, abrupt and heavy end, Eleanor slumped forwards to rain kisses on Mrs Hampton's face and neck. She felt her employer's wet hand pressed against her cheek and eagerly sucked her mistress's fingers inside her mouth to taste herself. Mrs Hampton watched Eleanor lick her fingers with lidded, wanton eyes. The intensity there almost frightened Eleanor. Mrs Hampton was so obviously fascinated by her new employee, and was clearly unable to resist stroking Eleanor's breasts as she eagerly sucked away at her mistress's fingers.

'Was that good?' she asked. Her voice had taken on a deeper tone, one thick with lust.

'Oh, so good, ma'am,' Eleanor said as Mrs Hampton withdrew her fingers.

Mrs Hampton kissed Eleanor again, at first tenderly, then with greater passion, and the two women, mistress and servant, were soon entwined on the bed once more.

That afternoon Eleanor and her mistress shared the intensity of passionate dreams and fantasies. Afterwards, Eleanor found she could think of nothing but Mrs Hampton and longed to see her again that day, even if it was just to receive a knowing look or the slightest of smiles, but as things turned out she didn't. Instead she was set the dull task of mopping the kitchen floor.

That wasn't so bad, though, she reasoned; it was mindless work and would allow her to slip easily into a dreamy reminiscence of what had happened earlier. Such reveries got her so hot that when she went outside to throw away the dirty water she gave a quick glance around and then squatted in the grass and played with herself. Her fingers went straight to her clitoris and worked fast, in case anyone should happen on her, and she wasted no time in having a hot, hard little orgasm, which left her guilty but relieved when she went back to cleaning the floor.

* * *

In the house above Eleanor, Tom withdrew from his window. He had been idly looking out at the yard when he'd spotted Eleanor coming out of the back door. His voyeurism was normally well planned and involved crawling through filthy old chimney runs, so to see her again sent a shiver of pleasure through his body, and to see her crouched below his window was a real treat. He had not been able to see much, sadly, but he had seen her hand working inside her underwear, and his prick had stiffened immediately. He was disappointed when she had picked up her little bucket and gone back inside.

But even though he had been denied a clear view of her fiddling little fingers, his imagination filled in the missing narrative, especially as he had first-hand experience to draw on when it came to Eleanor's private parts. He found he was desperately aroused, but when he twice reached for the bell that would summon someone from the kitchen, his hand uselessly fell away from it.

In the end he dressed himself in his smartest suit, went downstairs and told his mother that he'd be going out for the afternoon. He lied and said that he planned to go to the library to do some studying. Normally such a blatant lie would draw questions, for which he was amply prepared, but this time she had a faraway look in her eyes, and smiled and told him not to study too hard.

After leaving the house, Tom soon managed to flag down a hansom cab.

'Where to, sir?' the driver asked.

Tom told him to drive to the club. He had a yearning to be there this afternoon, and was pleased when the driver urged the horse to a good pace. Tom spent the journey thinking about Eleanor, wondering how best he could get her up to his room once more and how he should approach the matter of taking her again. He found the very idea of it gave him an erection so stiff it grew uncomfortable in his trousers.

When his father died the club had written to him offering their condolences. They had also suggested that the club might allow him to make use of his father's membership – to take over the reins, as it were. Tom had always assumed that a gentlemen's club was probably the most boring place in the world, and he had not replied. Then one day he had been nearby and in need of a brandy, so he had ventured inside. Walker, the genial doorman, had shown him to the bar, and then made it clear that the club offered other delights to the broadminded gentleman about town. It was those services he found himself urgently in need of.

Walker wasn't on the door that day. This was something of a let-down, as Walker was an absolutely capital fellow and blessed with the skill of guessing the nature of a gentleman's requirements on any given day. He could tell if a young man needed a drink, a quiet place with the newspaper to recover from a night's drinking, or what Tom needed today – a woman. There was always a woman available, and usually several to choose from. Instead of Walker an elderly man stood on the door, a respectable-looking sort. Tom greeted him and was pleased that the man knew who he was and showed him inside at once.

'What will be your pleasure today, sir?' he asked.

'A girl,' Tom replied simply. 'A pretty one.'

He was shown upstairs to an opulent chamber, where he sat on the bed and helped himself to a glass of port from a decanter. Tom was thinking of Eleanor, the maid who had treated him so firmly and with unexpected control. He felt slightly ashamed at the way he had let her do it – for surely he *had* let her do it? Had he chosen to resist he could have escaped easily, he a young gentleman and she a mere between-stairs maid.

Presently the door opened and a pretty little blonde woman came in. Her hair was the colour of new straw and she had bright-blue eyes. She was wearing nothing but a pale blue slip and boots with tall heels. When he beckoned her over she closed the door quietly and came to him.

'I am going to call you Eleanor,' he said.

She had probably been called just about everything in her time, from Aunt Bessie to Queen Victoria. She smiled and told him that was fine.

Tom then instructed her to raise her arms, and when she did so he slipped the little silky dress up and off her body. She stood before him with her hands on her hips, smiling at him.

'Do you like what you see?' she asked.

'I do,' Tom admitted.

She had tight breasts, quite large but beautifully firm. Her whole body looked fit and healthy and just as fine as could be. He admired her for a moment and then slipped his hand between her legs. She obligingly opened them and stood still while he groped her. The hair on her sex was almost as pale as that on her head, and shaved at the sides, leaving her lips mostly bare. He loved the sensation of her fur against the palms of his hands. After a while she began to moan softly, but her pleasure was of no consequence to him. He turned her around and ran his hands over her bottom, admiring her slender but womanly cheeks, as smooth and as finely muscled as the real Eleanor's.

'Bend over, Eleanor,' he told her.

\* \* \*

She knew exactly what was required and obeyed without hesitation. He stroked between her bottom cheeks and rubbed her anus with his fingertip. For a moment she expected to feel her anus roughly pushed open and explored, as some gentlemen are wont to do, but instead he slid his hand down to her vagina and slipped a finger inside her, all the way to the knuckle. It didn't matter how many times she felt a man push his finger in there; it always made her gasp a little with pleasure and surprise. He seemed to like that, and ran his finger in and out in hard little movements. She obliged him by backing up a little, holding her ankles firmly and rubbing herself against his open hand. At that he grunted with satisfaction and grabbed her firmly around the front with one hand as he struggled to undo his trousers with the other. She waited patiently. Not one to savour his pleasures, she thought to herself – this young man is keen as mustard.

Pulling his dick out, he took it in his hand and pushed it at her from behind. She was wet, not very wet, but enough, and she pushed back at him, encouraging him to penetrate her. He tried to slide his dick in her, but she could feel that it was curiously soft. Inwardly she groaned. Again he pushed it against her but it bent like a banana and wouldn't go in.

Clearly frustrated at his lack of stiffness, he told her to get up, turn around and then kneel in front of him. She did all of this willingly and took his cock in her mouth, but it wasn't enough. She'd had this happen before, and knew that the sensation of failure and his inability to get hard must be lingering like some dark shadow over him, as his cock still wouldn't come to erection.

'I never normally have this trouble,' he said uneasily.

She smiled up at him as she sucked, having heard it all before a hundred times. When it had first happened she had assumed she'd done something wrong, but now she didn't pay much attention. She tried a few of the tricks she'd learnt, but instead of making him harder it only seemed to make his cock shrivel in her mouth, until she had to hold it firmly between her lips to get any purchase on it at all. Determined to succeed, she began to roll his foreskin back and forth between her lips and to lick the head as it emerged, something she had found most men unable to resist. But still he failed to react. She stroked it in her hand as it went in and out of her mouth, but it sagged and flopped like a carrot that has been in the sun too long. At last he spoke up.

'You're doing it wrong. Eleanor would know how to do it properly.'

The girl took his cock out of her mouth and began to lick it, but she could tell his heart wasn't in it any more, and his cock had shrivelled completely. The only question was how to end this tricky encounter as gracefully as possible.

'Why don't you have a little rest?' she asked. 'Then we can try again.'

'You're no good at it, that's what the problem is,' he said.

She looked at him, doing her best to keep herself smiling politely.

'Perhaps sir has had a little too much excitement today?' she suggested.

'Perhaps madam doesn't know what she's doing,' he countered.

Her eyes flashed as she almost answered him back, but thought better of it.

'How about if I get on top of you?' she suggested.

'I don't think there's much point. You don't seem very good,' he replied haughtily.

She stood up, picked up her silky garment and slid it back on.

'Well, that's as you wish, sir,' she said with a shrug.

'Be off with you,' he ordered, tucking his penis back into his trousers, 'and don't come back till you know how to please a gentleman properly.'

Her cheeks had flushed a little but she was determined to stay calm. After all, it was a good place to work, and most of the men there left a generous tip. She would ask Walker to be sure not to put her with this young oik again, and all would be well.

'What are you waiting for?' the man asked angrily. 'Go on, get lost.'

'Aren't you forgetting something?' she snapped. 'I don't come for free, you know.'

He laughed and shook his head, lying back on the bed with his hands folded behind his head.

'You'll not get anything for that,' he sneered, 'not till you learn to do it properly.'

For a moment she hesitated and then, clearly to the man's surprise, she strode across to him and stood over him with her hands on her hips. She demanded to be paid, and told him that it wasn't her fault if he couldn't perform.

'I won't,' he said.

'Yes you will, you soft-cocked little ruffian,' she said angrily.

'What will you do if I don't?' he asked. 'Cry and beg me?'

She was furious now, and grabbed him by the lapels then dragged him up so that they were face to face.

'You pay me what I'm owed!' she yelled. 'Or I'll beat your backside black and blue, I will!'

'You wouldn't dare,' he goaded, but she could hear an uncertain tone in his voice.

'Wouldn't I?' she snarled. 'Well, maybe I wouldn't, or maybe it would be just what you need!'

She reached for the buttons of his fly, undid them and yanked his dick out. It was nearly hard.

'It isn't me that can't do it right,' she said hoarsely. 'It's you, you dirty little brat.'

She spat on his cock and he squirmed in her grip, but not for a moment did he try to push her away. Seeing his cock stiffen and his balls grow tight, she slapped his thigh, not hard but enough to make him give a little cry.

'Now get hard for me and put it in me!' she demanded.

The young man's cock was now as hard as it was going to get, and she didn't wait for him to fumble it into her opening, but climbed on instead and forced herself down on his shaft, pushing it all the way in.

'We better make this fast, hadn't we?' she jeered. 'Before you go all soft again. Think you can keep it hard for long enough?'

'Maybe,' the man replied, forcing a grin as she began to work her hips against him.

She wasn't in the least surprised when he began to come almost instantly, and nor was she taken aback as he continued to call her Eleanor and beg her to ride him harder as his spunk came out inside her body. Over her time as a working girl she had seen it all, and he was far from the only man who could only get a good hard-on with a fierce woman in control. Indeed, just two doors down she knew that a high-court judge of some reputation for ferocity himself would be meekly sucking his thumb, dressed as an infant, while one of her friends rocked him gently in her arms. And in another room further down the corridor her sister would be hard at work tying a rather rowdy young sailor to the bedspread and wiping lubricant between his trembling buttocks in preparation for a yet more subservient ordeal.

She'd seen it all, but that didn't mean she didn't still enjoy it. As Tom pumped the last of his juice into her she took over completely, rubbing herself on him until she had come once, bucking on his cock as the waves shook her body. She'd seen it all, but today was a rare treat and she hoped he'd be back. It was not an unpleasant thing to beat a gentleman and humiliate him. It could give a girl a special kind of thrill.

# Seven

*In which the gentle reader will be shocked by one servant's deception, and the particulars of another's shadowy past.*

Eleanor and Betty were watering the plants in the parlour when they heard heavy footsteps on the stairs at the rear of the house. They could hear Amelia talking and, judging by the tone of voice and the choice of stairs she had taken, it was clear she was talking to servants of some kind. They couldn't make out her words clearly but she was issuing instructions and they could hear mumbled agreement.

The parlour door opened and Amelia led in an elderly man in a bowler hat. He was wearing an old suit which might have once been black but had now begun to fade with age. It was worn and tatty, but had been patched up with all the skill he, or more likely his good lady wife, could manage. After him came a young man a little older than Eleanor. He was slim and blond and wore dirty overalls and a flat cap.

'This is Mr Goodberry,' Amelia announced, 'and his assistant. They are here to clean the chimney.'

Betty gave a polite little smile and a nod to each man. Mr Goodberry doffed his cap and gave his assistant a nudge as he pointed at the fireplace. The young man went back towards the rear of the house, quickly returning with a large sheet of tar-paper, which he began to set out beneath the fireplace.

'Do not distract them,' Amelia warned the girls. 'Mrs Hampton will be back in a few hours and I expect it to be finished by then.'

Mr Goodberry gave his assurances that they would be completed by then and asked if he might be shown the kitchen stove while his young assistant set about cleaning the parlour chimney. Eleanor was told to assist before Amelia went her own way, leaving Betty alone with the young man.

Betty looked him over as he knelt down unpacking the sheets which would save the expensive carpet from ashes and dust. He had a nice bottom, a firm small one, and though he was slim and boyish he had a compact body that spoke of good exercise. His hair was milky blond, which Betty found rather attractive. She had the feeling she knew him from somewhere, but decided he might have been to the house before, a long time ago, and turned back to her watering.

She was aware of his gaze on her as she stood on tiptoes to water the aspidistra. Betty normally liked to be looked at; she found the admiring glances she drew when she was walking down the street exciting. It was sometimes nice to see the hungry eyes of young men and even respectable gentlemen devouring her plump little body. But the assistant's look wasn't wishful desire, it was sly and unpleasant. Betty ignored him and began to gather up the watering cans.

'My name is Mark,' he said, still leering at her.

'Pleased to meet you, I'm sure,' she said automatically and made for the door.

'What's yours?' he asked.

'Mind your own business,' she said and went to push past him.

'Betty, isn't it?' he said, and she stopped.

There was definitely something familiar about him. She hesitated and looked at him leaning on his broom.

'It might be,' she said reluctantly.

'You was a lot friendlier last time I saw you, Betty, a lot friendlier.'

'And when might that have been?' she asked, but deep down she already knew.

'When you was on the street corner up at Whitechapel, selling your tuppence for not much more'n that,' he said, and struck by his own wit he chuckled.

'Those days are gone long ago,' she said, and made for the door, but he blocked her exit.

'Good-time Betty, that was your name,' he said. 'Out in the street near the Yellow Moon inn, weren't it? I remember you well. My friend had you up against the wall down that alleyway between, what was it – the chop-house and the Yellow Moon. Said you was a right little bargain and all.'

'It wasn't the Yellow Moon,' Betty snapped. 'It was the King's Head. The Yellow Moon burnt down months before I was there. And as for your friend, he can keep his happy memories to hisself, and I'll keep mine.'

He grinned and seemed to be considering it but Betty knew that he was about to demand sex.

'Think I'd like a reminder of what I missed out on,' he said, and put aside his broom.

'Them days are long gone. Like I said, I moved on. I don't sell myself no more.'

'Is that right?' he said slyly, and gave her a doubtful look. 'You get a reference off that old fella with a cork leg what sold you?'

Betty glared at him. 'No.'

'No, bet you didn't, bet you told her ladyship that you was a good little maid, bet you lied your way into the job, didn't you, Betty?'

'You don't understand,' Betty said, determined not to cry. 'I had to get out of it. I only did it a couple of times, because I had no choice. I had no money.'

'Some girls like to be sold,' he said pitilessly. 'That's all they's good for, ain't that right, Betty?'

'Shut up,' Betty said, and made for the door again, but he stepped in front of her, still talking.

'Now you get to sell yourself to me, and the price is nothing. Nothing at all, and if you want to keep your secret then you'll do as I say and on your day off you'll be round regular as the sun with some money for me. Some money and that thing what you sold on the streets.'

'Never,' Betty vowed. 'I'd go to the peelers before I'd do that.'

'And tell 'em what?' he demanded. 'That you don't sell yourself no more and the chimney sweep is after a cut of your wages? I don't think you'd do that; even if they didn't chuck you back out in the gutter, they'd be round here asking questions. Questions what would make Mrs Hampton look awful bad, make her feel stupid for hiring a little whore like you, questions what would see you slung out the back door and back into the gutter where you belong, quick as you like. Ain't that the truth?'

Betty felt like crying, but could do nothing but stare at the floor as if her own ruin were already laid out down there in vivid pictures. Satisfied that the deal was done the sweep cocked his head and listened. Downstairs Mr Goodberry could be heard faintly, talking to the cook.

'I'll expect you later then, Betty,' he said, fishing around in his grubby overalls for a card, which he gave to her.

She looked at it, wanting to tear it up in front of him, but she didn't dare. Instead she put it in her apron pocket.

'Be there at nine tonight,' he told her. 'Bring a pound, which is what I'll be wanting each month, and nothing need be said.'

'A pound?' she said, shocked. 'But I only earn thirteen a year!'

That was a lie. She really made fourteen, but she hoped he'd relent a little.

'A pound is fair,' he said. 'That's what you'll bring, but if you want to earn a little extra I know some lads what would like to remind you of the good times. Maybe there's things around here what your good lady won't miss either. I can help you with that an' all.'

Betty left him, crying as she went. He watched her go and then, with a wicked grin, closed the door after her and set about checking the chimney. His mind was racing with the possibilities the chance encounter had opened up. He had always dreamed of a woman at his beck and call, and he could see great possibilities for a girl like Betty to earn him a lot more than the pittance Mr Goodberry could afford.

Mr Goodberry was at work in the kitchen, and for a moment Betty considered tapping him on the shoulder and telling him what a vile man his assistant was, but that was tantamount to telling Mrs Hampton herself. Instead she went out through the back door and sat on the little step overlooking the washing yard, sobbing miserably. Presently Eleanor appeared, carrying a basket of clothes for the line.

'Betty, whatever is the matter?' Eleanor asked, putting the basket down.

'It's that young man upstairs,' Betty said, choking back her tears. 'He wants me to go to him tonight and do things, or he'll tell Mrs Hampton what I used to do.'

Eleanor looked at her friend with puzzlement. She clearly had no idea what Betty was talking about.

'Tell me,' she said.

'I can't,' Betty replied through her sobs. 'It's too awful.'

'Nothing's awful when you share it, Betty,' Eleanor urged, 'and you've been good to me since I walked through the door. You know I'll help you.'

'But it's so shameful,' Betty moaned.

'Come now, Betty,' Eleanor said. 'Aren't I the girl who you finger and lick till I'm near biting the pillow each night?'

Betty smiled and laughed despite herself.

'So tell me; you know I'm your friend,' Eleanor said.

So with reluctance Betty told Eleanor about the dark times down in Whitechapel and what she'd done to afford a meal and a roof over her head in the little room by the stable with the door that didn't lock and the roof which leaked. Eleanor sat and listened without saying a word. When Betty got to the part about the chimney sweep Eleanor looked at first shocked and then angry.

'Leave it to me, Betty,' Eleanor promised. 'I'll fix him.'

'Oh, Eleanor, it's all over, I'll be gone tonight,' Betty cried.

'You're not going anywhere, my dear,' Eleanor promised. 'I said I'll fix him and I will.'

Young Mark the chimney sweep was halfway up the parlour chimney when he heard the door open. He hoped it would be Betty back to sob and beg him to lower the amount he was blackmailing from her. He would argue a little, he decided, and then he'd finally let her barter him down slightly, but there would be other costs. He grinned in the blackness of the chimney. Oh yes, there would always be something else for Betty to pay.

'Young man!' a voice rang out. 'How much longer are you going to be up there? And you're making the very devil of a mess!'

He gave a start. The woman's voice wasn't Betty's. There was no cockney twang to it, and it had a hard, respectable edge.

'Begging your pardon, miss,' he replied, his voice muffled inside the chimney. 'I won't be long, but it's very dirty, needs more than a once-a-year clean if truth be told.'

'Don't tell me how often I need to have my chimney cleaned, you impudent young man!' the voice answered. 'And there's ash all over my carpet. Why isn't this sheet weighed down properly? Come down from there this instant!'

Mark hesitated. He was so far up the chimney that only his feet showed in the fireplace. He didn't want to climb back down but after a moment he saw he had no choice, and began to inch back the way he had come. The lower half of him appeared in the fireplace, but his top half was still inside the chimney. He began to turn around but the fireplace was narrow, and he realised he'd have to crawl out backwards.

'Sorry, my lady,' he said. 'I'll see to it right now.'

Something hard touched his bottom and he gave a little start. In the darkness he bumped his head against the stone wall and cursed under his breath. Whatever was against his bottom pressed hard between his buttocks. He froze.

'You stay where you are, young man,' the woman said, 'or I'll ram this poker right up your pert little backside.'

Mark gasped, unable to believe a lady would speak so coarsely. The poker eased off a little and he felt her hand snake around his waist and up to the buttons of his overalls.

'What are you doing?' he asked, feeling absurdly stuck and helpless.

She unbuttoned his overalls at the neck and quickly worked down from there. The poker was never far from his anus, and with his arms still up the chimney he found he could not stop her without freeing them, and that couldn't be done without backing into the poker. The overalls were held up by two straps which went over his shoulders. She fumbled in the dark and found them, then they were unhooked and to his shame his overalls fell down and were tugged smartly around his ankles.

The woman withdrew a little and swung the poker from side to side, bashing the insides of his thighs so that he was forced to open his legs a little wider. His underwear was tight and clung to his bottom cheeks, and his balls could be seen inside quite clearly. The poker pressed against them and he began to tremble. He had a horrible fearful moment where he felt sure the heavy metal poker would be brought up sharply to hit them, but it wasn't. Instead he felt it withdraw a little, and then it was discarded on the floor with a noisy clatter. He began to back out of the fireplace but when his bottom was sticking out a little more she stopped him by grabbing his underwear and hoisting it up by the seat. The pressure on his balls made him stop short.

'I'll clear it up!' he wailed inside the fireplace. 'Sorry, miss. I'll clean it right up. You'll never know it had been there!'

114

Her hands stayed on his underwear, but she had begun to unbutton them, and this time they were tugged down, not up, all the way to his ankles.

'You just hold on to that chimney and stay where you are,' she ordered. 'Not a movement, mind, or you'll get that poker where it's darker than that chimney, young man.'

Mark gulped and waited, standing stock-still, fearful for his prick and balls, yet a little excited as well. He heard her fishing around in the brass pot full of tools that stood next to the fireplace. She took something out, leaving him in fear of what it might be, and what she intended to do with it.

He didn't have to wait long to find out. A brush with a hard wooden handle came down roughly on his backside. He cried out, and again at a second stroke, staring into the inky blackness of the chimney as he was smacked. She beat his backside hard, each stroke making him jerk bolt upright, so that dislodged soot and cinders trickled down on his face and into his hair. He was no stranger to the inside of a fireplace, but standing in one with his pecker out and having his backside beaten was something rather different. She didn't stop with his bottom either, but took the brush to the backs of his legs and even his calves. When she finally stopped, she pressed the brush firmly against his backside, the wood cold and hard against his scrotum.

'Please, miss, I'll clean it up!' he moaned, not sure what else he could say.

He was blushing and shaking inside the chimney, and wondering why he had been punished so severely and in such a peculiar manner.

'You are a bad, rude young man,' she said, ignoring his promise.

'Yes, miss,' he whimpered.

His bottom stung from the beating he had received and he still felt very vulnerable. She ran her hand between his bottom cheeks and grasped his balls firmly. He moaned, half in pleasure and half fear as she took his little plums firmly in her hand. Her grip tightened and she gave a little downward tug on them that made him gasp, and another, to leave them feeling swollen and heavy.

'You should know your place,' she said imperiously. 'Don't you think?'

'Yes, miss. You're hurting me, miss. Please let me pull up my overalls.'

'No,' she answered. 'You'll come out of there this instant. Come on, back out of there, and I'd do it slowly if I were you, or I might give you a squeeze you'll never forget.'

He did as she said, feeling absurd and scared and excited all at once as he backed out from the chimney. She held his balls firmly as he did so and put a hand on his back as he emerged, so that he had no choice but to shuffle out bent almost double. He nearly tripped over the fire-grate and she laughed at that, a high, joyful, spiteful laugh.

Mark had never felt so humiliated in his life, but the worst was yet to come. She let go of his balls and he immediately cupped them; they were heavy now, and a little sore.

'Turn around, young man,' she commanded as she discarded the brush and picked the poker up again.

He did so, his hand over his private parts.

She was a beautiful woman, dressed in modest black and wearing fine pearl earrings and a white ivory brooch. A widow's veil covered her face and her hair was tied up behind her head. Standing in front of her, he realised that he had never been so exposed in all his life, even in those dreadful days when he'd

116

had to share a bed with another chimney sweep who had made fun of the way his dick had stood up in the mornings. This was far worse.

She had the heavy poker in her hand and was tapping it against her palm as a bobby taps his truncheon on the beat. He made to drag up his underwear but she put the poker beneath his chin, leaving a greasy black mark as she lifted his head.

'What do you think you're doing?' she demanded.

'Pulling them up, miss?' he ventured.

'I'm not finished with you, you little rat,' she said fiercely. 'Now listen to me. Betty is a good girl, a decent honest girl who got caught up in something she didn't want to do. She did what she had to, that is all, and now you come along into my house with your brooms and your dirty fingernails and think you can force her to pleasure you and to turn over her wages into the bargain? Is that what you think?'

There was no point lying, he knew that now. When he had first begun working for Mr Goodberry he had been a consummate liar, or at least he had thought so. But Mr Goodberry was apt to clamber up a chimney, sore joints or not, and check his work. Sometimes you just had to tell the truth and take your punishment.

'I didn't mean no harm, miss,' he said quietly, and it sounded false even to him.

The woman tossed away the poker and went to a high chair with beautiful stitching that depicted birds flying over a woodland scene.

'Come over here; come to me,' she commanded.

He reluctantly did so, keeping his hands over his dick and balls and shuffling with his overalls and underwear around his ankles.

'I'm going to teach you what happens to rude, blackmailing young men,' she declared. 'Be thankful

117

you're not being hauled down to the police station for what you've said to her. She's in tears down below stairs, crying because she thinks a little weasel like you is going to ruin her life.'

'I'm sorry, honest I am,' he moaned. 'I never meant no harm, honest.'

'Perhaps you'd like a spell in the jail?' she suggested. 'That's where you belong. They'd bend a pretty boy like you over in a moment. Would you like a hard cock up your backside from some rough sort?'

Mark shuddered. He had never heard a posh woman speak so bluntly, nor so coarsely. He went to her, standing with his hands over his parts while she looked him up and down. His skin was nearly hairless and he had rather feminine legs. There had been a time he'd been teased about them, and he felt very self-conscious.

'Bend over my knee,' she said.

For a moment he thought he had misheard her, but it seemed she was decided and there was little he could do to argue. He knelt over her knee and released his privates. She told him to grip the arms of the chair and he did so. For all his shame his dick felt wonderful pressed against her long dress, and though his balls ached they now throbbed with excitement too.

'You won't forget in a hurry.' She raised her hand and slapped him hard across the bottom, catching both cheeks at once. Mark tensed, and as he did so his cock contracted and then grew a little. He closed his eyes; he could not believe what was happening, and all over that silly little maid. She spanked him, not slowly and deliberately as she had done with the brush, but fast and hard. Each time her hand hit his buttocks he was pushed against her a little harder and his penis began to grow as it pressed against her leg.

118

By the tenth stroke his bottom was sore, and though he could not see it, he knew that it would have bright red hand marks across it.

At last she stopped to admire her work, tracing her fingers over the sore spots. Her hand then reached under him and found his penis, which was swollen now and as hard as one of his brooms. He flushed bright red as her fingers circled it and seemed to be measuring its girth. She withdrew her hand and hit him hard against the buttocks.

'You are in a state!' she declared.

'It was the rubbing,' he said fearfully. 'I didn't mean it to be like that, honest.'

'Stupid little bastard,' she said fiercely and gave him another hard slap.

His bottom was throbbing and tender and he began to cry a little.

'Get up,' she snapped. 'I won't have that – that obscene thing touching me a moment longer.'

He did so, climbing off her lap as carefully as he could, but as he got to his feet it rubbed against her dress, leaving a little wet streak. She saw it too.

'Disgusting,' she said. 'Look at yourself.'

He did so, not willingly but with deep shame. His dick stuck up, rock-hard, and the skin was tight and drawn back, so that the end stood out thick and purple. He had a long, thick dick, with a set of small balls that hung tightly underneath, and with it all showing he felt even more ashamed than the time his cousins, two crude teasing girls, had held him down and pulled it out when he'd awoken hard one morning. They'd touched it and teased him, squeezed it and fondled it. He'd wanted to love the experience but he'd hated it, because once they had touched it he knew he would be forever at their mercy and no longer the man of the house he pretended to be.

Afterwards, they had dressed him in a skirt to make him ashamed, and braided his soft blond hair and told him he was no man, because men were big and strong and not little sissies like him. He felt that shame and its strangely erotic sensations flood back as he looked down at his thick rod. She reached out and took it in her fingertips, lifting the head. He gave an involuntary moan and she laughed at him.

'You disgust me, but you amuse me also.'

'It was the rubbing, I didn't mean it to –'

'Be quiet!' she commanded. 'Empty it, right now, and I'll let you go.'

For a moment he stood staring at her in shock and then, understanding what she meant, he blushed furiously. He gingerly took it in his hand, as if he didn't know what to do with it. He couldn't look her in the eye but he felt her gaze on his cock as strongly as if she were still touching him, which made him tremble with both excitement and fear.

He began to tug, stroking his erection in his lightly closed fist. She watched with interest as he began to speed up his strokes, until he was hammering at himself with all his might. At that she giggled, a girlish sound that brought back shameful but wonderful memories. As he drew near to coming she slipped a hand under his balls and felt them.

'Such little things for such a heavy cock,' she mused.

He grunted and looked away in shame.

'I should have thought a big thing like that would have big fat heavy balls to go with it, but it seems not, doesn't it? Barely any hair either. Like a girl. So maybe there's not so much as a drop in those balls.'

The touch of her fingertips probing around his balls was the tipping point. He shot his load, a white splash of come that erupted from his cock and ran down his knuckles and over his fingers, save for a little that flew out further, striking her just below the breast. His heart was beating very hard as she laughed and drew her hand away from his balls.

'Oh my,' she said. 'Such a lot from such little balls.' And then she suddenly grabbed his hair, to pull his head closer to her angry face. He had to reach out and prop himself up by holding on to the arms of the chair.

'You've made a mess, young man,' she said. 'A worse one than the ashes you've trampled into the floor.'

'Sorry, miss,' was all he could muster.

'Clean it up,' she ordered. 'No, not with your hands, you idiot boy. They are in an even worse mess. Lick it up.'

He hesitated, but she had his hair tightly in her hand. She pulled his head down towards her, to bring his mouth to just below the breast, where the offending spot stained her dress. He began to lick, shamed and excited all at once as he tasted his own come, salty and still warm. She held his scruffy head in place until he had lapped up every last trace, the flavour of his spunk mixed with taste of the starch that had been applied to her dress and a residue of perfume, a day or two old but still strong on the fabric.

Still holding him, she undid her dress a little at the back and to his delight he saw she wore nothing underneath. She let a breast slip out and put his mouth to that too. 'You're just a big baby. Aye? Isn't this what you wanted? Mmm?'

He began to suck, slobbering inexpertly over her but guided by desire, squeezing himself between his legs as he mouthed on her nipple.

'That's it,' she muttered. 'You keep doing that, you little shit.'

121

She hitched up her dress and found her crotch. When he saw she wore no underwear he reached for her, but she slapped him away.

'You're going to learn how to be a good boy, aren't you?' she asked.

'Very!' he promised, drawing away from her tit for a moment.

'Good,' she replied, and she began to toy with herself, stroking between her legs in quick hard movements.

She didn't let him touch her, but she did let him watch. He saw her fingering herself, first along her slit and then deeper, with two fingers in her hole while he licked and flicked and pressed against her nipple with his tongue. She began to moan and rise from the chair, which he took to be his signal to touch her, but again she slapped his hands away. But she kept hold of his cock, hard once, more stroking it with her free hand as she toyed with herself. Then she was jerking and writhing in pleasure at the work her hand had done, and at the height of it she drew him tightly to her and filled his mouth with tit.

It was over in a moment – a sudden flash of pleasure, no more. To his disappointment she let go of his cock and pushed him away, leaving him looking at her in wide-eyed bewilderment, his erection still sticking up hard in front of her, ready for more.

'Get your clothes back on,' she commanded, 'and get back to work. I want this done fast.'

'Yes, miss,' he said, hastily pulling his overalls and underwear up.

'And you be sure never to speak to my Betty again,' she instructed.

'No, miss, never.'

She buttoned up her dress to the throat and rose from her chair, then strode out of the room, leaving him in shock. When the door was closed he quickly fastened his overalls and, mindful of her instructions to get to work quickly, cleaned the chimney out with more dedication than he had put into a job in quite some time.

The lady in the veil reached the master bedroom and collapsed on to the bed. She took off her veil and then the dress. When she had carefully returned each item to the wardrobe she slipped on her servant's uniform and went to tell Betty the good news, that her friend was free from blackmail and that she'd wager the chimney would be the cleanest it had ever been.

It was fortunate that Mrs Hampton was delayed a little longer than she had planned. When she returned she found Eleanor and Betty in high spirits, cheerfully polishing the mantel and standing shoulder to shoulder like the two oldest friends in the world. She even favoured them with a smile as she glided past on her way upstairs.

# Eight

*Wherein the lady of the house receives news of a sad
departure and Eleanor makes a decision.*

Amelia knocked softly on the door of the master
bedroom and crept quietly in. Mrs Hampton was
sitting at the side of her bed with a book in her hands,
but looked up and smiled as Amelia closed the door
behind her.

'You're late,' she declared, looking at the clock on
the mantelpiece.

'I'm sorry, Mistress,' Amelia replied. 'You know
how I hate being late.'

Mrs Hampton did indeed; Amelia was a punctual
person, but more than that she knew what happened
when she was late for her special appointments with
the lady of the house.

'Come over here and bend over my lap,' Mrs
Hampton commanded.

Ordinarily Amelia would have hurried over and
taken her spanking, but today she lingered near the
door. Mrs Hampton at first thought her maid was
playing that most exciting of games – the reluctant
submissive. Sometimes Amelia pretended she was not
going to be obedient and that she'd refuse, or
struggle. Mrs Hampton liked that very much; she
enjoyed forcing her maid over her knee and holding

124

her arm behind her back with one firm hand while hauling the girl's drawers apart with the other. Sometimes she even enjoyed restraining the girl on the bed and ordering her to pull her own underwear open. But today Amelia seemed distracted and tense, and there was something about her eyes that troubled Mrs Hampton.

'My dear,' she said. 'Whatever is the matter?'

Amelia came to her, knelt down and put her head on Mrs Hampton's lap. She gave a long sad sigh and for a moment didn't answer.

'Amelia!' Mrs Hampton exclaimed. 'Tell me, what is the matter with you?'

'A letter arrived this morning,' Amelia said sadly. 'It is terrible news.'

Mrs Hampton stroked her maid's hair lovingly and bent down to kiss her cheek.

'Tell me, Amelia, what can be so bad?' she asked.

'It is my father,' Amelia said. 'My mother wrote to me to say that he has finally run off with one of the little whores he had working for him behind the bar at the café. He has run away and will never come home and she is all alone, and she needs me to help her run the bar.'

Mrs Hampton gave a sigh and continued to stroke Amelia's hair.

'Shh, now, don't cry, Amelia. Perhaps if I was to send her some money, might that help?' she asked.

'Oh Mistress, thank you, but she needs my help,' Amelia said. 'I must go. I am so sorry. I do not want to leave you and I know I promised I would serve you all my life, but now I must go home. Please forgive me.'

'There is nothing to forgive,' Mrs Hampton said, and closed her eyes to think on this news. Eventually she spoke, while trying to keep the tremor from her voice. 'I will draw some funds from the bank to help you when you arrive back at home. Your duty is to her, and I do not hold your choice against you, but I shall miss you terribly. You know that, my dear. More than I can truly say.'

'And I will miss you terribly too, ma'am. This breaks my heart. It truly does.'

They embraced briefly, but before she could become engulfed in her tears Mrs Hampton sent Amelia away and instructed her to pack.

When Amelia had left the room, she rose from her chair and paced the floor with a hand to her forehead like a woman about to faint.

When she had heard the news her first impulse had been to take the girl, to possess her and use her with a greater passion than ever so that the beautiful young creature would never have been able to leave her. Yet she could not. The sadness of it dragged at her heart. But it was not just melancholy that afflicted her. She was also gripped with a fear that stemmed from her own implacable self-interest. Because she was a woman with needs, dark severe needs that not just any girl could meet. Experience had taught her this long ago.

And she would have to find a replacement. If she didn't her lust would eat her alive from the inside out, as it had done before she had discovered the joy of dominating younger women.

She sat down and knotted her fine white hands together. While she mourned the loss of Amelia the realisation slowly dawned upon her that maybe all was not lost after all.

Amelia sat on the back step outside the kitchen and dried her eyes. She had made a solemn vow to Mrs Hampton, and one which she had felt sure she could honour. More than that, she had wanted to honour it. Mrs Hampton had shown her a new way of life which excited her greatly. It was a life of submissiveness, of being a sexual toy, and it had been a journey she had taken to with much enthusiasm.

Just as she gave another heartfelt sigh and blotted her eyes, the back door opened and Eleanor came out, whistling cheerfully. She had a basket under her arm full of wet washing to be pegged out.

'Oh!' she said, 'Amelia, what are you doing out here? What is the matter? Are you crying?'

'Get on with your work,' Amelia snapped back. 'It does not concern you! And do not call me Amelia. If I've told you once I've told you a hundred times!'

'Sorry,' Eleanor said, and started down the path towards the washing line, but then hesitated, stopped, and put the basket down to go back.

'Whatever it is, perhaps talking about it would make it less bad?' Even though Eleanor said this cautiously, she could still surprise herself by how much and how quickly her confidence had grown here. There was something about this house that allowed her to blossom in ways she could never have imagined herself capable.

She didn't like Amelia very much, but she'd learnt that sometimes people were fierce because they were unhappy or unsatisfied, and she seemed to have acquired a skill at pleasing others whilst also pleasing herself. And this ladies' maid looked very unhappy indeed.

Amelia looked up, meaning to give a curt reply to the nosy little thing, but her emotions got the better of her when she saw the genuine sympathy in the girl's pretty eyes. It made her begin to sniff again, and then to weep, and before long she found herself telling

Eleanor about the letter and about the pact she had made with Mrs Hampton, the deep sexual pact which made her a toy for her mistress. She even admitted how pleasing it had been for her. Once she started it was as if she couldn't stop; she'd never confided in a single soul before. But this pretty little thing seemed to understand everything. And so she told her of the first time Mrs Hampton had bound her wrists to the bed and used her, of the toys and clothes which her mistress had introduced her to, things the new maid had probably never heard of and was unable to fully comprehend. But Amelia had to let it all out, as if she were saying goodbye to the whole life and her sadness with it.

'Oh, Amelia,' Eleanor said when the ladies' maid finally stopped and lifted a handkerchief to dab at her eyes. 'It sounds as if you were her slave, not her servant!'

'A willing slave,' Amelia replied. 'When you give yourself up so completely you feel free; you do not have to worry about what to do, because you are told. You do not have to think for yourself, because someone else is doing that for you. And when you are told what to do you know you are pleasing to her, because she has told you exactly what she wants.'

Eleanor sat and listened intently. She began to remember moments when she too had been made to do things, and when she had made others do things for her. She remembered Amelia, fierce and hot, forcing her to bend over to be spanked. She remembered being so humiliated when Amelia had shaved her that she had felt hot pinpricks of shame and excitement. She also remembered Tom, and the feel of his balls in her hand, and the chimney sweep over her knee with his hard cock pressed against her when she had dressed as Mrs Hampton.

She dared not admit those things to Amelia, especially her masquerade as their mistress. Yet she yearned to; she wanted to tell Amelia that she understood her feelings, from both sides. Being in charge was good, very exciting, but it was nothing compared to the heat she had felt when she herself was the object, the toy.

'Now I have to leave her,' Amelia went on, 'and I swore I never would. Who is going to replace me? That is what I want to know. My poor mistress; now she will have nobody, nobody to serve her as she needs.'

'Oh, poor Amelia,' Eleanor said. 'You must think of your own mother first, for I am sure that is what Mrs Hampton would want. I'm sure she will find someone, too.'

Amelia dried her eyes and smoothed back her hair. Loose strands of it had fallen over her eyes, giving her a fey girlish look that Eleanor thought ravishing. Now she could quite understand their mistress's obsession.

'She will never find someone as dedicated as me,' Amelia declared.

'I could do it,' Eleanor said quickly, and immediately regretted her words.

Outraged by the suggestion, Amelia glared at Eleanor.

'What makes you think you could do it for her?' Amelia demanded. 'It is not just about a quick fumble at night-time before bed, you silly girl. It is about giving yourself, completely and utterly, to someone. A person who can have you anyway and for as long as they want. It is about doing things you do not know you will like because that is what is commanded of you. You could not even begin to understand such a thing.'

Eleanor flushed and replied, 'You may think that, but I know Mrs Hampton likes me. Just the other day we played together when I was undressing her. She was soft and gentle, but I would not have minded how she was with me. You are not the only one who adores her.'

The words fell heavily on both of them. Eleanor could not believe what she had said, and it was only when the words were out that she realised how fully she meant them. Yes, she adored Mrs Hampton, wished she could spend more time with her, and if that meant that her backside was tanned pink or her slit stroked while she was tied down – oh, what a thought – then so be it. She lowered her eyes briefly as she thought of her own submission, then turned and glared at Amelia, challenging her to argue.

'What?' Amelia said. 'What is this you are telling me? She took you?'

Eleanor had expected to be challenged on an entirely different front, with Amelia denying that anybody else could possibly have such feelings for Mrs Hampton. It had not occurred to her that their illicit encounter would cause Amelia to grow so cross that her pretty plump cheeks would flush and her eyes would turn as hard as flint.

'When was this?' Amelia demanded.

Eleanor didn't reply. Amelia stood up and hauled Eleanor to her feet by the scruff of her neck.

'Tell me!' she demanded. 'I am her toy. I am her plaything. How did you tempt her away?'

'I didn't!' Eleanor protested. 'I was undressing her and she wanted me.'

Amelia had obviously heard enough. She dragged Eleanor by the collar of her uniform and spun her around to face the wall, then gave her a shove so that the maid could only stop herself hitting the wall by putting out her hands. Amelia then covered and encircled Eleanor's wrists with her own hands, to secure her against the wall.

'You are not worthy to touch her,' Amelia said. 'You are a dirty little slut, you and your wet little pussy. You made her do it!'

'No, I did not!' Eleanor protested. 'I want to please her, as you did.'

Amelia grabbed Eleanor's hair and pulled her head back so that the maid could feel hot breath against her ear lobe.

'You are not good enough!' Amelia snarled. 'You are too common.'

'Maybe I am not good enough as you see it,' Eleanor answered, 'but I will bet that when you have packed your bags it will be me she calls upstairs.'

At that, what few remaining threads restrained Amelia's temper all snapped at once. She seized Eleanor's dress in both hands and wrenched as hard as she could, to tear a seam and send a button spinning away to the ground.

'Get off me, you stupid bitch!' Eleanor snapped and, with all her strength, shoved Amelia away.

But Amelia was back on Eleanor in a heartbeat, pulling at her hair and jerking her from side to side. Eleanor slapped out in turn, her open hand catching Amelia hard against the cheek. Amelia let out a cry of anger and tugged Eleanor off balance and to the ground.

The rain had soaked the little yard and mud splattered over Eleanor's smart uniform and up her arms. She scooped up a wad of it and shoved it in Amelia's face. She then tried to struggle to her feet but Amelia clung on, turning her on to her side by pulling hard on her hair, then forcing her head down into the mud.

Climbing on to Eleanor's back as a rider sits on a horse, Amelia began to push Eleanor's face deeper into the mud, while taking one of Eleanor's wrists with her free hand and wrenching it up in a grip behind her back.

'Get off me!' Eleanor cried out, spitting mud from her lips.

She redoubled her efforts, but she was helpless, pinned down by the other girl's weight.

Amelia grabbed Eleanor's dress with both hands and began to beat her whole body against the muddy grass. The dress ripped open all the way down the back, the buttons, which had been straining at her initial onslaught, pinging off into the dirt. Eleanor squirmed under her, wriggling to make some room to fight back, and even though Amelia's large thighs were firmly locked around her middle, in her rage at the injustice being meted out she pushed back with all her might and managed to unbalance her tormentor, who slid sideways and removed her weight from Eleanor's back.

Then they were struggling wildly, their hands grappling and grabbing at each other, sometimes slapping, sometimes clawing, until Eleanor managed to gain a firm purchase on Amelia's dress. With a powerful yank she pulled the ladies' maid's dress asunder, ripping the cloth at the front. The slip underneath tore too, and one large rounded breast fell out.

Amelia gasped in shock and anger, before retaliating by snatching the front of Eleanor's dress and pulling as hard as she could too. It did not rip, but with the back of the garment fully open it came away, forcing Eleanor's arms together as it slid off. The lower half of the dress was still on, but on her top half the new maid wore only her chemise. Amelia forced

Eleanor's hands down on to the ground and rolled back on top of her. The ladies' maid's skirt had rucked all the way up to her hips and her lacy French drawers were dirty with mud and open, leaving both bottom cheeks bare.

'Little trollop!' she snapped. 'I'll murder you!'

Eleanor struggled to free her hands but could not, so she began to rock from side to side, trying to unbalance Amelia again. Amelia anticipated the tactic this time and laid her full weight against Eleanor's body. Her tit, exposed and dangling free, brushed Eleanor's cheek, giving the maid a sudden, wicked idea.

She nipped Amelia's nipple, just a quick sudden movement that caused the ladies' maid more surprise than pain. Amelia quickly hauled herself up into a kneeling position, pulling her breast away to protect it.

Letting go of Eleanor's wrists, Amelia made a desperate snatch at Eleanor's chemise. She gave it an almighty pull and the straps broke painfully against Eleanor's shoulders before it came away. Eleanor found her breasts exposed. Her nipples were hard and excited, making Amelia laugh, at which Eleanor lunged for the ladies' maid's hair, catching it and twisting hard. The move nearly unseated Amelia, but she regained her balance and snapped her hands over Eleanor's wrists, forcing her down on to her back again.

'You little tramp!' Amelia said with a hiss. 'You are nothing but a common slut!'

'At least I'd fetch a price!' Eleanor retorted.

Amelia bent down and put her mouth over Eleanor's right breast. The new maid struggled but Amelia had her nipple in her mouth and closed her teeth over it. It hurt, but the pain was nothing compared to the agony when Amelia pulled her head back and stretched the nipple from her breast – then it brought tears to her eyes and a long anguished moan from her soiled mouth.

Amelia sat back, triumphant.

'You can't change what will happen, you horrible little bitch!' Eleanor spat. 'You can bite my nipples till they turn purple, but when you leave I'm going to go to her, and offer myself in your place, and she will accept me!'

Amelia gave a cry of anger and reached out to grab Eleanor's tit, squeezing it hard, then struggled to her feet. Eleanor sat halfway up and wrapped her arms around Amelia's legs. She pulled and Amelia's feet slipped in the wet grass, to bring her crashing down on to her back. Eleanor quickly got to her knees and again they struggled, pulling hair and biting at each other's flesh.

Amelia's rage had reached its peak. She was sweating and red-faced, her normally immaculate hair wild, while her expression was positively feral. And through the almost inhuman strength that came with such anger, she managed to get Eleanor on to her back again, and at her mercy.

Eleanor was reminded of a picture she had seen of Joan of Arc standing at the head of an army. It was from a school book she had read years ago. Joan had looked absolutely ferocious, and had been wielding a broadsword large enough to chop a man in half. The connection made Eleanor laugh, despite the madness of the situation.

'What are you laughing at?' Amelia demanded.

One of Amelia's breasts swung freely about, and its soft partner was only half obscured by her tattered dress. If she was aware of it she no longer cared. She had her fists clenched and she was gritting her teeth.

'You, you stupid bitch,' Eleanor said breathlessly. 'I'm laughing at you, you with your tit hanging out and your skirt up around your middle.'

'Laugh all you want!' Amelia snapped. 'But she'll never be yours, not ever! Especially if I beat you till your face isn't pretty any more.'

'Is that what you want, then?' Eleanor said. 'You want her to be alone always? Want her upstairs so lonely that she cries herself to sleep? I bet that's what she did before you came along, back when Mr Hampton was off on his journeys, putting his thing in strangers.'

'What do you know about that?' Amelia demanded. 'You don't know anything, you stupid fool.'

'I know that she needs someone!' Eleanor shouted. 'Can't you see that too? Don't you think it's cruel to leave her and deny her someone who would really care for her, really do all she could to replace you? Are you that stupid and selfish?'

'You couldn't do it,' Amelia answered. 'You wouldn't be able to do it, not the way I did it, because you're just a stupid country girl.'

'Maybe,' Eleanor said, 'but which would be better – me, who wants to do it, or a stranger who only does it for money?'

Chest heaving and hair stuck to her muddied cheeks, Amelia looked down on Eleanor. Disgust and anger still clung to her face, but she had worn herself out.

'So give me a chance,' Eleanor said. 'It would be for the best. You know I'll look after her. Train me, teach me how to please her.'

The expression on Amelia's face grew more severe, and Eleanor prepared herself for a blow. But it never fell. Instead, Amelia clambered to her feet and stumbled away from the mire they'd been rolling through. Panting, she turned to face Eleanor. 'Come here, then. And let's see how you like being used. We'll see if you are worthy. Get up.'

Eleanor climbed to her feet and stood with her hands at her sides. She now wore nothing but her soiled drawers.

Amelia clicked her fingers and pointed at the earth before her.

Eleanor moved closer and, for a moment, feared she would be wrestled to the ground again, but Amelia evidently had other ideas. Instead, the ladies' maid held her arm and led her down the garden.

'Let me get my dress, Amelia!' Eleanor said. 'I'm nearly naked!'

'If you want to serve her, to really serve her, that is how you will be for most of the time,' Amelia said. 'Or have you had enough already?'

Eleanor pulled herself free from Amelia's grasp, tugged the mud-splattered drawers off her hips and down to her ankles, and then stepped away, naked. It was only mid-afternoon, and though the garden was walled other houses still overlooked them, but Eleanor didn't care. Amelia grinned and nodded, as Joan of Arc might have acknowledged a worthy foe, Eleanor thought. She smiled back.

Amelia led Eleanor over to the washing line and told her to put her hands on it. Eleanor hesitated for a moment and then did as she was told. Amelia took a pair of stockings from the end of the line and tied Eleanor's wrists to the line with them. With Eleanor firmly secured to the washing line, Amelia took a moment to tuck her breast back inside the remains of her dress before taking up position behind the helpless maid.

'Stick your bottom out,' she ordered. 'Open your legs.'

Eleanor did as she was told, and hung her head to look at the ground in an effort to overcome the terrible shame and sense of sin mingling with her feelings of arousal. Amelia walked away, and for a moment Eleanor feared she would be left there, naked and hanging from the washing line.

She need not have worried. Amelia returned with the carpet-beater in her right hand. She must have found it outside the back door, where only an hour earlier Betty had used it to knock the dust from an old rug that lived in the parlour. Eleanor watched her approach and her bottom tensed in anticipation.

'You don't want the whole street hearing you cry out, do you?' Amelia asked.

'No,' Eleanor said quietly.

Any hope that the carpet-beater was just for show evaporated. She was to be beaten, and beaten hard enough to make her cry out.

'Speak properly, let that be the first rule,' Amelia said, running her hand down Eleanor's bare body.

'What should I say?' Eleanor asked.

'Mistress,' Amelia replied. 'You should address the one you serve as Mistress.'

'No, Mistress,' Eleanor said.

'Better,' Amelia announced. 'Now I intend to beat you, hard, but the moment you start screaming there will be people looking out of the windows. They'll look out first to see what is going on, and then they'll look because they want to watch. So you better keep your mouth shut.'

'I will, Mistress,' Eleanor promised.

'I doubt that very much,' Amelia replied, glancing around, then giving a little cluck of satisfaction. 'So I will have to take measures against your cheap little mouth.'

She walked a little way back towards the house, where she picked up Eleanor's muddy drawers.

Bundling the soiled garment into her hand, she came back and offered the soiled drawers to Eleanor's face.

'Smell them,' Amelia commanded.

Eleanor bent forwards, balancing as best she could while holding the line, to sniff at the drawers. She could smell mud and sweat, but also the pungent scent of her own arousal. Amelia gave a chuckle of amusement and pressed the drawers against her victim's nose and mouth. Eleanor struggled but was taken by the hair and held tight as the dirty material was pressed to her lips.

'Open your mouth,' Amelia commanded.

Eleanor reluctantly did so and Amelia at once held her by the jaw and forced a large fold of the drawers into her mouth, leaving the remainder hanging out. The taste of wet soil dominated over that of her own musky arousal, and so much of the material had been pushed into her mouth that she found herself gagging.

Amelia then retrieved an old pair of the cook's stockings on the line, took one and wrapped it twice around the makeshift gag before tying it off behind Eleanor's head.

'How do you like that?' Amelia demanded.

Eleanor tried to speak, but only managed to produce a muffled grunting.

'Say it properly!' Amelia snapped.

Again Eleanor tried, and again she could only make incoherent noises. Amelia laughed and stepped back, swishing the carpet-beater through the air, unseen but so close to Eleanor's backside the new maid could feel the air moving. Eleanor hung still, her hands and wrists firmly tied and her mouth gagged, wondering if anyone was looking out at her, and sure she would die of shame if they were. She resolved not to look and find out, closing her eyes and hoping that her submission would be enough to prove she was Amelia's rightful heir.

Amelia took her time getting ready, evidently savouring Eleanor's shameful pose. Then she slapped the carpet-beater down on Eleanor's raised buttocks, hard enough to make the girl give a muffled cry through her mouthful of soiled cotton. Again Amelia struck her with the carpet-beater, and again Eleanor cried out, this time jerking in pain as well, the blow leaving one leg trembling uncontrollably.

'Is that too much for you?' Amelia said, and laughed.

By way of proving that it wasn't Eleanor went up on tiptoes. The washing line sagged under her weight as she held herself trembling in anticipation of the next stroke. Amelia gave a grunt of annoyance and began to beat Eleanor's backside with furious blows, each one stinging madly but quickly superseded by the next, as the ladies' maid swung again and again. Eleanor nearly fell to her knees from the sheer force of the beating, and the washing line sagged as she slumped down, her shins brushing against the grass, but she forced herself up again, trying desperately to maintain her position as she was beaten.

When Amelia finally stopped, both of Eleanor's legs were trembling uncontrollably and her bottom looked very sore indeed. Amelia inspected the smacked flesh with interest, noting that the carpet-beater had left large red marks the size of saucers all over Eleanor's bottom. Amused, but still determined to break the maid, she changed the angle of the beater in her hand. Instead of bringing it down on Eleanor's buttocks she instead placed it under her spread legs and pressed it against the maid's shaved vagina. Eleanor gave a little whimper and half turned.

'Enough?' Amelia asked.

Eleanor couldn't reply with her mouth stuffed to capacity with the soiled knickers, but shook her head instead.

'Surely that is enough for you?' Amelia asked in astonishment.

But again Eleanor shook her head.

'I'm going to slap you between your legs unless you nod,' Amelia warned.

Eleanor mumbled something unintelligible but defiant. Amelia laughed. She had warned Eleanor, and now it was time to introduce her potential replacement to the sensation of a slap in her most sensitive place. It wasn't something Mrs Hampton usually did, but Amelia was still angry and determined to make Eleanor give in – anything else would feel like losing to the little brat of a girl.

Amelia lowered the carpet-beater a little, letting it play down Eleanor's thighs until it reached her knees. She noted with satisfaction that Eleanor's legs were shaking harder than ever and that her bottom cheeks were clenched tightly together.

Eleanor was clearly not indifferent about what was to be done to her, for all her defiance. Amelia made a mock swipe, letting the beater stop just before her victim's lips, and the new maid flinched and grunted through her mouthful of muddy underwear.

'Stand still,' Amelia instructed.

The tremor in Eleanor's legs slowed down, and the expression on her face was terrified but determined.

The ladies' maid then struck Eleanor's bare vaginal lips with the beater, bringing it up in one sudden movement. She did not do it hard, just enough to make the other girl squeal and writhe on the line. A second smack and Eleanor's legs had begun to twitch and kick uncontrollably. After the third she could no

140

longer stand. Her lips stung furiously and all the strength had gone out of her legs.

She slumped down, her arms outstretched on the line, clearly unable to support herself, and trying vainly to press her thighs together to protect her sex.

Amelia stepped close, watching with no pity; all she felt was a sense of glorious revenge. Eventually she pulled the stockings off and tugged the drawers from Eleanor's mouth.

'Can't you even take a few gentle smacks?' Amelia taunted. 'You are weak, Eleanor. Far too weak, I fear, for Mrs Hampton. Time for you to give up. You have reached your limits, girl.'

Eleanor said nothing. Instead she struggled to her feet, and to Amelia's amazement she parted her legs and exposed her slit once again.

'What are you doing, you silly girl?' Amelia demanded.

'If you wish to beat me, then do so, Mistress,' Eleanor gasped.

'Don't be silly!' Amelia retorted. 'I am done with you, because you cannot accept the pain.'

'Then why am I hanging on the line with my legs open, Mistress?' Eleanor asked. 'I am weak, but if it is your wish to beat me I shall accept it as best I can.'

'But – but does it not hurt you too much?' Amelia asked.

The anger was gone from her voice, replaced by curiosity and wonder.

'Of course it does, Mistress,' Eleanor answered, 'but you are the one to decide when it stops. And maybe you should feel me.'

Amelia did just that. She put her hand on Eleanor's backside and the freshly beaten maid flinched at the touch. The skin felt hot and oddly thick, while welts were rising in a dozen places. She let her hand slide under Eleanor's rear, seeking out her lips. She felt the wetness at once. Eleanor was not just wet; she had come, and come very hard. The juice was welling up at the point where her lips parted, and as Amelia investigated deeper she found that Eleanor's opening was soaked. She dipped a finger in and Eleanor made a harsh hissing noise of gratification.

'I do not believe it,' she said.

'Well, Mistress?' Eleanor asked. 'Will you train me now? Teach me your ways? Give me a chance. You know I am worthy of her. Even if it makes you spit, you know it.'

Amelia untied Eleanor's wrists, and when she was finished she helped the naked girl to her feet and hugged her close. Yes, she would train her with what little time she had left. Eleanor was a worthy replacement, even though it was not Amelia's place to pick and choose. She would teach her all that she knew, but it was up to Mrs Hampton to make the choice. Perversely, her anger sated on the little maid, and now becoming respect, Amelia felt a strange sense of pride at having been asked to train her successor. She looked into the girl's dirty little face, gave a sigh of pleasure and kissed Eleanor deeply on the lips.

The two girls went inside, with Eleanor wrapped in a sheet, and ran quickly to Amelia's room. With surprising tenderness Amelia drew Eleanor over to the bed. When she was seated Amelia patted her knees encouragingly and Eleanor looked fearful, clearly worried she would be beaten again. She did not hesitate, though, but lay over Amelia's knees and obediently opened her legs on instruction. But Amelia didn't want to beat her, and found instead a jar of ointment, which she dabbed smoothly and gently against Eleanor's bruised bottom.

\* \* \*

Eleanor lay there for an hour or so, being soothed and listening to Amelia talk of the services she provided for Mrs Hampton. And as she listened, Eleanor did not protest when the older girl slipped her fingers inside her, nor when she was gently guided to her knees in front of Amelia, the girl who had beaten her and made her wear her own knickers in her mouth.

# Nine

*In which Mrs Hampton makes full and proper use
of her servants.*

Mrs Hampton woke up to a soft knocking on her
door. She opened her eyes and arched her back a
little, enjoying the warmth of the bed.

'Come in,' she called.

The door opened to reveal Amelia, a breakfast tray
carefully balanced in one hand. Behind her was
Eleanor. Both looked as pretty and innocent as could
be in their little black and white uniforms. Their hair
was neat and their legs looked divine in their smart
black stockings. Mrs Hampton smiled and sat up in
bed as Amelia directed Eleanor to plump up the
pillows behind her.

'Good morning, Mistress,' Amelia said. 'I hope
you slept well.'

'I did, thank you,' Mrs Hampton replied. 'Why
have you brought Eleanor with you this morning?
Have my servants not got enough work to do?'

Amelia smiled and put the tray on the bedside
table, then sat down on the bed. Eleanor stood at the
end of the bed with her face lowered.

'I must leave soon, my lady,' Amelia said sadly,
'and someone must replace me. Young Eleanor has
persuaded me that she is most eager to take my

position. If she is to do so, then with your permission I must show her how to attend you.'

Mrs Hampton responded with surprise. Even though Amelia was to leave her service she could not tolerate such boldness. Grabbing the girl's arm, she pulled her over the bed so that her little round bottom was sticking up in the air.

'Who are you to decide who does and does not serve me?' Mrs Hampton demanded.

'But Mistress, you know how much I adore you!' Amelia protested.

'Enough of that, you impudent girl. Pull up your dress and we shall see what happens to girls who put on airs above their station, shall we?'

Amelia had undertaken punishment on her bottom since the day she had arrived and clearly knew exactly what was expected of her. She reached behind herself and drew her skirt up to her waist, then folded her arms in front of her on the bed. Mrs Hampton nodded her approval.

'Eleanor,' Mrs Hampton commanded, 'open Amelia's drawers, fully.'

Eleanor gave a little start. She had been staring, evidently mesmerised by the sight of the fierce Amelia so easily brought to heel, but hastened to obey.

Mrs Hampton smiled to see Eleanor fumble at Amelia's underwear, her unsteady hands fiddling with the buttons, and then with a swift pull the drawers were open and down around the maid's thighs. When it was done Eleanor looked at Mrs Hampton, her dark eyes full of apprehension. Amelia was partly sprawled over her mistress's legs, and waited patiently for her next move.

'Fetch me the cane from my night stand, Eleanor,' Mrs Hampton ordered. 'I won't have such insolence under my own roof.'

Again Eleanor did as she was told, bringing the malacca rod to Mrs Hampton and offering it to her.

'No, I think you shall do it this time, though I'm sure you are partly to blame for this,' Mrs Hampton declared.

'Me?' Eleanor asked, clearly shocked at the suggestion.

'Yes,' Mrs Hampton continued. 'I am sure young Amelia has been quite strict with you, perhaps unfairly so. She is a fiery little madam at times, as I should know. It is I who have had to tame her, or at least try to curb her wilder instincts. Has she been strict with you?'

'Yes, Mistress, on many occasions,' Eleanor admitted.

'I do not doubt it,' Mrs Hampton replied.

'She took down my underwear and spanked me,' Eleanor admitted. 'She also shaved me bald in the most private place out of pure spite.'

Mrs Hampton smiled at that. She knew where Amelia had got the idea of shaving a girl as punishment from well enough, but said nothing.

'One must be careful not to tell tales, my dear. But you were right to be honest with me. Now give her six across her bottom,' she instructed. 'And an extra two each time she moves.'

Eleanor tightened her grip on the cane in her hand and gave it an experimental swish through the air. Mrs Hampton watched with approval as the new maid moved into position to punish Amelia. The cane came down hard, again and again, not pausing even as Amelia yelped and raised her leg a little at each stroke. After the fourth blow Eleanor paused. She touched her victim's red backside and smirked as Amelia shivered beneath her. The fifth she gave harder still, then the final stroke, a stinging fast strike that hit Amelia below the curve of her backside and caught her vagina, made her cry out and shoot forwards at the sudden pain.

'That was well delivered, Eleanor,' Mrs Hampton remarked with approval, 'and fully deserved, Amelia. The next time you come to me in the morning with suggestions above your station, or even the faintest trace of impertinence, you'll have your privates spanked until they turn red. Even on your last day. I'll make no exceptions. One must have standards. And that goes for you too, Eleanor. I simply won't stand for any nonsense under my own roof from headstrong and wilful girls.'

'Yes, Mistress,' Amelia whimpered, her fingers still clutching at the bedclothes, and Eleanor echoed the words.

Mrs Hampton signalled that Amelia should rise, pull up her drawers and pull down her skirt. Amelia did as she was told and gave Eleanor a sharp glance. Mrs Hampton noted the look on Amelia's face and realised with a shock that she had already accepted the fact of her departure. It was best she was leaving – the two maids would never be able to tolerate each other for long, and Mrs Hampton's allegiances were already shifting. Yet the effrontery of the offer still shocked her, and she decided to stand firm.

'She likes it,' she told Eleanor by way of explanation. 'That is why she likes to serve me, and that is also why she is suited to such a position and you are not. I appreciate the offer. It is brave of you if nothing else, but a replacement will be found from an agency. I quite look forward to seeking that girl out; perhaps one who has some experience of the darker human desires. Do you understand me, Eleanor?'

'Please, Mistress, I like it too,' Eleanor whispered.

'Nonsense,' Mrs Hampton remarked coldly. 'You know nothing of such things.'

'She does, Mistress,' Amelia said. 'Of that I may assure you.'

'Amelia, do you wish to be travelling home in such discomfort that you are obliged to remain standing for the entire journey?' Mrs Hampton demanded.

'No, Mistress,' Amelia said quickly, 'but it is my duty to tell you that Eleanor does like to serve you as I do. She wants to serve you very much. Show her, Eleanor.'

Mrs Hampton watched in astonishment as the new maid turned around, placed her legs apart and began to raise her dress. Underneath she wore no underwear, as was common with the poorest of the working classes, so that her bottom was left quite bare. Mrs Hampton could clearly see the marks of a severe spanking upon them.

'She asked for it, and wanted more,' Amelia announced.

'Pass me my orange juice, Amelia,' Mrs Hampton ordered. 'And as for you, my little thing, I suggest you pull down your dress and stop acting so foolishly. Any girl in the world can be bent over and spanked, and perhaps even like it, but you have not the faintest idea what I should need from my personal maid.'

Eleanor turned around to face her mistress, her skirt still lifted to her waist and her bald slit and bare thighs exposed, perfectly framed by her raised dress and black stockings.

'Perhaps my lady doesn't care to look at me. Is that it, Mistress?' she asked, her voice meek and yet steeled with impudence. 'Don't you like to see me like this?'

Mrs Hampton had just taken a sip from the orange juice handed to her by Amelia, and nearly spat it out in shock at the girl's tone.

'What has the world come to?' she demanded. 'There was a time when serving girls knew their place. They did not walk into their mistress's room before she had even had a chance for breakfast and start offering themselves to her. I have seen far too many young girls for one more to excite me to the point of making a rash decision such as this. Now be gone, the pair of you, or I shall get out of this bed and make you regret your impetuousness.'

'Not even when I do this?' Eleanor asked innocently.

Mrs Hampton was about to shout at the maid when she saw what Eleanor was doing. Her hand had reached down between her legs and she was idly pushing her labia from side to side, stroking her index finger against her clit and looking directly into Mrs Hampton's eyes.

'Good heavens,' Mrs Hampton declared, 'I have never seen such a wanton display in all my life.'

'I cannot help what I am, ma'am. And I'm very grateful to be in a place where my nature can be indulged and guided by my betters.'

Mrs Hampton narrowed her eyes, a sly smile creeping to the sides of her mouth. 'Very well. If you are determined to make a slut of yourself, do continue.'

All three could see that Eleanor's lips were starting to get very wet. Evidently determined to make a show of herself, she pushed a finger a little way inside her slick hole and then drew it out and tasted it. Mrs Hampton put down her glass and turned a little in her bed so she could watch the display on her side. Eleanor stood before her mistress, shamelessly stroking herself more and more firmly and deeper and deeper until the sound of her fingers working at her wetness were loud and the sucking sound each time

149

she withdrew her fingers quite obscene. When she parted her fingers and rubbed either side of her lips, pulling them open, she exposed her tiny pink clitoris. As one finger worked on the tiny bud she began to emit soft little cries that rose with her excitement. She let her head loll forwards and her hair fell in front of her face as she worked her fingers faster and faster, stroking firmly at her little opening until her bottom had begun to tense and her legs to shake.

'Come closer,' Mrs Hampton said quietly.

Eleanor took a few steps forwards and stood bracing herself with her knees against the bed. Amelia stood behind her and gently took hold of her dress, taking it from her grip and raising it until it was above her breasts. Mrs Hampton watched with fascination as the young girl stood with breasts and crotch bared, her fingers working hard at herself. Soon Eleanor's legs began to shake again as she came with cries of joy and lust.

As she reached her peak, Amelia gently reached around her and pulled Eleanor's hand away so that Mrs Hampton could see the creamy fluid running down the maid's thighs and on to her immaculate black stockings, staining the material.

Eleanor stood still for a moment as Amelia exposed her to her mistress's gaze, her head hanging forwards, and then looked up and gave Mrs Hampton a little smile.

'Well, well,' Mrs Hampton said.

'Do you believe me now, Mistress?' Amelia asked. 'She is so keen to serve you, and I doubt very much you could find a better girl.'

'She is quite shameless, that much is evident,' Mrs Hampton said. 'But it takes more than a mere slut to provide the services I require, as you very well know, Amelia.'

'You did not enjoy what I did then, Mistress?' Eleanor asked.

'Of course,' Mrs Hampton answered. 'It was very entertaining, but I will make my own arrangements. Certainly I do not need you two scheming madams to make my decisions for me. Now be off, before I decide to give you both a dose of the cane.'

'Did I not arouse you?' Eleanor begged, now clearly close to tears. 'Did I not make you at all excited? Am I just an interesting diversion, for all my loyalty and desire?'

Mrs Hampton looked at the girl. She could see that what she had done had taken some courage, but she would not be pushed – giving in now would show serious weakness of character.

'You are a pretty thing, but I prefer blondes,' Mrs Hampton remarked.

Eleanor stood for a moment with her mouth open but said nothing. Mrs Hampton waited to see if the maid might cry a little. To have a young girl with her tits and slit bare, sobbing for approval, never ceased to be exciting.

'I don't believe you,' Eleanor whined. 'You are a cruel woman!'

'Oh, I can be,' Mrs Hampton replied. 'You are pretty but lack that special quality I have come to appreciate in Amelia. And, if you must know, your little display barely moved me.'

'Liar!' Eleanor blurted out. 'I know you liked it. I could see it in your eyes!'

'I have already made allowances for your candour, my girl,' Mrs Hampton warned. 'But watch your tongue. If you ever suggest I am a liar again I shall simply put you out on the street.'

But Mrs Hampton was having difficulty maintaining her stern posture. She had loved Eleanor's performance and had every intention of giving the girl a chance now that she had shown her mettle, but she was reluctant to back down in front of Amelia, and knew in any case that it would increase her power to make the maid beg to be her slave. It was also enjoyable, almost as much as seeing the girl cry.

'What on earth do you think you are doing?' she cried out suddenly as Eleanor snatched the sheets and blankets from the bed with one quick motion. Exposed, she sat up in bed, and glared at Eleanor in anger and astonishment.

The maid ignored her mistress's question and walked around to the side of the bed. Mrs Hampton watched with fascination as the young maid took hold of her mistress's nightdress and yanked it up to her waist, all the while looking her firmly in the eye as if daring her to protest. She did not; it had been a long time since anyone had dared move a hand against her and, despite her profound shock, she found it strangely pleasurable. Even as the gown was hauled above her bottom and her little patch of dark pubic hair was uncovered she held her peace, and even found herself allowing her legs to be parted, exposing the hairy bush between her thighs.

'Give me that pillow,' Eleanor instructed Amelia.

Amelia was standing at the side of the bed, clearly amazed at what she was seeing. She blinked at the command and stared blankly at Eleanor.

'The pillow,' Eleanor repeated. 'Give it to me.'

Amelia gently pulled the pillow from behind Mrs Hampton. She looked afraid that she would be scolded or grabbed and punished, but her mistress just lay there, watching Eleanor with both surprise and amusement. Eleanor took the pillow.

'Lift up your legs please, madam,' the maid instructed.

Mrs Hampton laughed at her.

Eleanor grasped the woman's heels and lifted her legs with one sudden jerk, so that they were at right angles to the bed with the soles of her feet facing the ceiling, then, with surprising strength, she lifted Mrs Hampton's bottom enough to slide the pillow underneath. Mrs Hampton's surprise changed to astonishment and her mouth came open to admonish Eleanor, but the maid wasn't finished.

'Not excited?' Eleanor asked. 'We shall see, shall we?'

Working with brisk efficiency and a great deal of strength, Eleanor hauled Mrs Hampton's thighs wide open, displaying her sex, which was quite clearly wet. With a soft chuckle the maid climbed on to the bed, to kneel between her open thighs. She began to kiss the pale flesh, her tongue moving slowly upwards.

After only a moment Mrs Hampton let out a soft moan and lay back as Eleanor's mouth found her sex, kissing her outer lips. The pillow propping up her bottom gave Eleanor a wonderful angle from which to tease her mistress, allowing her to kiss the turn of Mrs Hampton's bottom and the opening of her sex, right up to the tiny, engorged clitoris.

As Eleanor's tongue found that most sensitive part of all, Mrs Hampton found she could hold back no longer, letting out a long moan as her hands gripped the sheet.

Eleanor licked for a moment more, then withdrew her tongue. 'Are you truly not excited?' she asked. 'You seem quite wet to me, Mistress, and quite eager.'

'Don't stop,' Mrs Hampton implored.

'Then you do like me?' Eleanor demanded.

'Of course I do; now continue,' Mrs Hampton replied.

'Will you take me on as Amelia's replacement, then?' Eleanor insisted, her fingers now toying with Mrs Hampton's swollen lips.

'Stop teasing me, you little harlot,' Mrs Hampton demanded. 'Lick me deeply, girl. Lick me firmly with that delicious little tongue, at once.'

'Oh, I might,' Eleanor teased, 'once you admit that you desire me and you want me to be your new special maid.'

'I shall not be blackmailed,' Mrs Hampton began, then broke off. 'Oh yes, that is nice, keep doing that. A little firmer now, push your fingers inside me. Come, now, don't be a tease, push your fingers inside.'

'Then I have the job?' Eleanor asked innocently.

'No, not yet. I shall decide in my own good time,' Mrs Hampton whispered, 'but don't stop.'

Eleanor drew a wet finger from Mrs Hampton's slit and offered it to Amelia. The smiling ladies' maid bent over and sucked Eleanor's finger into her mouth, making approving noises as she did so.

'It seems mistress is more than a little excited,' Eleanor said.

'Very,' Amelia agreed. 'Indeed, I think she is making a mess of that pillow.'

'Oh, you wicked girls!' Mrs Hampton cried. 'Very well, since you want it so badly I shall give you a chance, but if you are not as capable as you seem, I shall dismiss you and you can return to your normal duties. That is all I will offer. Now see to me.'

'As you please, my lady,' Eleanor said softly. 'You shall not be disappointed, I feel sure of it.'

Eleanor used her thumbs to push Mrs Hampton's lips open, brushing her pubic hair aside with her fingertips and holding her open like that for a long moment of anticipation. The older woman was

154

breathing hard, her chest rising and falling as she watched the pretty young maid pause with her mouth just a tiny distance from her vagina. Then Eleanor gave her what she wanted, what she craved and desired, until all control was lost and she would have acquiesced to any demand made of her by the simple country girl who worked downstairs.

Eleanor placed her mouth over her mistress's pussy and pushed her tongue deep inside, just as she had done with Betty. The taste of arousal was deep and unmistakable, a wonderfully slick and rich texture that suggested an urgent need from within.

Mrs Hampton placed her ankles upon Eleanor's hips and pushed forwards to bring her sex and Eleanor's mouth more tightly together. She began to rock forwards and backwards on the bed, and her pubic hair brushed against Eleanor's cheeks and nose as the new maid licked and pushed her tongue in deeper and deeper. The wetness all about Eleanor's chin and mouth tasted so good she found herself pausing to lick it up before going back to her task.

Only as Mrs Hampton grew close to orgasm did Eleanor place the tip of her tongue against the woman's firm clitoris and flick it as fast as she could. Mrs Hampton lost every trace of ladylike composure that instant, and begun to buck and writhe on the bed, crying out in ecstasy with her hands clawing at the bed sheets like a woman possessed. She began to swear, little half-formed words that she could barely get out as she shook and convulsed. Her orgasm was so powerful that her juices didn't just run from her, but sprayed out in a quick jet that went mostly into Eleanor's mouth but also splashed against her cheeks and chin.

For a while afterwards Mrs Hampton lay panting on the bed, her long shapely legs trembling from the force of her explosive ejaculation. She had closed her eyes and laid her head against the mattress, muttering and moaning as small aftershocks ran through her body.

Eleanor climbed on to the bed, her knees either side of Mrs Hampton's legs, and kissed her mistress' stomach, then laid her head upon it. Mrs Hampton gave a happy sigh and put her hands over the girl's head to stroke her hair. Amelia sat on the edge of the bed and lay against Mrs Hampton too, watching her doze for a moment with a look of pure bliss on her face.

Mrs Hampton then opened her eyes and gently guided Eleanor to her, drawing her up so that the maid was kneeling over her mistress with her bare lips tickled by Mrs Hampton's own dark patch of hair. They kissed, and she must have been able to taste herself on Eleanor's lips – a flavour that made her body shiver with excitement again.

'You will find being my maid quite a challenge, young lady,' she said sleepily.

'I hope it is a challenge I can meet,' Eleanor said. 'I do not understand it completely but I thrill to serve you, my lady.'

'What about you, Amelia, are you jealous?' Mrs Hampton asked. 'Do you feel neglected?'

'Of course. But I am happy also, my lady,' Amelia answered. 'Because I want you to be happy.'

'Come and lie down with me,' Mrs Hampton said. 'The pair of you, come and curl up with me, you pretty things, and we'll sleep a while. You have left me quite worn out and I haven't even risen from my bed yet.'

Amelia and Eleanor lay down at either side of the lady of the house, their hands on her smooth stomach and their heads against her breast. Within moments they were all asleep, and none of them woke until the rattling of a carriage on the road outside jerked them from their pleasant dreams.

'Sleepy, Eleanor?' Mrs Hampton asked.

'Oh yes, Mistress,' Eleanor said, sitting up.

She looked at Mrs Hampton and then Amelia and saw the wicked look on their faces. Mrs Hampton grabbed one wrist and Amelia grabbed the other, then they held her down firmly on the bed.

'You have been a cheeky little thing today, haven't you?' Mrs Hampton said.

'A little, Mistress, yes,' Eleanor admitted.

Amelia smirked. 'She has been quite the little troublemaker. What should we do with her, ma'am?'

'I think she has been indulged enough and needs to be reacquainted with who is in charge here,' Mrs Hampton said. 'And I have just the tonic for that.'

Amelia reached under the bed, keeping a firm grip on Eleanor's wrist, and brought out Mrs Hampton's special toy – a length of firm rubber shaped like a penis. She handed it to Mrs Hampton, who showed it to Eleanor's wild, bright eyes. Eleanor then turned her head to one side and gave a little moan.

'Oh Mistress, not with that,' she pleaded.

Mrs Hampton ignored her, and ran the dildo down Eleanor's body, over her breasts and down along her belly. Then she ran the head of it over the maid's crotch and Eleanor raised her leg to block its progress.

But Amelia knew just what to do, and placed her own knee in between Eleanor's legs to keep her thighs apart. Mrs Hampton then climbed over Eleanor and dipped the toy between her lips. She drew it out, wet, and bent Eleanor's arms up and over her head before pressing it into Eleanor's mouth.

'Suck it,' she instructed.

Eleanor tried to turn her head away. She was excited but also felt obliged to struggle, although resistance was pointless. But Mrs Hampton pushed her mouth open with the menacing black dick-toy, forcing Eleanor to let it into her mouth, and then drew it out again. She writhed in their grip, but while pretending to struggle she also found herself pushing her body up towards them.

Amelia giggled. Running her hand down the new maid's belly, she felt Eleanor's growing excitement with her finger.

'I think she likes that,' Mrs Hampton said.

'She does, Mistress,' Amelia agreed.

'Let's see how she likes it in her,' Mrs Hampton said.

She took the toy and rubbed its length over Eleanor's bare crotch, sliding it between the maid's lips and against her clitoris, before pushing it inside. As the big toy pressed into Eleanor's body she continued to struggle, hoping they would pin her down and increase the intensity of their coupling.

Amelia read her signal, and pinned Eleanor's legs apart with her body weight. Mrs Hampton followed her example and stretched her torso across Eleanor to hold her helpless as she was fucked.

Eleanor continued to wriggle and squirm as the thick, hard dildo worked inside her, her pleasure rising quickly, and more quickly still when Mrs Hampton began to twist the dildo inside her, stimulating the sensitive spot deep within. At that she began to moan and buck up and down on the bed, struggling not to break free but to push herself on to the great rubber dick.

Both Amelia and Mrs Hampton were laughing at the state to which they'd brought Eleanor, and they kept her firmly pinned down, with the dildo moving inside her until her wriggling body began to approach orgasm. When she came it was with a sharp hiss and her back locked into a tight arch, with wave after wave of ecstasy running through her, while every sensation seemed greatly magnified, from the overwhelming pleasure of her well-filled hole to the faint rustling of the goose-down pillow beneath her head.

When at last it was over, Mrs Hampton bent over Eleanor and kissed her, briefly slipping her tongue into the maid's mouth before she pulled away.

'I am truly sorry to lose you, Amelia,' Mrs Hampton said, 'but I think this little kitten is going to fill my bed nicely.'

'I am glad,' Amelia replied. 'She has much to learn, but I am sure there is no finer teacher.'

Eleanor sighed and closed her eyes. She felt full of bliss as Mrs Hampton and Amelia lay down beside her and stroked her hair. She had achieved what had become her greatest desire.

Eleanor was downstairs that evening when she was summoned by the ringing of the parlour bell. She went upstairs and stopped in surprise to see Amelia standing in the hall with her cases at her side.

'Amelia?' she asked. 'Are you leaving already?'

'I must,' Amelia replied. 'My mother needs me, and Mrs Hampton has been good enough to allow me to leave directly.'

'Oh, Amelia,' Eleanor cried. 'Well, thank you. I am grateful, you know, for making me your replacement.'

'I feel you earned it, little slut that you are,' Amelia replied, with one eyebrow raised haughtily.

Mrs Hampton came out from the drawing-room. She looked beautiful with her hair up and her long flowing white and cream dress trailing behind her.

There was a bunch of flowers in her hands and Amelia looked as if she might cry when her mistress handed them to her.

'Amelia, my sweet,' she said, 'your carriage will be here at any moment. I hope you like your flowers.'

'They are lovely,' Amelia replied, and had to wipe away a tear.

'We shall come and visit you soon, I promise,' Mrs Hampton told her.

Before Amelia could reply they were interrupted by the sound of knocking at the tradesmen's entrance downstairs. They hugged and then without a word Amelia picked up her cases and began to walk downstairs. As she went Mrs Hampton tucked a small package into her pocket and gave her a smile and waved goodbye.

The carriage driver was a cheery old fellow, always happy to talk to anyone who cared to listen, or at least half listen. He packed Amelia's cases on to the roof and then helped her inside before resuming his seat. The servants and, if he wasn't mistaken, the lady of the house stood outside on the steps, waving, but the young girl in his carriage gave them only a quick glance before turning away. He set the horses trotting towards the station and called down to ask if his passenger was comfortable. She replied that she was but fell silent again. He thought he could hear a little sobbing, so he too didn't speak for the rest of the journey, content to leave her to her own thoughts. He wondered if perhaps she was a disgraced maid sent away, but her fond farewell suggested otherwise.

In the back of the cab Amelia opened the package given to her by Mrs Hampton. Inside was a pair of scandalously short and lacy drawers which she recog-

160

nised as a pair of Mrs Hampton's finest. She put them
to her face and breathed in the delicious aroma of
arousal that they held, then put them in her pocket.
Also in the package was a thin leather collar tied
around a fat roll of banknotes. She undid the collar
and held it in her hands; it was worn with age and
cracked a little but as she ran her delicate fingertips
over the studs she smiled and remembered happy
times when she had worn it.

When the carriage arrived at the station she got
out, handed the driver one of the notes from the roll
and wished him well. He blinked at the note and
called out for her to wait, as he couldn't possibly give
her change for such an amount. She just smiled and
waved, leaving him standing there turning the note
over and over in his hands and grinning from ear to
ear. With that amount, Amelia reflected, he must
have earned enough to purchase his carriage and
horses outright twice over.

Mrs Hampton wasn't in such a fine mood. She retired
early and refused Eleanor's offer to join her. Eleanor
felt emotionally exhausted too and curled up with
Betty in the little servants' room downstairs. Soon
they were fast asleep and didn't even wake when the
cook and her lover nearly broke the kitchen table
making love with the frenzied enthusiasm that only
new lovers or those who seldom get time alone know.

# Ten

*In which Mrs Hampton goes riding.*

Eleanor was chatting to Betty about the departure of
Amelia when the bell rang to summon her. She gave
Betty a little kiss on the cheek and a squeeze on the
bottom and ran upstairs. Mrs Hampton was seated in
her tall chair with her hair up, wearing a delightful
jacket and a long dress, both made of tweed. On her
feet were a pair of small pointed boots of the finest
soft leather, which matched her gloves perfectly.

'You rang, Mistress?' Eleanor said as she closed the
door.

'Yes, I shall be going riding today,' Mrs Hampton
declared.

'Oh, how lovely,' Eleanor replied. 'Shall I call for
the groom?'

'No,' Mrs Hampton said airily. 'I thought a little
fresh air would do you good, so you shall come with
me today.'

Eleanor felt elated, and she couldn't hide her
delight, but Mrs Hampton seemed not to notice.
Shortly afterwards a carriage driven by a rather
hungover-looking man arrived to take them out into
the country. Eleanor tried to start a conversation with
Mrs Hampton several times as they drove, but the
lady seemed preoccupied and would say little in

return. Eventually they were out of London and into the countryside, the sun shining and the sky blue and clear. Eleanor did indeed feel better for being out of the town, but she also felt a little uneasy; she didn't like to be leaving the house, and felt a tiny bit uncomfortable. She assured herself she was worrying over nothing; if Mrs Hampton meant to dismiss her she would not go to the trouble of dropping her in the middle of nowhere.

The carriage pulled into the drive of a large house set in ample grounds, and Mrs Hampton announced that they would get out there. The driver turned around in his seat to ask if she was sure, and told her that there was no extra charge to take her to the door, but the stern expression on Mrs Hampton's face spoke volumes. When she gave him a handful of coins he looked mildly disappointed but wished them good day and turned the horses, driving them off down the path at a trot.

'Such beautiful animals, are they not?' Mrs Hampton remarked. 'Noble creatures, unlike man.'

'Yes, Mistress,' Eleanor said.

'Have you ever wondered what it might be like to be an animal, Eleanor?' Mrs Hampton asked, and with that she began to walk across the fields towards a large barn.

'An animal, my lady?' Eleanor asked, almost running in her efforts to keep up.

'Are you deaf this morning?' Mrs Hampton asked, and then spotted a woman emerging from the barn and waved and called out to her.

The other lady saw her and waved her parasol in greeting.

'Come on, do hurry, Eleanor,' Mrs Hampton said. 'I want you to meet my friend Emily.'

Emily was tall and slim, with straw-blonde hair neatly tied up and topped with a sun-bonnet. She was wearing a long summer dress and shawl and her little rosebud mouth gave her the look of a woman who was rather amused by life. Mrs Hampton greeted her with a warm hug and a kiss on the cheek. Eleanor stood behind her mistress with her eyes downcast. She had hoped to be the centre of attention today.

'And who is this?' Emily asked.

'This, my dear, is my new maid,' Mrs Hampton replied. 'A pretty little thing, isn't she?'

Much to Eleanor's surprise the young lady walked right up to her, put her index finger under Eleanor's chin and lifted it up.

'A pretty face, certainly,' Emily noted.

'Yes, she looks so innocent, doesn't she?' Mrs Hampton replied. 'Although appearances can be deceiving.'

Eleanor felt herself blush. She was cross that she was being discussed as though she weren't there, but thought it best to remain quiet. The other woman ran her hand approvingly down the new maid's side and seemed amused at her nervousness.

'Have you broken her in yet?' Emily asked, and watched as Eleanor squirmed with embarrassment.

'A little,' Mrs Hampton replied. 'I've taught her a few things and from what I can tell she's learnt a little of the art of lovemaking from my little slut of a tweenie maid, and Amelia of course. You heard she has left?'

'Already? Oh, you poor thing. We'd better make sure this little madam is trained up as soon as possible, then,' Emily said. 'Come then, Eleanor, follow us.'

Eleanor had no idea what to expect. She was stunned that the other lady seemed to know all about Mrs Hampton's use for her, which she had always assumed would be a well-kept secret. It seemed not to be, and the thought that her secret services for her mistress were both known and discussed shamed and aroused her at the same time.

The barn into which she was taken had hay on the floor and some stalls, but not a hint of the strong scent of horses.

'Do you like my stable?' Emily asked her.

'Yes, it's – very nice,' Eleanor replied.

'Good. Did you ever ride on someone's shoulders when you were younger?' Mrs Hampton asked.

'On their shoulders?' Eleanor asked.

'Yes, or perhaps on their back?' Emily suggested.

'I think so, my lady,' Eleanor replied, purposefully directing her answer to Mrs Hampton rather than Emily. 'When I was little.'

'And what about other people, have you given other people a ride on you?' Mrs Hampton asked. 'On your back, I mean, not in your hole. I know you have done that.'

'Well, yes, I suppose, when I was young,' Eleanor replied.

She was blushing deeply at the subject matter and hoped they would be alone again soon, far from Emily and her amused little smile.

'Get undressed then, dear,' Mrs Hampton said simply.

For a moment Eleanor imagined that Mrs Hampton had not spoken but that instead she had read her mistress's thoughts, like the carnival men sometimes pretended to do with simple-minded folk. But no, it seemed as though she *had* spoken, because she repeated herself, only this time far more sternly.

'Here?' she bleated.

'Yes, of course here,' Mrs Hampton snapped. 'Where else do you imagine I might mean? Don't keep us waiting.'

'But, but mistress –' Eleanor began to moan.

'Unless you are not suited to being my servant after all,' Mrs Hampton suggested. 'Perhaps you would be better used downstairs washing pots and scrubbing floors, as you began?'

'The poor little thing isn't ready for this,' Emily said with mock sympathy. 'I told you that you should have let me find you a girl, one who's already been broken in.'

Eleanor flushed with shame but began to unbutton her dress. The two women turned their full attention to her, and as she pulled the dress off Emily took it from her, folded it in half and placed it on a hay bale. Eleanor could not look either of them in the eye, and was hoping Mrs Hampton would order her to stop as she tentatively removed her shoes and then her stockings, to leave her standing in front of the women in only her chemise and bloomers. She stopped, but Mrs Hampton clicked her fingers to indicate that Eleanor should take off her chemise.

Ever more reluctant, Eleanor unbuttoned herself at the front and shrugged off the garment, which Emily took. Knowing she was very unlikely to be allowed to keep her drawers, Eleanor unfastened them and let them drop to the ground rather than suffer the indignity of being told to do so. After stepping out of them, she picked them up and held them loosely in her hand, covering herself. Emily held out her hand and Eleanor passed her drawers over, leaving her stark naked and red-faced with embarrassment, her eyes fixed firmly on the ground.

'She colours up prettily, doesn't she?' Emily remarked.

'Very,' Mrs Hampton replied. 'She is a shy little thing at heart, at least until she's been warmed. Come, Eleanor, let us look at you properly. Straighten up, and put your hands behind your head.'

Eleanor looked at Mrs Hampton with imploring eyes but saw no mercy there, so she slowly raised her hands and put them behind her head. Emily and Mrs Hampton stood in front of her, appraising her form.

'She has nice titties,' Emily said, 'small, but shapely. Do you remember that girl at school? What was she called? Portia, wasn't it? She didn't get hair till she was seventeen.'

'Oh yes,' Mrs Hampton responded. 'She had the sweetest little breasts, very like Eleanor's. Oh, how I loved to squeeze those. Weren't nights in the dormitory simply wonderful?'

'Oh, quite,' Emily agreed.

Emily reached out and ran a hand over Eleanor's breasts, pausing at the nipples and giving them a little squeeze to make them hard. Eleanor shut her eyes, forcing herself to accept the stranger's touch for the sake of her mistress, even as she was turned around and bent down over a bale of hay. The hay was uncomfortably spiky, but that was nothing to the discomfort of having her bare bottom and the rear lips of her sex on display to the two women.

'How short her pubic hair is. Do you shave her?' Emily asked.

'No,' Mrs Hampton replied, 'my maid did that. Isn't it ever so smooth, though?'

Eleanor felt her lips being pushed apart, but held absolutely still, even as they explored her bottom, touching, pinching and probing where they pleased, until she was trembling with shame and need. She had no idea which of the women was doing what, but was unable to disguise her response in any case, and grunted as two fingers entered her. Biting her lip, she vowed to be silent when she heard the women giggling at her reaction. She wished she could control her arousal but she could not, and despite the shameful situation she was in she felt herself grow wetter and wetter.

'Let's get our little mare saddled up, then,' Emily declared at length.

Eleanor was guided upright by the two women and led into one of the stalls. There were saddles and all kinds of riding gear there, but even when she saw them what had been said meant nothing to her.

'Down,' Mrs Hampton ordered.

Eleanor began to turn to ask her mistress what she meant, or planned to do, but at a sharp slap on her bottom she decided she was in no position to argue. She quickly got down on her hands and knees and waited nervously as Emily selected some leather straps and a halter from the pile then walked behind her. Suddenly Eleanor realised that they meant to use the harness on her, and she almost rose to protest. Being spanked and serving her mistress with her fingers and tongue was one thing, but this was depravity on an altogether different scale.

But the harness was being put over her, and she closed her eyes, reminding herself of what Amelia had said about needing to surrender absolutely to her mistress's will. Now passive, she allowed the thick leather straps to be fastened around her middle and neck, opening her eyes only when something hard was pressed to her lips.

'Open wide,' Emily, who'd moved in front of her again, said in the most mocking tone imaginable.

Eleanor's initial relief that they meant her mouth gave way to resentment as she realised they meant to put a bit in her mouth. It was made of wood and had leather straps. She took it reluctantly and bit down on the sour wood, knowing what was expected of her. Emily spent a moment adjusting the buckles of Eleanor's bridle to make it tight, then produced a curious object, a horsetail made with a little rubber end. Eleanor looked down at the ground as Emily walked behind her and patted her backside.

'Aren't you going to look pretty?' Mrs Hampton asked as she gathered Eleanor's hair up and began to braid it.

Unable to reply, Eleanor cast her mistress a pleading glance, which was ignored. Her bottom was patted and she realised that they meant to push the tail's rubber end inside her. She gave a little moan, shaking her head and shivering, but a spit-wet finger had already been applied to her anus, opening the little hole. The finger withdrew, and Eleanor braced herself as she felt the rubber press against her. As she bit down on the wood inside her mouth it was pushed in. She gasped and bucked a little but Mrs Hampton held her hair firmly and the plug was pushed deep, to leave her trembling.Her shame was close to unbearable, and yet so was her arousal, and her naked little nipples felt hard as Mrs Hampton reached under her breasts and slipped a length of leather between them, then tied it to a collar around her neck.

'Shake your bottom, little pony,' Emily instructed.

Eleanor hated Emily just then. She turned her head a little to look up at Mrs Hampton but saw no sympathy in her mistress's eyes. Instead, Mrs Hampton seemed very amused at Eleanor's situation, and judging by her cruel smile she was enjoying herself immensely. Eleanor obliged, swinging her pert bottom from side to side, which made the tail swish against her thighs, tickling her. The rubber end had been firmly pushed inside, and the tail stayed in place. Emily clapped in pleasure at the sight of Eleanor's display.

'Let's hitch our pretty little pony up then, shall we?' Emily said.

Eleanor tried to turn round to see what was to come next, but found the harness they had attached to her made it very difficult to look anywhere but straight ahead. It was so constricting and firmly fixed to her calves and wrists that she couldn't stand up if she tried. She listened as something that creaked was pushed behind her, and then they were fixing it to her harness.

'Let us see if you can pull it, then,' Mrs Hampton said. 'She is strong for her size, so I expect so. Walk on.'

Too full of shame and resentment to want to oblige, Eleanor stayed still. Only when she felt the crack of a riding crop against her backside did she begin to crawl. They had fixed a cart behind her; she couldn't see it but she could feel its weight. It had four wheels and a small seat; the wheels supported its weight and it was quite easy to pull it along. Yet for all that Eleanor felt utterly humiliated. She had been degraded to the level of an animal, and a beast of burden at that. She dared not stop, because the riding crop stung mightily, and even though she sensed that they were enjoying her shame she would not give them the satisfaction of failing.

They guided her outside, much to her horror, as she could not tell if there was anyone else in the paddock to witness her degradation. She kept her head down and pulled the little cart obediently behind her. Each step made her tail swish down against her bottom cheeks and she was ever conscious that her movements were completely constricted, while her body was fully on display to both women.

'I shall fetch my mount,' Emily announced. 'I fear that your little pony isn't going to be much of a racer, though.'

'You may be surprised,' Mrs Hampton replied.

'She is of country stock and they breed them for endurance there, or so I hear.'

Eleanor and Mrs Hampton were left alone and she looked up at her mistress, as far as her harness would allow. Mrs Hampton came to Eleanor's side and patted her hair, which was wound into a mane and pulled firmly up from her neck. Eleanor stayed still, trying to convey her discomfort with her eyes, until Mrs Hampton dipped into her pocket and pulled out a sugar lump, which she offered in the palm of her hand. Eleanor looked away but Mrs Hampton took the strap of her bit and pulled her head back so she was forced to look at her mistress.

'Is this too much for you, my little pony?' Mrs Hampton teased. 'Do you want to go back to cleaning floors and mopping up like the little serving girl you are?'

Eleanor could not speak, but shook her head vehemently.

'Is your tail comfortable?' Mrs Hampton asked.

Eleanor looked away; she could feel the shaft between her buttocks and the ball in her anus. It was impossible to remove it by shaking it out of herself, as it was wedged well in and furthermore held in place by straps. To be wearing such a thing up her bottom was the crowning humiliation, and she began to wish she had not been so bold in coming forward to assume Amelia's position. But it was too late to change her mind now, as her pride would not allow her to be returned to the kitchen, and she still craved the wicked attentions of Mrs Hampton.

When she heard Emily's voice raised in command she at first assumed it was directed at her, but then came the creaking of another carriage and she realised with sudden horror that Emily had her own mount. She also realised what Emily had meant when she had mocked Eleanor for being unfit for racing. They intended to race her against another girl across the paddock.

'Climb up, then, my dear,' Emily said.

Mrs Hampton climbed into Eleanor's cart.

'Walk on,' Mrs Hampton instructed, and as Eleanor hesitated the riding crop smacked down on her naked bottom.

Eleanor heaved the cart forwards. It was lighter than she had expected, and she was glad that Mrs Hampton was a slender woman.

'You haven't a chance, my dear,' Emily laughed.

'A pound says you are wrong,' Mrs Hampton said.

'You are feeling brave!' Emily said and laughed again. 'I'll tell you what, I'll be sporting and give you a minute's head start.'

'We don't need that long. Give us thirty seconds and we'll be well away.'

'Thirty seconds then; are you ready?'

'Yes, we're ready.'

'Then go!'

Eleanor felt the cruel kiss of the riding crop against her thigh and began to crawl as fast as she could, terrified of the stinging strokes. The wet grass left her hands and knees muddy and she was grunting with effort as she bore the cart onwards. Mrs Hampton was laughing in her seat, geeing her on and calling back to Emily to catch them up if she could. Eleanor heard the sound of the other cart moving and Emily urging her pony onwards. It must have been more used to its task than her, she thought, as she could hear it gaining on her. Still she crawled as fast as was able, feeling the halter dig into her shoulders and her bare breasts dangling free and shaking as she went. The hateful plug with the tail attached seemed to be growing warmer and warmer at each movement, and it felt like a hot cock inside her as she struggled on.

The noises of the other cart were drawing closer. The crop smacked down on Eleanor's flesh once more and she struggled to go faster. Yet soon she could see the hands of the other pony moving up along the grass to her side. Mrs Hampton gave her legs another lash to urge her on.

'Come on, you lazy mare, faster! They're going to overtake us,' Mrs Hampton called out.

'Go on, go faster,' Emily urged her own mount. 'Overtake her.'

Eleanor could not see to her sides very well because of the blinkers which were part of the headpiece and collar, but she could see that where hands had been visible there was now a whole arm. She concentrated on the tree at the end of the paddock which she guessed must be the finishing line, but at a sudden shove at her hip she realised that the other human pony was trying to push her aside. She used her bare shoulder to shove back, but found the flesh of the other pony surprisingly hard, and chanced a look to the side. What she saw surprised her so much that she nearly lost all co-ordination.

He was a young man, no more than 22 or 23 years of age, and also completely bare except for his halter and straps. His teeth were firmly holding the bit and his face was covered except for the mouth and chin by a black leather mask. It even had ears, large floppy comical-looking ears that waggled as he crawled. Eleanor felt renewed determination not to lose and forced herself forwards, but she lacked his strength, her hands slippery with grass, and each small forward movement made her shoulders ache. He overtook her, then drew ahead with a spurt of speed, far enough for her to see his backside and his penis and balls dangling between his legs, small and tight with the cold fresh air. His genitals were shaved bare and tied with a length of cord that led back to the cart, and he too had a tail, a rich chestnut-coloured one that was as firmly fitted as her own. His penis and testicles juddered and shook with the motion of his crawling.

Eleanor trotted after him, but his powerful legs and determination were the deciding factor, and he made it to the tree with three cart lengths to spare.

'Bravo!' Mrs Hampton cried.

Eleanor came to a halt, panting at the exertion, but Mrs Hampton was determined to drive her on to the finishing line. Two more whip cuts were applied to her bottom and she started forwards once more, but Emily had dismounted already and was stroking her young slave's chin approvingly by the time Eleanor reached the tree.

'A valiant effort,' Emily conceded.

'Yes, well done, Eleanor,' Mrs Hampton agreed.

Eleanor was in no mood to be praised but was thankful when Mrs Hampton dismounted her and turned her towards the stables. Much to her dismay she was led ahead of the young male and could feel his gaze on her private parts, which even with the cart behind her were very much on show. The two ladies chatted on the way back to the stables and Eleanor picked up on the name of a club to which they both belonged – The Cauldron. Emily asked her mistress if she intended to bring Eleanor to the club or if the arrangement was only temporary. Eleanor snorted at that but Mrs Hampton said nothing in reply, and Eleanor sensed that the two women were communicating silently instead. She would have loved to know what Mrs Hampton was signalling to her friend, for she feared that she would be excluded.

Eleanor felt a moment's annoyance at herself; what was driving her to want to participate in such depravity?

She was relieved when the cart was unhooked and waited patiently for the harness to come off too. On the one hand she was eager to be released from the humiliation of the bondage they had forced her into, but on the other she felt deep pleasure that she had trouble understanding. While she waited for them to finish undoing her bonds she came to a realisation: it was the lack of control that was so sexually stimulating. You didn't know what was going to happen next, and that was exciting, but more than that you didn't have to think, because that was done for you, as Amelia had explained. Yes, it was true that she was being used, but wasn't she really the centre of attention in it all as well? Then there was Mrs Hampton herself, fierce and unyielding – yet she could control Mrs Hampton as much as the lady controlled her. She had shown that in the bedroom, and she knew that without her Mrs Hampton's most desperate needs would go unsatisfied. The only thing that really troubled Eleanor was that she feared she would not meet her mistress's expectations. If she were to be rejected now, that would mean all her efforts had been for nothing. For all that she'd been put through, she remained determined to end up as Mrs Hampton's plaything and knew she would do whatever it took.

'I believe I owe you a pound,' Mrs Hampton said to Emily.

'How about just giving my little mount a treat instead?' Emily suggested.

'That's very kind of you,' Mrs Hampton responded.

Eleanor shied a little, worrying that she herself might be the treat for the male pony, but Mrs

Hampton came to stroke her hair and pat her head while Emily fiddled with the young man's straps. As soon as he was loose Emily guided him towards Eleanor, whose worst fears were confirmed. She was to be mounted, but Mrs Hampton had taken a firm grip of her hair and kept her in place as the male pony was brought close. Eleanor struggled as he placed his hands on the small of her back, but even without her mistress's firm grip she would have been too weak to resist, both in mind and body.

He mounted her, his cock pressing against her body. It lolled soft between her bottom cheeks at first, but as he began to rut between them it grew rapidly larger. Emily bent down and pulled Eleanor's tail to one side. A hand guided the male pony's dick, now hard, against her opening, rubbing it against her lips. She could hear his breathing becoming short as he was stimulated against her sex, and then he was being guided in to fill her hole.

Eleanor clamped her teeth on the bit to stop herself crying out as her fucking began. His penis filled her, its long length sliding in and out as she knelt helplessly before him, moaning and shaking her head. She longed to lie down so he could enter her with his whole weight pressing on her back, but she could not move that way. Instead she pushed down her head and lifted her bottom, offering herself to him so that his cock went deeper and his belly smacked against her bottom cheeks as he thrust in and out.

Soon she felt her orgasm building, and a helpless sob came from her as it coursed through her body, with her bottom pressed hard against him and her swollen lips spread out around his erection. He did not pause a stroke as she reached her climax, which only seemed to spur him on to more frenzied efforts. Emily reached beneath him to grab the young stud's balls and give them a firm squeeze, letting him know that she wanted him to empty his testicles at that precise moment.

He had been gripping his bit with his mouth up until then, and finally let himself orgasm. A deep warmth filled Eleanor and his penis became immediately a little more limp, like a hose with the pressure reduced. Even then he did not slow his pace, but kept his cock pumping inside her until at last it had gone completely soft. Emily released his balls from her grip and with her crop drove him away to his stall, although Eleanor barely registered that he'd gone. She was so completely exhausted that she nearly fell when her harness was unhooked, but maintained enough dignity to sink slowly to the ground instead.

Mrs Hampton had never stopped stroking Eleanor during the fucking, and now whispered soothingly in her ear as she began to undo the harness. Naked once more, Eleanor was allowed to collapse in the hay and sleep while the two women walked and talked out on the field.

In the carriage home Eleanor could barely look her mistress in the eye without blushing deeply. She had not been given the chance to clean herself up, and so her thighs were still covered with the other pony's ejaculation as well as her own mess. Mrs Hampton did allow her to rest against her breast, though, and under the cover of a blanket Eleanor slid her hand as directed between her mistress's legs and saw to her need, which had grown urgent.

'Did you enjoy yourself today, Eleanor?' Mrs Hampton asked.

'I don't know if I enjoyed it, my lady,' Eleanor whispered. 'But anything that makes you this hot between your legs pleases me greatly.'

Mrs Hampton kissed Eleanor's cheek and then turned her face to her maid and kissed her full on the lips, her tongue sliding into her mouth. They kissed until Mrs Hampton was driven to distraction by the twitching motion of Eleanor's hand, and then she gripped Eleanor's wrist hard lest it move away, and started to orgasm. When Eleanor withdrew her wet fingers she put them straight into her mouth and sucked them eagerly.

'What is The Cauldron Club?' Eleanor asked.

'Servant girls shouldn't listen to the talk of ladies,' Mrs Hampton replied haughtily.

'And servant girls shouldn't be ridden like beasts of burden with a rubber shaft and horse tail in their unmentionables,' Eleanor suggested.

Mrs Hampton laughed. 'Well, perhaps not, my little plum pony, but don't ask questions or I'll make that tail part of your uniform.'

'Please tell me, Mistress,' Eleanor begged.

'Very well, then. It's a club for ladies and gentlemen who wish to indulge their pleasures in private, with like-minded people,' Mrs Hampton explained.

'Did you take Amelia there?'

'Sometimes.'

'And will you be taking me?'

'Perhaps.'

'Please,' Eleanor urged. 'I really want you to. I want to be a part of everything. I want to learn what you like, and be by your side. Why don't you think I am ready? Please take me.'

Mrs Hampton sighed, and instead of answering she held Eleanor to her side. Before they were quite home the maid felt her hand guided back to that dark, wet warmth between her mistress's thighs.

Tom had decided to go out, despite the fog. There was something exciting about the way it smothered the streets and turned everyone into ghostly figures. He walked into the night not knowing where he was going, guided solely by his erection. On either side of him fine town houses loomed in the mist. There were few people on the streets tonight, and that suited him fine. Tom's voyeurism had begun when he first discovered the joys of spying on the staff, but he now enjoyed it in small everyday ways too. He could not pass a window without glancing in, or an alleyway without a little peek down its length. It was just in his nature, and nothing thrilled him as much as a stolen look at a private moment, so as he walked he kept his eyes and ears open.

As he passed the gates of a large house he spotted a chink of light at the window, and after stopping for a moment to check he was alone on the street he walked brazenly up the driveway and paused by the bushes outside. His heart was beating hard as he crept to the window and peeked inside. He was disappointed to see nothing but an elderly man reading his book by gaslight.

Tom quickly walked back to the road and picked another house. He knew it was dangerous, but if the peelers caught him they would surely believe his cover story that he had become lost. After all, he was a respectable young man and not the sort of riff-raff who burgle and rob; but more than once he had heard the barking of dogs or the sound of feet and had had to dash into the night. Such risks were part of the thrill for him, but he knew they might have a destructive end if he could not find an alternative source of fun. It was an addiction, though, and when it took hold he could not control it.

He crept down an alleyway and climbed over a low wall into a back garden. There were lights on in the house but they gave only a faint glow behind heavy curtains. He was halfway across the garden to the back door when he heard the bolts being drawn back. His heart leapt into his mouth and his skin frosted all over. He looked around desperately for somewhere to hide, then spotted the privy, a wooden building with low bushes around it. He made a run for it and managed to get inside before the back door opened.

His heart was beating madly as he heard the door of the house open and then close, and he vowed this would be the last time he went out at night spying. The footsteps drew closer and he felt his balls tighten with fear. He took stock of the privy, desperate for somewhere to conceal himself, but all he could do was crouch down in the shadows. They were headed towards him, and he cursed himself for picking the worst possible hiding place. Where else would someone be going in the dead of night but the privy? He waited nervously in the dark, hoping against hope that they wouldn't come in.

The door opened and a man in his long johns stepped in. He was clearly in a hurry, and had his buttons undone even before the door was closed. Luckily for Tom the privy was in almost total darkness and the man's need was urgent. He took out his penis and began to piss into the bowl with a sigh of relief. Tom was shaking with fear as the man gave his cock a shake and tucked it into his long johns.

Impossibly it seemed he had somehow escaped detection. But at the very peak of his hope and relief, the man suddenly gave a cry of surprise, stepped back, tensed with anger and then hauled Tom to his feet.

'What the hell are you doing in here?' the man demanded. 'Well? What's the meaning of this?'

'I'm sorry, I, er – I was caught short,' Tom said desperately.

The man was taller than Tom and a good few years older too. He had a broad chest and thickly muscled arms. There could be no escape, and Tom began to shake with fear.

'You came to rob me, didn't you?' the man asked. 'Tell the truth.'

'No, sir!' Tom said, and to his relief the man seemed to believe him, probably on account of his accent and obvious grooming.

'Then what are you doing here, boy? Speak up or I'll drag you to the station.'

'I told you, I needed to pee.'

'Liar! There's an ale-house across the street. Much more convenient, wouldn't you say? How could you have overlooked it? Mmm? Deciding instead to trespass?'

'I never meant any harm, sir,' Tom said in a meek and tremulous voice.

'Lurking in outhouses to spy on men when they pee, eh?' the man said.

'No!' Tom protested. 'No, not that. I'm not, you know – queer.'

'Is that so?' the man said, folding his arms over his large chest. 'Kneel down, boy.'

Tom dared not argue. The man guided him to his knees, facing his captor, and Tom knew at once what he was going to have to do. He still couldn't see the fellow's face in the shadows, and despite his fear and guilt and shame, some deep part of him warmed to life at the very indecency of what was about to take place.

He had played with other men on occasion, but only ever when they had shared a girl, and that was different – or at least that's what he had always told himself.

The man unbuttoned his long johns and let his cock slip out. It was as thick and muscular as the rest of his body, and Tom gave a little gulp of apprehension. The man lifted his dick with two fingers and let the tip touch Tom's chin.

'Open your mouth,' the man told him.

'Please, no. For God's sake. Let me go. I beg you.'

'It's the law or my cock. Your choice,' the man said, with a hint of derisive amusement in his stern words.

Staring at the fat cock being offered to his mouth, Tom swallowed. Part of him wanted to do it – the shame of the act was so strong – but it was only when his head was pulled roughly into the man's crotch that he could force himself to open his mouth. The cock went in, broad and already quite hard. Laughing, the man took hold of Tom's hair and forced his head back.

Tom found himself looking directly up at the long body of the man whose cock was in his mouth, with the heavy balls resting on his chin. He knew he had no choice, and began to work his head backwards and forwards, pulling the big cock into his mouth with stronger and stronger strokes.

The man grunted with pleasure and let his hand fall away from Tom's hair. He needed to steady himself against the privy walls as Tom sucked him deeper into his mouth, working his cock as though his life depended on it, at first unwillingly and then with a growing pleasure he could not deny.

'Let me see yours,' the man commanded, his words breathless and raspy with pleasure.

Tom hesitated, but when the man's body tensed he quickly unbuckled his trousers and exposed his cock, which to his utter shame had begun to grow hard. The man looked down with satisfaction.

'You like that, don't you?' he asked.

Tom could not answer because the man had his hard cock in his mouth, but then he didn't have to

182

answer – his half-stiff dick was all the response the man needed. As Tom sucked, the urge to take his own treacherous penis in his hand was growing. He struggled to resist the temptation, but then the final humiliation was inflicted upon him as the man approached the time for flooding Tom's mouth with spunk.

It would be soon, Tom knew. The man's cock was rigid, so close to orgasm that Tom could taste the semen leaking into his mouth. And then it happened.

Tom's mouth suddenly expanded and filled with thick, salty come, which he was forced to swallow as the man held tightly to his head, grunting and shaking as he forced his penis as deep as it would go.

After several gulps it was over and the man released his head. In the darkness, Tom could feel his grinning scrutiny.

'You need to come, don't you? the man scoffed.

Tom shook his head vehemently, but his cock said otherwise, now almost at full erection even though he hadn't touched it.

The man laughed. 'Go on, do it then, you little sissy.'

Again Tom shook his head, but the need was growing stronger and the man's derision only served to make it worse. Still the man blocked his exit, and Tom knew he would not be released until he'd obeyed the brute. With a shame-filled sob he took his cock in his hand and began to masturbate, kneeling in the darkness at the feet of a man whose spunk he could still taste in his mouth.

Tom couldn't look the man in the face as he tugged at himself, but his cock was hard and he knew he would have no difficulty coming. Even as he wanked he was telling himself that he was no homosexual, and it was true. The thrill came not from contact with another man, as contact with a woman thrilled him, but from the unbearable humiliation of having had to suck another man's cock. With that thought he could contain himself no longer. His cock jerked and with a great spasm he shot his spunk on to the floor.

'You liked that, didn't you?' the man said again.

'Yes,' Tom admitted miserably. 'Can I go now, please?'

'In a moment,' the man answered, and walked from the privy.

Tom hesitated, wanting to run but still confused by his own reactions and wondering what the man was going to do. He was guessing that the man intended to give him a few shillings for his services, and he knew he would accept because it would add another layer of humiliation. But what the stranger had in mind was worse still.

As the man came out from the house Tom saw that he was carrying a handful of some soft material, which proved to be a pair of extravagantly lacy women's drawers and a set of stockings. The man was sneering as he ordered Tom to put them on.

'Women's clothes?' Tom stammered.

'Just put them on,' the man ordered. 'It will remind you of what you are, a boy who takes his pleasure in sucking men's cocks.'

When Tom stumbled out of the man's house some hours later he was wearing not his own underwear but lacy drawers and slippery silk stockings. It all felt tight inside, tickling his penis and caressing his legs with every step. The sensation nearly brought him to his knees in dark semi-private places more than once on his shameful journey home. And by the time he had reached the privacy of his own room he was achingly erect, and went straight to his bed, where he

184

pulled himself to a sobbing, gasping orgasm through the slit in the lacy drawers as he thought of how it had felt to be forced to take a man's penis in his mouth.

# Eleven

*In which Eleanor is shown her place, on the stairs.*

The early-morning sun was a pale glow that did little more than tint the dark sky. A thick fog was forming over the city and the air had turned a dirty grey. Those who could avoid venturing outside stayed indoors as the fog and smoke swirled down through the streets of London. The bustle of the city had slowed in the face of the dark and foreboding weather, and few carriages could be seen or heard on the streets. The house felt hemmed-in and isolated, and the drab dampness outside seemed to seep in, giving the house a melancholy air.

Eleanor busied herself on the top landing, polishing the floor on her hands and knees, so lost in thought that she didn't hear the footsteps on the stairs behind her. She was thinking about how she'd been so rudely used on the previous day, tied like a beast and forced to compete in a game of such cruel perversity she doubted anyone respectable would even believe such things happened. Had it not been done to her, she herself certainly wouldn't have believed such tales, even after her introduction to the pleasures of submission and Sapphic love.

As her mind dwelt on the depravities she'd been made to suffer, her body automatically and unthinkingly continued with the familiar routine of house-work. She knew vaguely that when the floors were done she'd replace the newly beaten rugs and then go back downstairs and start folding the laundry, but in her mind she could focus on nothing but Mrs Hampton.

Only slowly did she begin to sense that she was not alone, and it was some time before she became certain. She could feel the presence of someone behind her on the stairs, looking at her, but she resisted the temptation to look around to see who it was. Whoever it was had crept up on her by stealth and obviously didn't want to be seen. Maybe it was Mrs Hampton, perhaps eager for an excuse to begin some new game.

She continued to clean the floor, but now pushed her bottom up in the air a little as she did so. Her uniform skirt was tight against her flesh, and as she bent over on all fours she knew she would be making a show of her figure, with her bottom like two rounded balls beneath her dress, and a little of her stockings on show too.

The watcher stayed still and quiet, encouraging Eleanor to wiggle her bottom as she worked, in teasing invitation to touch, and perhaps even to smack. With any luck her mistress might then take her to the bedroom and spare her an afternoon's work in favour of being licked to ecstasy, or perhaps dishing out a brisk spanking.

As Eleanor rubbed away her breasts swayed, and she became increasingly conscious of their movement, with her nipples brushing lightly against the cotton of her chemise. Behind her, she could hear her mistress's breathing, and she decided to provide something worth looking at – something which might warrant a punishment.

Spreading her knees a little, she began rubbing with greater vigour, making her breasts jiggle within her chemise and wiggling her bottom in a manner she was certain would be distracting.

Sure enough, she soon felt a hand touch the hem of her uniform, raising it as she worked. Her excitement began to grow, but she was keen to play the game and pretended not to notice, even as her skirt was turned up to expose the seat of her drawers. A finger slipped her underwear to the side, stroking her bottom cheek, then the whole hand was on her, squeezing her buttocks before straying down to her sex lips.

At that she could hold back no more, and with a little moan she let herself loll forwards so that her bottom was fully available, her long hair covering her face. She was being manipulated, roughly spread apart and fingered with sharp little thrusts. Then the other hand was on her breasts, briefly, before moving to the buttons on the back of her uniform. She started to raise her head but it was pushed firmly back down.

Eleanor gave a contented little sigh and closed her eyes, content to be taken there and then if it pleased her mistress, and determined not to seem disobedient or unreasonably shy in case Mrs Hampton was put off. She need not have worried, though: her lover had no intention of backing away, not with her so open and eager. She moaned as two fingers penetrated her, and again as they began to work in her hole.

Her legs felt weak as her underwear was pulled fully to one side to expose her, so that Mrs Hampton could watch her probing fingers at work. Eleanor put up no resistance as she was manipulated, even when she was pushed down to the floor and her drawers yanked wide, bursting their buttons so that the garment fell around her knees. Her bottom was now fully naked, and as she was pushed gently but firmly to the ground and her legs hauled apart she knew that no detail of her sex was concealed.

Eleanor lay still, panting and pressing herself against the wooden floor in little jerks that rubbed her clit against the ground. She felt feral and wild, in need of taming and taking and fucking with the big rubber dildo. It was a glorious feeling, so simple and full of need. She was held firmly at the hips as Mrs Hampton moved up between her thighs, to once again explore her bottom and probe the willing hole between her thighs, then jerk her dress up higher still, and her chemise with it, covering her head and allowing her breasts to fall naked to the slippery floor.

The smell of the polish was intoxicating, and she felt light-headed and dizzy as her lover fondled her body. Two fingers dipped into her slit and rubbed her, and she began to squirm on the floor in her excitement, completely abandoned to Mrs Hampton's touch. She groaned with pleasure as nimble fingers found one nipple then tugged and rolled it, pulling at it until it was rock hard. Her pert little bottom was slapped hard and she gave a gasp of surprise and pain, but forced herself to push it up for more.

Her mistress began to spank her, and as the playful slaps rained down on her bottom Eleanor struggled playfully. She began to turn around, wanting to kiss the lips of her lover, but instead she was forced down on to the floor and mounted, her neck bitten and kissed. As she writhed and struggled in mock resistance something pressed between the cheeks of her bottom, something hard and rubbery, but also hot. With a cry of surprise she realised that it was not her mistress's dildo at all, but a penis, and that she was about to be fucked where she lay.

Twisting violently around, she confronted her molester, her mouth opening wide in shock and her hands going to her breasts and sex when she saw that it was Tom.

'Oh my goodness, it's you!' she cried.

Tom laughed and said, 'Who did you expect?'

Eleanor could not answer, at least not truthfully, as she could hardly admit to him that she expected his mother.

'You knew I'd be back for you, didn't you?' he challenged. His speech was slightly slurred, thick with lust.

'Yes,' she said meekly, 'I suppose I did, but – but I have to finish my work.'

'You are such a hot little thing,' he said. 'So hot down there.'

He pushed his cock against her bare leg, and Eleanor tried to get up but was pushed quickly back down.

'Stay as you are,' he demanded, pressing forwards to pin her down on the floor. 'I was enjoying our game, and so were you, and now I'm going to take you, right here.'

'You can't!' Eleanor protested. 'Let me up.'

Tom grabbed her by her hair and twisted her around, exposing her bottom once more. She gave a little cry of frustration and anger as his cock pressed to her bare bottom cheek, but he held her in place.

'Is that what you want? To be left in that state?' Tom demanded. 'And me in this state also?'

'I don't know what –'

'Left like this?' Tom asked.

His free hand slipped down to his cock and he ran it against Eleanor's backside. A thin trail of wetness touched the cleft of her bottom and she gave a hot little moan.

'You see,' he said. 'You are as hot for me as I am for you. Now let's fuck.'

'Stop it! I've got work to do; let me up!' she protested.

'You were happy enough to let me get you in this state,' Tom sneered. 'Who did you think it was? Mr Coleman, come to have you like the little common serving wench you are?'

'No!' she protested. 'Not Mr Coleman, that's – that's disgusting!'

'Who, then? Betty, with her busy little tongue? Come upstairs to slide your dress up and help herself to you?'

'A better prospect than you, at least,' she retorted. 'Now get off me, Tom!'

His dick was touching her between her bottom cheeks now, rubbing against the smooth soft curves and getting ever closer to her moist hole. Eleanor grabbed his wrist to stop him rubbing himself against her, but it didn't work and she snatched at his cock instead.

'Oh no, not this time,' he said, keeping a firm grip on himself but still rubbing between her cheeks.

She could feel his urgency and knew that he could not last much longer, and would shoot his hot juices over her bottom with just a few tugs.

'I'll just have to report what you've been doing up here,' Tom said sadly. 'With your bottom stuck up and your wet little slit all ready for whoever might want you. What a slut you are!'

'No, you will not report me!' Eleanor begged.

'Then let me take you,' he urged. 'Come on, you can hardly deny you wanted it, and you still do.'

This time Eleanor had no answer. Tom chuckled and quickly rolled her on to her back. Her hair fell in front of her face and she blew it away with an impatient puff, looking up at him. He was kneeling over her now, leering down at her with his cock in his hand, pulling it as he waited for her response.

Eleanor didn't know what to do. The thought of being reported for playing the slut was unbearable, as Mrs Hampton was hardly likely to want a personal slave who went around encouraging others to take her at all times. Tom didn't know about that, of course – he thought she was scared because she would get the sack for being a slut – but it made little difference. She knew she would have to surrender, a choice made easier because it was what her body wanted, but she could not bring herself to say the awful words.

'Gone quiet?' Tom enquired. They both knew he had won.

He let go of his dick and grabbed the edge of her uniform, to pull it up and off, leaving her with nothing on but her ruined drawers, which were still around one ankle, her stockings, shoes, and her chemise, which had been turned up and pulled over her breasts. He gave a satisfied nod as he admired her nakedness.

'So pretty,' he said. 'So pretty I may just have to take you now, with or without your permission, right here on the floor.'

'You can't, Tom,' Eleanor protested. 'You can't.'

'Why not?' he demanded. 'I'm hard enough, as you can see, and you're wet enough, for all your protests.'

He'd begun to jerk his dick, seemingly unable to contain his excitement a moment longer. His head rolled back a little but he was still looking down at her, clearly relishing the sight of the fine hair between her legs and her swollen lips.

'Open your legs for me,' he ordered.

She shook her head and tried to sit up. He used his knees to force her legs a little wider apart. His eyes were nearly closed now and his hand was moving very quickly, almost shaking instead of sliding up and down. She was fascinated despite herself, her pride the only thing that stopped her parting her legs completely and letting him inside.

'Another way, then,' he grunted.

He took hold of her hair and drew her closer to his busy hand. Tiny drops of his juice fell against her cheek and the side of her neck as he forced her face closer to his cock.

'Open your mouth,' he commanded. 'Let me do it in your mouth.'

Eleanor's mouth was slightly open already; she was watching his masturbation closely, mesmerised by it. He needed no further encouragement, and forced his hard member against her lips. Eleanor gave in, taking his cock inside her mouth and letting her lips run down to the base of his shaft. She began to suck, gently at first and then firmly moving her head up and down its length. As she did so the tip of her tongue sought out the underside of his cockhead and stroked it.

Tom's bottom clenched in ecstasy and he grabbed on to her hair with both hands so tightly that she couldn't move at all. He was coming, his balls as hard as marbles as his orgasm sprayed into her mouth, coating it and running down her throat. She felt as though she might drown in it, but he held her firm until she had swallowed every drop. At last he let go of her hair and with a gentle push let her slide down on to the floor.

'Get on with your work,' he said, buttoning up his fly.

'You can't just use me like that!' Eleanor said, wiping her mouth. 'You dirty little boy.'

'Oh I can, and I will,' Tom said. 'Any time I like. That's what you servant girls are for.'

'So you mean to leave me in this state?' she asked.

Tom's eyes travelled down her slender body to look at her hands, one on top of the other and both pressed against her pussy. The sound of her stirring herself was unmistakeable, and their eyes met over her naked body.

He laughed. 'Wanton, that's what you are. You let girls lick you down there.'

'And I bet you like watching that,' she teased. 'Don't you like watching that, Tom? When a girl is down on her knees licking me? I think you probably do – almost enough to bring your cock back to attention, isn't it?'

'Get on with your work,' he said absently.

'I am, Master Tom,' she replied. 'That's what us serving girls are for, isn't it? This is our work, fucking and teasing and sucking. I can still taste you in my mouth.'

'You made me do that, you little slut,' Tom said cautiously.

Eleanor's back arched.

'Wanton,' he whispered.

She gave him a sly smile.

'I can't help it,' she said. 'It is my nature. When I touch myself deep inside – just, oh yes, there, it feels so good. Different. I don't think even –' she caught herself just in time, having nearly said Mrs Hampton's name '– even Betty doesn't know about this place.'

She took his wrist and placed his hand over her crotch. The wetness seeped between his fingers.

'You're so wet,' he said.

'Of course I am,' she replied. 'What do you expect when you make me suck your cock and swallow your stuff? You wanted me, and you've got me now. I'm all yours, I need you to fuck me.'

'I can't. My balls are empty.'

'Let me see.' She began undoing his buttons.

His dick was slightly erect – she could feel it against her fingers as she undid the last of his buttons – and he was wearing no underwear. All the better, she thought. She pulled his dick out, and found it still wet from her mouth.

He watched, fascinated, as her slippery fingers moved up and down his cock. She gently pulled the skin back and trapped the head between her thumb and forefinger. He gave a little cry of surprise and pleasure as she yanked it towards her mouth.

'Let's get you ready, Master Tom,' she said, and put her lips to it.

For all her inexperience she knew what felt good. Her tongue was like a snake around the length of his stiffening dick, sliding under and over it. Her hand reached around to his backside and her nails dug into his bottom cheeks. She parted his backside and teased him with her finger.

'What are you doing?' he moaned.

She just glanced up with a wicked look in her eye. His dick was harder now, nearly as strong and firm as it had been in his fist. When he was totally hard she took him by the shoulders and pushed him down, letting his cock slip out of her mouth. He pulled his trousers down to his ankles and climbed on to her, his stiff dick ready once more.

Eleanor lay back. She could smell the rich aroma of the floor polish and Tom's sweat as he guided himself into her. His hot temper had cooled and now he seemed to be experiencing every sensation with fresh wonder. She smiled up at him and kissed his mouth, her tongue slipping inside to meet his own.

Tom began to increase his speed, now raised up on his hands, and he was gasping with each stroke.

195

Eleanor began to orgasm, her body writhing on the floor, and they came together, their bodies pressed tightly to each other until both were done.

He rolled off her and lay on his back, panting with his hand around his softening penis. Eleanor hastily got up and grabbed her clothes.

'This has to be our secret,' she told him.

'Perhaps,' he said. 'So long as there's a next time.'

'There won't be a next time, not if I can help it,' Eleanor said as she rearranged her clothing.

They both knew she was lying.

'You took me by surprise,' she went on. 'That's the only reason I let you.'

'You looked so perfect bent over on the floor like that, who could resist?' he said, and gave his cock a little stroke.

Despite her conflicting emotions Eleanor was smiling as she carried her cleaning bucket downstairs.

# Twelve

*Wherein the reader is introduced to the forbidden pleasures of The Cauldron Club.*

Betty and Eleanor lay in bed together kissing and touching each other until the cook roused them with a loud bang on the door. They reluctantly got up and slipped their uniforms on, chatting and joking before they went to work. Eleanor took young Tom his breakfast that morning, but remained cautious in case he tried to grope her or worse. She needn't have feared; he seemed very quiet and took the tray without a word.

Next she took Mrs Hampton's tray up, and was permitted to stand by the bed while her mistress ate. Eleanor loved it when she was allowed to stay in the room while Mrs Hampton had breakfast. It reminded her strongly of why she liked the older woman. Mrs Hampton tucked into her food with gusto and pushed aside anything that didn't meet her high standards. When she had finished she mopped her mouth delicately and opened the newspaper with a flourish, but read for only a moment before casting it aside and glancing at the window, where the dull grey light showed through a crack in the curtains.

'Another day of fog,' she remarked.

'Yes, my lady,' Eleanor replied. 'They say it's so

bad in the East End that people are getting sick from the vapours.'

'It is the night of The Cauldron Club as well,' Mrs Hampton said. 'It would be a shame if the weather were to keep me away. I missed last month for no better reason than the visit of my puritanical sister.'

Eleanor had never heard her mistress speak of her sister and couldn't imagine Mrs Hampton bending her will for anyone, but she said nothing.

'We will be heading towards the West End anyway,' Mrs Hampton told her. 'The fog may well be a little lighter.'

'Do you mean you are taking me after all?' Eleanor asked.

Mrs Hampton beckoned Eleanor over and slipped her hand behind the maid, against the backs of her legs, to run it up her thighs to the hips. She slid her hand up the thin cotton slip to touch the girl's bottom, squeezing her cheeks and tickling the slit between her thighs. Eleanor felt her heart skip as she was pulled in for a kiss. Mrs Hampton's exquisite lips brushed hers and their tongues touched, even as her mistress's hand pushed between the maid's legs. Eleanor could not hide her wetness. Just kissing Mrs Hampton left her in a state, and she could feel that her lips were already swollen and hot.

'Such an eager little thing, aren't you?' Mrs Hampton said as she pulled her mouth back.

'Yes, Mistress. Always, Mistress, for you,' Eleanor said in a low husky voice.

'Yes, you are coming with me to The Cauldron Club,' Mrs Hampton told her. 'Be in my room at seven, as I wish to pick what you wear tonight.'

Mrs Hampton's fingers were still between Eleanor's thighs and starting to slip inside her very slowly. She couldn't help but push herself down on them. Encouraged by the response, her mistress quickly worked her fingers in and out, fast enough to elicit hard little moans and make Eleanor hold on to the arm of the chair for support.

'I hope you are feeling brave, my little toy?' Mrs Hampton asked.

'I will try,' Eleanor promised.

'Be here at seven. Now go,' Mrs Hampton said.

Eleanor felt Mrs Hampton's fingers slip back out of her and gave a cry of frustration and deep longing.

'No more,' Mrs Hampton instructed. 'Save yourself for tonight. One last thing, clean my fingers. You've left them soaked to the knuckle.'

Eleanor obediently knelt down in front of Mrs Hampton and took the woman's long, slender fingers in her mouth. She sucked them and licked between them, and when she had cleaned them she kissed the fingertips.

'Good girl; now go and get on with your duties,' Mrs Hampton said, and stood up.

She stroked Eleanor's hair and patted her head and then left her maid kneeling on the carpet, trembling with the urgent need to be fucked and taken. Eleanor even considered following her mistress upstairs, but did not dare. Instead she got unsteadily to her feet and checked that nobody was about to come in. Sure she was alone, she took the napkin from the table and pressed it beneath her dress. When she took it out she found the imprint of her wet lips could be clearly seen. It was tempting to masturbate, but her mistress had given her an order and she was determined to obey. Smiling despite herself, she went back to work.

Naturally the day dragged horribly. Every time she looked at the clock the hands seemed to have moved only five minutes forwards. It was an intolerable wait. She even asked the cook for extra duties to keep herself busy, but that didn't help. Her eye kept going to the clock, where time seemed determined to tease her. Little by little, though, the day passed, until finally it was nearly seven. Eleanor washed herself and let Betty brush her hair, then gave her friend a little kiss on the cheek and skipped upstairs with her stomach a hive of busy, wicked sensations.

Mrs Hampton was waiting in her room, sitting on the bed with all kinds of clothes laid out before her. She was wearing just a short silk slip and stockings with garter belts. Her hair was a little wet, and she was brushing it as Eleanor closed the door behind her.

'Hello, Eleanor,' Mrs Hampton said. 'Let's get you dressed up, shall we? Slip your clothes off.'

Eleanor did as she was told. She loved to be bare in front of Mrs Hampton; she especially liked the way the woman's eyes ate her up and then savoured every inch of her. Mrs Hampton waited until Eleanor was naked, then picked out a corset from the bed. It was a beautiful colour, a deep wine red with little gold flowers embroidered in a swirling pattern. The stays were white and gleamed with polished age.

'Do you like it, dear?' Mrs Hampton asked.

'Oh, Mistress, it is beautiful. Did it belong to Amelia?'

'No, my dear, I found it just for you. Don't you think it matches your hair? Try it on.'

Eleanor took the corset from Mrs Hampton and put it around herself. The material felt wonderful close to her skin. She loved the way it cupped and lifted her small breasts and encased her hips, and it had a section that was raised so that it didn't cover her private parts.

Mrs Hampton turned Eleanor gently around and patted the maid's bare bottom appreciatively. She

tightened the laces, urging Eleanor to breathe in and
stand up straight. Each tie that was pulled into place
made Eleanor more upright, and she felt her breasts
pushed firmly up and her waist held in.

Once the laces had been tied off, Mrs Hampton
took Eleanor over to the full-length mirror and stood
behind her. Eleanor marvelled at the wasp-thin waist
the corset gave her, and the way it made her look so
feminine. She was grateful she didn't have to wear
one all the time, but she loved how it made her look.
Mrs Hampton picked out a pretty silk skirt for her
and told her to put it on. It went all the way down to
her ankles but was split up one side as far as the knee.
A few days ago she would have protested at the idea
of strangers seeing her in such immodest attire, but
since then she had crawled through mud wearing
nothing but a few leather straps for modesty, and this
seemed charmingly innocent by comparison.

A long red coat with a pretty little hood was picked
out for her, and then Mrs Hampton showed her the
boots she was to wear. Eleanor had never seen
anything so lovely in all her life; they were knee-high
and of black leather, with as many stays and buckles
as her corset. She was thrilled to try them on; they
even had heels that made her leg muscles go tight and
firm when she stood up in them. Mrs Hampton
helped her lace them up.

'Don't you look the prettiest thing?' Mrs Hampton
said with some pride.

'I've never worn anything like this before, Mistress;
thank you,' Eleanor said.

Mrs Hampton left her to brush her hair. When she
returned, Eleanor turned from the mirror and was
unable to think of anything to say, her mistress
looked so beautiful.

'Don't you like it?' Mrs Hampton asked.

'Oh my lady, you look so wonderful!' Eleanor said.

Mrs Hampton had chosen a long black dress that left her arms bare, with gloves to match and elegant boots with pointed toes. Her hair was up, but a few strands fell loose with a slight curl in them, giving her a look of potent sexuality that Eleanor found both exciting and intimidating.

'Put on your coat, my little love toy,' Mrs Hampton said. 'Let's see what you think of The Cauldron.'

The weather had not improved at all, and the cab ride took them through streets dense with fog. There were few people on the road and those they passed seemed in a hurry to get indoors, while the carriage driver was silent all the way, as if trying not to inhale too much of the damp, dirty air. The two women sat close together, the fierce expression on Mrs Hampton's face clearly preventing the driver from trying to strike up a conversation.

Eleanor was thankful. Her stomach was fluttering again and her new clothes made her feel beautiful and sexy, but also vulnerable. She wanted to savour the moment instead of wasting it making small talk.

The cab came to a halt and Mrs Hampton paid the man and helped Eleanor down. The cab clattered off, leaving them outside a nondescript-looking house set slightly back from the road. Huge gothic gargoyles glared down at them, and the smoke and fog clung to their bodies before being blown away by the wind, which rose then fell again, as if imitating Eleanor's nervous mood.

Mrs Hampton knocked on the door three times. A small grate slid back and an eye peered out, then the door was opened. The woman who let them in was dressed in a skin-tight costume with ostrich feathers at her rear. In her hair there were more feathers, tall ones dyed silver and gold and yellow and red, which stuck out like a crown. She did not speak, nor could she, for her mouth was gagged with a length of stocking. Instead she gave a little bow to Mrs Hampton and stood aside. As Eleanor walked in she found herself staring at this strange young woman, whose costume was so tight that her pussy lips could be seen beneath it, as well as the curve of her breasts and her nipples, which stuck out hard and erect. She led them down the hallway, her tail feathers moving rhythmically as her bottom swayed. The hallway was lit only by a few stubby candles, which cast little more than a dim glow, showing an impression of the layout before them but giving little else away. They were led into a larger room, where the walls and floor were bare brick and flagstones. It looked as if it should be a cold place, but the many candles within seemed to warm it so much that Eleanor felt a little faint. There were candelabras set at intervals down the room, and under each one Eleanor could see a gathering of people talking quietly. As her eyes adjusted to the gloom she saw them more clearly, and blushed to see what they were doing.

Eleanor and Mrs Hampton removed their coats and handed them to the silent servant in the extravagant tail feathers. Closest to them were three pretty young girls wearing the most fashionable and expensive clothes. They could have been the daughters of nobility, judging by their stylish attire. Yet if they were from such aristocratic stock, and they did look as if they might be sisters, then they had surely lost all sense of good breeding. The trio, despite their style, were down on their knees with their mouths open while a man in a dark suit and fez masturbated fiercely in front of them. Every few moments he would pause and hold his balls so that his proud and thick member would stand up tall, and the three girls would eagerly fight for the chance to swallow it for a moment before he pushed them away and carried on pleasuring himself. Eleanor glanced over at Mrs Hampton and saw that her mistress was looking elsewhere, so she followed her gaze and gave a little gasp of surprise. It seemed the whole room was alive with furious sexual activity.

Under the next candelabra she could quite clearly see a young lady naked and tied to a wheel. The wheel was turning slowly, driven by some mechanism hidden from view, and around the girl an enthusiastic audience had gathered. They were drinking from tall glasses topped with ice and fruit and were teasing her by dropping the ice on her body. She wore a blindfold and could not judge where the next sensation would come from. As Eleanor watched, a candle in its wrought-iron holder above began to dribble, and a spluttering of hot wax ran down the base of the holder and landed directly on the girl. She bucked in her straps, straining at the wheel and moaning as the wax spattered down on to her shoulder, and then as the wheel turned it ran on to her arms and then fell on to the wheel itself. The flow began to trail off, but there were still a few drops left for her thighs and vagina as the wheel turned her completely around. The girl lifted her head and cried out, less a cry of pain than of bewildered, desperate lust. Eleanor couldn't take her eyes away from the scene. One of the audience took a piece of ice from his drink and tossed it on to the girl's belly. It made her twist against her restraints, and as she rose the sliver of ice ran down towards her pussy lips, meeting the hot juices there and slowly melting away as she cried out to be fucked hard. She begged for it, demanded it, pleaded for it, but those gathered around her simply left her there, pumping her thighs upwards and arching her back, offering herself to anyone who would take her and sate her terrible yearning.

Yet that was not the most perverse thing on show: everywhere the eye travelled there was a display of sinful pleasure. On a small platform against a wall a woman of some size lay on a day-bed being fed grapes and wine by men dressed in short togas. She was wearing just a long white sash of material that covered one breast and part of her leg; her other large breast hung loose, and one man was enthusiastically sucking and kissing it. Other groups were visible beyond this, and it seemed to Eleanor that each was competing with the next for the sheer perversity of their amusements.

'Come, I want a drink,' Mrs Hampton said.

Mrs Hampton guided Eleanor to the bar, which was against the far wall and near a small orchestra composed entirely of naked and masked musicians. Eleanor was fascinated by them, but Mrs Hampton managed to regain her attention by giving her bottom a swift slap.

'Oh, I'm sorry, Mrs Hampton,' Eleanor said. 'I was lost in thought. There's just so much to see!'

'I said, what do you want to drink?' Mrs Hampton asked.

'Oh, I don't know – what should I have?' Eleanor said.

'Two of my usual, please,' Mrs Hampton said, and the barmaid, a pretty little thing with streaked hair and a spiked collar, brought them two tall glasses full of ice, over which she poured a richly coloured drink from a jug.

'Have you had Pimms before?' Mrs Hampton asked.

'No, Mistress,' Eleanor admitted.

'Poor thing, you haven't lived. Come with me. I want to show you something.'

She led Eleanor to a quiet corner away from the musicians, where a few people were chatting to each other and drinking. There was a large X-shaped wooden cross set into the floor, fixed together with iron bands. Where the arms spread at the top there was a collar of metal and leather. Mrs Hampton guided Eleanor towards it and they set down their drinks on a nearby table.

'What is it?' Eleanor asked.

'It's for bad girls,' Mrs Hampton said. 'Bad girls like you.'

She took one of Eleanor's wrists and lifted it up to the top of a beam, slipping it inside a metal cuff padded with leather. Eleanor began to breathe hard, growing ever more nervous and excited. Mrs Hampton walked behind her and took her other wrist, then put that in another cuff, closed both and fixed them securely in place with bolts. Eleanor knew what was coming next, and sure enough Mrs Hampton knelt behind her, pulled her legs roughly apart and fixed her ankles in place. She left her facing the stone wall, her back to the room.

Mrs Hampton stood back and admired her work, then moved out of view. Eleanor waited a moment and then tried to turn to see what was happening. Mrs Hampton was nowhere to be seen, and Eleanor was gripped with a sudden panic, knowing that, tied up as she was, anything could happen to her.

'Mrs Hampton?' she whispered. 'Mistress?'

There was no answer, but she heard a man say 'Bravo' and some clapping, increasing her fear until she was wriggling in her cuffs, only for relief to flood through her at the sound of a light laugh from her mistress. Mrs Hampton put her hand on Eleanor's back and leant close to the cuffed maid.

'Are you ready, little one?' Mrs Hampton asked.

'What for?' Eleanor said.

'You'll see. Hold still, now. I'm accurate but not perfect.'

Eleanor had no idea what to expect but Mrs Hampton showed her, lifting a coiled whip of supple, plaited leather, which she rubbed against Eleanor's face. The maid gave a little gasp.

'Oh no, not that.'

'Be quiet and hold still; that is my advice,' Mrs Hampton said and walked away.

Eleanor stared straight ahead at the stone wall, wondering how many other girls had stood here trembling powerlessly. Had Amelia been spread so completely here too? She heard a crack of the whip behind her and saw it lashing down on the ground to her side. There was applause, and Eleanor resolved to keep very still.

The first whiplash fell short, snapping loudly behind her. She could feel all eyes on her now; even the musicians had stopped. The whip came again, this time so close she could feel the air move as it passed. The lash cracked on the floor, making her try to jump, but of course she could not – she couldn't move at all. She tried to force herself not to flinch as the whip cracked once more, but again it missed, and again her body jerked in fear.

A few light sounds of amusement reached her from the crowd, increasing her fear and frustration until she could feel the tears starting in her eyes, but Mrs Hampton calmed her by laying one gentle hand on her bare shoulder. Immediately Eleanor felt better, soothed by her mistress's touch, even as her beautiful skirt was unfastened and slipped off to leave her legs and bottom bare to the audience.

'Did you really think I would risk tearing such a beautiful garment?' Mrs Hampton asked softly.

'I do not know, Mistress,' Eleanor breathed.

Mrs Hampton gave a quiet cluck of amusement and stood away again. Eleanor felt her bottom tighten in anticipation of the whip, and again, her cheeks clenched over and over, much to the amusement of the watchers. At last she forced herself to be still, out of sheer embarrassment, and at that very moment the lash snaked out, catching the crest of one naked bottom cheek to make her gasp and jerk in her bonds.

Polite applause and a few muttered compliments greeted the shot, while Eleanor was left to calm down, shivering in her bonds. Again the whip struck, landing with perfect accuracy on the helpless maid's other cheek, to leave her with twin blemishes that graced the alabaster skin of her bottom. The audience once more clapped their appreciation. Eleanor braced herself for further pain, but Mrs Hampton came to her once more, to stroke her maid's bottom and kiss her cheek.

'You are very brave,' Mrs Hampton said.

'Oh, Mistress! I am so scared,' Eleanor gasped, 'and it hurts so very much.'

'You will find it warms you,' Mrs Hampton assured her. 'Now, let us slip this corset from you.'

Eleanor had felt at least slightly covered with the corset on; now she feared her back would be whipped, but she knew she would achieve nothing by protesting. Mrs Hampton loosened the lacing and eased the corset open at the front, her hands lingering briefly on Eleanor's breasts before removing the garment altogether. With it off Eleanor felt even more vulnerable. She had nothing on now but her boots and stockings.

'You've hardly touched your drink,' Mrs Hampton remarked.

'I had little chance to drink it, my lady,' Eleanor said quietly. 'Please take me down.'

'Of course, once I've had my own drink,' Mrs Hampton replied.

She stepped away and Eleanor was left hanging in the straps, much to her surprise and horror. It was mere moments before people started to come and look at her. She felt a hand on her bare shoulder, then another, smaller and more feminine, snaking down her back and on to her bottom to touch the warm spot where the whip had found her.

'Such a nice little bottom,' someone remarked, a woman's voice. She was answered by a man.

'Yes, look at her anus – very tight.'

Eleanor flinched. Someone had parted her bottom cheeks and was showing her off to their friend. She felt crimson shame flush her face, and was glad they could not see it. New hands found her legs, running fingers down the sensitive skin and squeezing her calves through her boots. Then someone reached around her and began to explore her breasts, groping her and pulling at her nipples, while the first man or possibly his lady began to tease her anus with a feather.

As they touched her body her embarrassment slowly began to fade, to be replaced by erotic sensations, until she felt she was floating, drifting away from what was happening and experiencing only the sensual feeling of being used. Her whole body tingled and felt like one organ, some huge sexual organ that reacted to every touch and poke with wild excitement. A hand slipped between her legs and ran over her most private parts. She felt the wetness run down their fingers. She didn't know if it was a man or a woman touching her and she didn't care; she just wanted those fingers inside her.

'Fuck me,' she moaned.

There was laughter, and someone put an ice-cube down her back. She gave a breathless shiver and then moaned and tried to push her lips down on the questing fingers of the mystery figure. But the fingers withdrew momentarily, only to return with more force as a thumb pushed at her clit. She cried out, pleased, like the woman on the wheel she had seen, but they laughed at her, still touching her and teasing her body.

'Fuck me, I need it – fuck me, please,' she heard herself saying.

A man pressed himself against her. She could tell it was a man because she could feel the impression of a hard cock against her flesh. He must have then unbuttoned his trousers and taken his cock out, because in moments she felt the unforgettable sensation of hard male sexual muscle rubbing against her bottom.

'Please, please do me,' she cried.

She felt his cock push between her legs, rubbing against her opening. It was very thick and hard, bigger than she had ever seen or felt. He pushed it a tiny way inside her, so that only the tip of the head was in her, and she called for more. She begged, pleaded, cried out and nearly wept to be fucked before he let the whole head inside her. At last he took her by the shoulder and around the waist and forced it in her. He was rough with her, not waiting for her to get used to it before fucking her hard and deep. She let her face fall forwards at each stroke, her entire body jerking and her pussy already tightening on his cock. He was close, almost straight away ready to come, and she wasn't far behind.

He put his hand over her mouth and gripped her shoulder as he began to come. She could taste the salt of his sweating palm over her mouth as he exploded deep inside her. He held himself there until she felt she would burst, only to suddenly pull back and let a gush of his juice and hers squirt from her body.

With her body spread open she knew that the watchers could see every detail of the state she was in. Interested observers began to touch her swollen lips and feel for her clitoris, which was so delicate and sensitive that the slightest of touches made her whole body shake. She felt someone's tongue lap up the man's come that had dribbled down her leg, and she longed for them to plunge their tongue into her too, pushing her bottom out and begging for it even as a familiar voice spoke behind her.

'I can't leave you alone for five minutes, can I?' Mrs Hampton said and laughed.

Eleanor let herself be untied and almost fell into her mistress's arms. Mrs Hampton guided her over to a pile of cushions and let her fall back into them.

'Oh, it felt so good,' Eleanor sighed. 'I love it when I'm out of control. Why is that? Why is it so good?'

'Everyone is different, Eleanor dear. I am how I am and you are as you are. You get the same thrill and pure pleasure when tied up and being fucked or whipped as I do when I am in charge. It is the perfect arrangement, is it not?'

'It is. I am so happy. I never knew I could feel so – so aroused. Oh, Mistress, what is that?'

Mrs Hampton had a little box in her hands. It was the same shape as a shoe box, but a little smaller. She smiled and handed it to Eleanor.

'Open it.'

Eleanor did so. Inside was a collar of red leather, set with spikes. A small silver tag bore her name.

'If you are mine then you must wear that when we are together, so that you remember your place,' Mrs Hampton said. 'Here, let me put it on you.'

'I love it, thank you,' Eleanor said.

'Let's go home. What do you think?' Mrs Hampton asked. 'An early night, just you and I.'

'Oh yes! I would love that. Shall I go and fetch my clothes?'

Mrs Hampton laughed and her eyes glinted with wicked delight. Eleanor gave a moan that was half apprehension and half pleasure. The evening wasn't over yet.

Mr Pendleberry and his wife always took a constitutional walk of an evening, which he believed to be essential for the digestion. Mrs Pendleberry was unenthusiastic about it but she knew better than to drag her heels. Mr Pendleberry was a stickler for routine, as she had found out over the course of their long and rather tedious marriage. Still, at least he kept a roof over their heads, she reflected as she hurried along at his side, even if he did drag her out to walk with him whatever the weather. As the pair marched along at a brisk pace Mr Pendleberry tipped his hat, and his wife peered into the fog to see whom he was greeting. At first she mistook the woman at the lamppost for one of those awful women of the night they sometimes saw. She hoped not, because whenever they did spot one her husband would spend ages afterwards praying for their souls and detailing the depravity of their acts to her. Sometimes he even wrote to his member of parliament. As it happened, though, it was nothing but a lady out walking her dog.

'Terrible weather,' Mr Pendleberry commented.

'I hope it lifts soon,' the woman agreed. 'It makes my poor little missy ill at ease.'

Mr Pendleberry peered down at the animal on the lead. It was quite a big dog by the look of it – one of those foreign breeds, no doubt.

'They say it will be in for another night then lift,' Mr Pendleberry announced, 'and my barometer says much the same.'

'Oh, are you a scientific man, then?' the woman asked.

The animal was shuffling around in the fog, pulling at the lead, but the lady gave it a sharp tug and it seemed to accept that she meant to stop for a while.

'Oh, I wouldn't say that,' Mr Pendleberry said modestly.

He was tempted to tell her that he was no less than the senior partner of a thriving chemist's shop, but thought better of it. Instead he introduced his wife, who wished the stranger a good evening.

'Good evening to you too,' the lady said.

'I think your pet has finally decided it's safe to do its business,' Mrs Pendleberry commented.

Mr Pendleberry scowled. Trust his wife to make a show of him in front of a lady of breeding, he thought. Whatever must she be thinking now? A man whose wife refers to the most basic and crude animal functions in the street. To avoid further embarrassment he bid the lady goodnight and quickly guided his wife by the elbow off up the street. It was true, though; he could hear the animal pissing against the lamp-post as he walked away. The fog did strange things to the acoustics of the street, he thought as he walked. If he hadn't known better he would almost have thought the animal gave a human sigh as its urgent urination ended.

# Thirteen

*In which the lady of the house makes a decision which
pushes her maid to desperate lengths in order to prove her
loyalty and determination.*

Eleanor found out about the party quite by chance,
which made her very cross. It was the cook who
informed her that all servants were to be given two
nights off. This sudden act of generosity was because
Mrs Hampton was having a soirée on the second
evening and said she would be hiring outside staff for
the occasion.

'But where will you go?' Eleanor asked Betty.

'Probably find myself a warm bed with a gentleman
to fill it,' the tweenie maid answered. 'Cook and her
lover will be off down to the coast as Mr and Mrs
Smith, as always. Why don't you come out with me?
I never end up short of somewhere to stay.'

'But why does Mrs Hampton want us out of the
way?' Eleanor asked.

'So us servants don't see what goes on at her
parties, which is probably not unlike what goes on at
her club. You still haven't told me what happened, or
why you didn't sleep downstairs last night.'

'This isn't right,' Eleanor said. 'I don't want to be
kicked out; I want to stay here.'

'Not for me to say, but I don't think we're sophisticated enough for her guests,' Betty said. 'Come out with me and enjoy yourself.'

'Thank you, Betty,' Eleanor said, 'but no, all the same. It's not that I won't enjoy being with you, but I feel Mrs Hampton doesn't think I'm good enough for her, and I should be here.'

Betty hugged her and gave her a kiss on the cheek.

'Don't be silly, Ellie, you're beautiful and I know she likes you a lot. It's just that some of her friends are probably hoity-toity nobs, you know how it is – us lot aren't good enough for them sometimes, not for what they get up to. It ain't down to how you look or how much she likes you.'

'I suppose not,' Eleanor said sadly.

Just then Mr Coleman came downstairs, looking flushed and annoyed. He had an envelope in his hand which he was tapping against his palm in agitation.

'Everything as it should be, Mr Coleman?' the cook called from the kitchen.

'No,' the butler replied, 'and it never is with that woman.'

The cook beckoned him into the kitchen and spoke to the girls.

'You two stop standing around and get some work done. Come on in here, Mr Coleman, you poor thing. Sit down and I'll make you a nice cup of tea.'

'I wonder what that's all about?' Eleanor asked as the kitchen door closed behind the butler.

'Something to do with the party, I suppose,' Betty said.

'Cook, we're going upstairs to clean the grates now,' Eleanor called, and she took Betty by the arm as they went out into the stairwell.

'What are you on about, Ellie?' Betty asked. 'I've already done 'em.'

'Never mind that,' Eleanor whispered. 'Just stamp upstairs and make a lot of noise. I'm going to listen to what they're saying.'

'I don't stamp,' Betty said. 'I'm like a bleeding ballerina, me.'

'Go on, get off upstairs, silly,' Eleanor said, and gave her friend a hug.

Eleanor sneaked back into the servants' parlour and hid behind the dresser. She could hear the cook clattering with pots and pans in the kitchen.

'You know how I feel about it; I ruddy well hate going there. If she wants it doing then why doesn't she go herself?' Mr Coleman was saying.

'Oh sweetheart, I know, but think of our lovely time away and a couple of good nights in bed by the sea,' the cook said.

'Well, you know I'm as keen as you to get away, but that isn't the point. What if someone sees me? Doesn't look very good, does it, me going into a whorehouse? And goodness knows what's written in this letter I'm supposed to give over, could be anything.'

'It'll be what she wants for her party, that's all.'

'Yes, and what is that? What if it's something illegal or something? Suppose there's trouble? You know who will end up behind bars for it – not her, that's for sure.'

'It's never been a problem before, my sweet; I think you should just go and deliver it and get it done with.'

Mr Coleman gave a surly grunt.

'She did say she wanted it delivered as soon as possible so I best go soon. Damnable shame the fog has lifted now, I would have rather gone under cover. I might go this evening.'

'There you go, then, go up there when it gets dark and nobody will see you. Don't worry, it will be worth it for the treat I'll give you. I'll do that thing you like.'

'You saucy little pudding,' he said, and Eleanor could hear them kissing.

She withdrew to the stairwell and sneaked upstairs to join Betty. Her mind was racing and she felt furious. So Mrs Hampton intended to exclude her and hire in some prostitute? It was an outrage and nothing less, after what she had done for her mistress. She would fix things, she decided – she would fix things so Mrs Hampton never sent her away again.

As the day went on Eleanor became more convinced that Mrs Hampton wouldn't send her away after all, and that at some point she would tell her she was invited too. After all, she had trusted her at the club. But no word came, and when darkness fell Mr Coleman slipped on his coat, checked he had the envelope and sneaked out.

'Betty, I'm going out,' Eleanor said.

'Out? Oh, Eleanor, don't get in trouble.'

'Just cover for me,' Eleanor said, and promised she would be back soon.

She followed Mr Coleman down the street at a discreet distance, keeping away from the gas-lamps wherever she could. As it happened Mr Coleman was in far too much of a hurry to notice her. He eventually came to a rather run-down-looking house near the market and rapped on the door. Eleanor could see a man in the shadows when the door was opened, and watched Mr Coleman hand over the letter. Without a word he turned on his heel and began walking back up the street. Eleanor ducked into an alley and watched him walk past. When the coast was clear she went home and climbed through the window into the bedroom she shared with Betty. Betty was already asleep, so Eleanor curled up around her and lay with her eyes closed but her mind racing.

The next day was cold and bright and the household was in a bustle as the servants readied to leave. Eleanor was the only one not in a cheerful mood. She moped around and sat on the stairs, and even when Betty came and dragged her into the bedroom for a kiss she didn't cheer up. Betty urged her to come out drinking, but Eleanor had a different plan and wouldn't be dissuaded. In her heart she felt sure Mrs Hampton would call for her, or at least offer some explanation, but she heard nothing until late afternoon. All of the servants were called up to the hall, where their bags were stored. Mrs Hampton was ready with a little purse of money for each of them, and a smile to wish them a pleasant time. She instructed them to be back by early afternoon two days later. Eleanor silently fumed as she was given her purse, and then Mrs Hampton bustled them out of the door. The cook and Mr Coleman said a hasty goodbye and headed off in separate directions, fooling nobody. Betty implored Eleanor to come with her, but she wouldn't hear of it. Instead she said goodbye, and with a wave set off in the direction Mr Coleman had walked the night before.

Arriving at the house, Eleanor knocked on the door and waited. She felt very nervous but also determined and full of anger. She would not be sent away, not after everything she had been through and done. The door opened and a man in a suit with embroidered lapels opened it.

'What the bleeding hell do you want?' he demanded.

'I'm Mrs Hampton's maid,' Eleanor said. 'I've come about tomorrow night.'

'Oh yes? What about it?' he said.

'There's been a change of plan,' said Eleanor.

'Yes? What's that then?' he said.

'Well, I'd need to see what was in the letter first,' Eleanor said.

'You're not fooling no one, love,' the man told her. 'What is all this?'

'Look, I just need to see that letter,' Eleanor pleaded.

'Go on, be off with you,' he snarled. 'I don't know what your game is, but what my customers ask for is private and that means none of your business. Now go on, be off with you, whoever you are, and leave me in peace. I've got my hands full tonight as it is.'

'I'm Mrs Hampton's maid,' Eleanor insisted. 'I know she has asked you for something or someone for tomorrow night, but I don't want you to send them. It's a girl, isn't it?'

'What if it is?' he asked.

'Send me instead,' Eleanor begged.

The brothel owner laughed heartily and shook his head.

'Why would I want to do that? There's nothing in it for me, is there? I send someone who is wanting to sneak into her house, who may or may not be her maid, and next day she's sending for me to give me a right earful. She probably wouldn't use me any more, or worse yet I've got the peelers banging on my door because of you.'

'I'm not here to cause any trouble,' Eleanor said. 'It's what she would want if she only realised. Send me instead; I'll make it worth your while.'

She opened the little purse and showed him the collection of coins inside.

'Nothing doing,' he said. 'What I'd lose from business would be more than that.'

'Then I'll pleasure you myself, in any way you desire,' Eleanor promised.

'Love, I've got a dozen girls inside what answer to me; do you think I'd be so easily swayed by you, pretty though you are? A dozen of them, sweetheart, and when I want more I just take a walk down the Whitechapel and pick any of 'em what takes my fancy.'

'What do you want, then?' Eleanor pleaded.

'Nothing from you,' he said. 'Now bugger off.'

Eleanor noticed that a thin-faced girl had climbed the stairs behind the man and was waiting patiently to talk to him.

'Mr Johnson?' the girl said meekly.

'What is it?' he asked, trying to close the door.

Eleanor quickly got her foot in it.

'The sailors – they've got awful rowdy down there, Mr Johnson.'

'Don't call me by my real name, you silly girl,' Mr Johnson barked. 'Don't worry, they're just randy and drunk. The three of you should be able to handle them.'

'The girls don't want to,' the girl said. 'Kick them out, can't you?'

'And lose their money? You know how much sailors drink and like to fuck when they're back on leave. Send another three of the girls down there. And you, get off my doorstep, you're bad for business.'

'I'll be worse if I stand here crying and telling passersby what a cruel man you are,' Eleanor said. 'And about how you send innocent young ladies down there to deal with rough sailors. Not much of a gentleman, are you, and I bet some passing bobby would like to hear about you and your lovely little house here.'

'Now you just watch yourself, missy,' he warned.

'You do that and you're going to get in a lot of trouble. Nobody threatens Elliot J. Johnson.'

'Oh, that's your full name, is it?' Eleanor said with contempt. 'Well, Mr Elliot J. Johnson, I'll offer you a deal. I'll spend the night here and take care of your sailors for you and you tell me what was in that letter.'

Mr Johnson stood on the doorstep, looking from right to left down the street. There were many respectable gentlemen out walking, and at the end of the road a bobby was chatting to a flower girl. Any moment now he judged the policeman would start strolling down the road towards them. The girl at the door seemed mad enough to start crying and wailing just as she'd threatened if he didn't do something quickly.

'She just wants a girl for tomorrow night, delivered to her in a mask. That's all,' he said. 'Must be a masked party she's having. Happy now? Going to leave us in peace?'

'Fine,' Eleanor said, 'then I shall be that girl, and in the meantime I will take care of your sailors.'

Mr Johnson hesitated, wondering if the girl was a fool, mad or playing him a trick, but the policeman had begun to walk towards them, and it seemed best to let her in. 'Well, if that's what you want,' he said, and ushered her through the door.

The three sailors were roaring drunk. They had been at sea for nearly two months and hadn't seen a woman in all that time. Despite sodomising each other vigorously they were in need of something more feminine, singing and calling for a woman when the door opened and the young lady slipped in. They fell silent for a moment and then let out a whooping cry of delight. She was far prettier than the normal girls they were sent, with long auburn hair brushed straight down, and as an extra kick she was dressed up like a maid, wearing black stockings and a little uniform complete with frilly white pinny. The boatswain slapped his thigh and waved her over.

'Come on over here, my pretty. I've got a seat for you.'

'Hello, boys,' she said, and gave them a smile and a wink.

She went and sat on the boatswain's knee and put her hands around his neck. He immediately began to grope at her breasts and bottom while kissing her, first on the cheek and then the mouth.

'Hey, we're paying too,' the first mate said. 'Don't hog her.'

The second mate agreed, and tipped the remainder of his bottle of rum down his throat.

'You'll all get your turn, boys, don't worry,' she said.

The boatswain continued to fondle her, squeezing her breasts. He could feel her nipples, tight and hard under her clothes. She gasped at his strong hands, and as he kissed and felt her the more sober of his companions, the first mate, lifted her ankles and began stroking her legs. From his sounds of appreciation they clearly felt good to him, the material of her stockings thin and soft. He ran his hand further up her leg, slipping his hand under her dress and stroking her thigh. She opened her legs obligingly so that he could put his hand between them. He gave a grunt of pleasure to discover there was barely any hair on her sex.

'She's nearly bald!' he exclaimed.

'Yeah?' the second mate drunkenly slurred. 'Not like that one in Spain?'

'God, no!' his friend said. 'Here, 'ave a look.'

He pulled up the girl's dress and the two of them leant over her, admiring her thin line of hair. One of them reached down and stroked it, but she held the kissing boatswain tightly to her without a glance in their direction. His friend pushed her legs further apart. She was wet all right, no doubt about that. There was a dark patch of wetness on the boatswain's leg, and her labia were sticking out and touching his thigh. The girl moaned when a finger went inside her, but rather than resist she only opened her legs wider to let it in. Soon she was being fingered enthusiastically by the second mate while the boatswain kissed her mouth and neck and the first mate unbuckled his trousers.

'Me first!' he said.

'Get out of it, I got her first,' the boatswain said. 'Order of seniority, that's how we'll fuck her.'

'We aren't on the ship now,' the first mate said, and laughed.

The boatswain took out his cock. It was only half hard, because he had been drinking himself into a stupor, but he was excited by the girl's tongue and wanted to feel it around his bell end. She held it in her fist and pumped it, tugging it into life and pulling the skin tightly back. He gave a rasping moan and kissed her neck before putting his hand on her back and guiding her down. The angle she was sitting at made it impossible to take his cock all the way in her mouth without slipping off his lap, so she gently took the second mate's finger from her pussy, stood up and bent over in front of the boatswain.

She sucked his cock into her mouth and began to rock her head back and forth, pulling at the root of it and giving the head a long slow lick as she came upwards. The boatswain swore extravagantly and put his head back – he had laid in his bunk many nights dreaming of this. The first mate staggered to his feet with his trousers around his ankles and stood behind her. When she felt his hands on her hips she opened her legs and pushed her bottom backwards. She grinned with delight as he took a firm hold of her and pushed himself inside. The force of his cock filling her made her suck the boatswain hard, clamping her lips tightly over him. He grabbed her hair and began to move her up and down, controlling the speed at which his cock slid in and out of her mouth. The first mate was pumping her hard now, his balls slapping against her inner thighs, and she tried to match the rhythm with her mouth.

The second mate suddenly pulled her dress right up over her tits, so that they dangled and jiggled as she sucked. He put a rough hand under her and squeezed her flesh, pulling her breasts towards him and trying to hold them both in one hand. He put the other hand on her back and stroked her skin, down to her bum. His friend's cock was banging into her just beyond his fingertips, and his presence seemed to drive the first mate to new heights of arousal, judging by his increased tempo. The drunken second mate fumbled with her breasts a little longer and then pressed his dick against her hot side. He let it slide against her skin for a moment, the heat of it making her squirm with pleasure, then he began to jerk it, pulling himself as hard as he could.

He hadn't seen a bare pair of breasts in such a long time, and devoured the details – the way their little pink nipples stood out so hard, and the way they quivered as she was getting pounded, while the way the girl looked when she was being taken at both ends, cocks in her mouth and cunt at the same time, was something altogether new for him. The manner in which she was taking both of his friends so willingly was suddenly too much, and he began to come. Months of pent-up frustration spilled out of him, a hot flow of white passion that splattered over the girl's side and breasts, touching her nipple before beginning to drip off. At that she gave a gasp and gripped the boatswain's cock in her hand, pumping it into her mouth as she sucked.

The boatswain was close, his dick rigid and his balls incredibly tight. The maid used her fingernails to grip the swollen balls and applied just the tiniest bit of pressure. Much to his shock the boatswain found himself crying out and began to come in her mouth. He had not expected it so suddenly, but he could no longer contain himself as it began to pump in great spurts from him.

The maid swallowed it, still sucking him hard as if unsatisfied. He obligingly held her face in one hand and took his prick with the other, then began masturbating furiously against her lips. She flicked out her tongue and licked the end of his cock to catch the last of his seed. It splashed over her face and mouth, running across her cheek and lips.

The man behind her reached his peak at the same time. His fingers locked on her hips and his thrusts became more frantic before he jerked free to spray ropy jets of come over her bottom. At the sensation of having her bottom coated in spunk the girl began to come too, her fingers busy between her legs as she moaned with delight into the boatswain's lap.

'See how messy you've made me,' she said to the sailors, touching herself languidly as she shook with the aftershock of her orgasm.

'We like it like that,' the second mate said. 'You been here a long time?'

'Me?' the girl said innocently. 'It's my first night.'

'Bloody hell, a virgin!' the second mate said with delight. 'I'm not missing my go on that.'

The maid smiled, turned to him and knelt down, her mouth closing around his cock. He groaned with pleasure as she massaged his soft shaft with her tongue.

The other two men reeled away and found a fresh bottle of alcohol. Some of it spilled over the girl sucking between their comrade's thighs. No sailing man can abide such a waste, and one sailor was soon holding her while the others licked it off her flesh. Their tongues swept over her back and neck, down her backside and over her legs. Her stockings were around her ankles, her pinny hanging untied and her dress rolled up under her arms, leaving plenty of bare flesh for their attention. They laughed as they poured more drink over her, lapping at the naked skin and laughing and squeezing as they did so.

As they licked her body she worked the second mate furiously with her mouth, bringing him slowly erect once more, and before long the others were also ready for second turns with her. Soon the boatswain had entered her from behind, slapping her bottom and singing a shanty at the top of his voice as he fucked her, while the first mate beat time with the bottle on the floor and rubbed his cock on Eleanor's breasts.

Driven by her eagerness and stamina, aroused more than they could ever recall, they laid her upon the floor and used her for hours. They took turns, one fucking her while the others pushed their cocks into her mouth at the same time. And though she could barely fit two inside at once, she did her best to accommodate them, sometimes holding one and licking the other and at other times holding them together over her and rubbing and kissing them while her pussy was pounded by a third.

Her appetite seemed to know no limit, and they were as greedy as she was willing, until the writhing mass reached a point where the energy of the sailors had been conclusively sapped and they could no longer arouse themselves. So instead they pulled the blanket from the creaky single bed, laid it on the floor and put her upon it.

She lay there naked for them while they arranged themselves around her. They all wanted to be touching her constantly.

Eleanor too was content, though she ached and was in a terrible mess. Semen, alcohol and male sweat seemed to have blended into a glaze over her skin. More importantly, she was to be delivered to her mistress for her party. She sighed in her sleep, and though the three sailors all about her snored she didn't stir once.

The four of them slept through the day, tangled together and bare on the brothel floor. When they awoke, late in the afternoon, they were bleary-eyed and hungry. Eleanor wrapped her pinny around herself and left them, returning with a jug of water and some toasted bread and butter. They tucked in and sat her on their knees, and when they had finished eating they sang to her, a cheerful collection of songs about women and the high seas that was as ribald as it was out of tune.

Eleanor eventually said goodbye, kissing each of them on the mouth and stroking their hair. When she was gone they gathered up their clothes, got dressed and argued over the bill. When it came time to pay they were shocked and delighted to learn that the girl was free and that she had already paid for their drinks. It would be a night long talked about on board and, like many of their tales, not a word of it would be believed by their fellow sailors.

# Fourteen

*In which a maid of some considerable determination sets out to win her heart's desire by whatever means necessary.*

Mrs Hampton's guests began to arrive at seven in cabs and private coaches, elegantly dressed in dinner jackets and formal gowns. When they knocked on the front door there was no butler or servant of any kind to greet them. The outside staff Mrs Hammond had hired had done their work and been dismissed. She herself opened the door and welcomed them with open arms.

The gas-lamps had been turned off inside and replaced by the light of hundreds of candles of various colours and shapes, throwing flickering shadows as the guests came inside and discarded their coats. Mrs Hampton mingled with them, offering drinks and chatting to them all, making sure that nobody was left out, for she was a dutiful hostess.

'Where is that delightful maid of yours?' an eminent man of politics asked Mrs Hampton.

'Haven't you heard?' Emily said. 'She's gone back home, to France.'

'Oh, you poor thing!' The man addressed Mrs Hampton. 'She was a true treasure.'

'I have found a replacement, though,' Mrs Hampton told him, 'or rather, she found me.'

'Where is young Eleanor tonight?' Emily asked. 'Is she here somewhere?'

'No, not tonight,' Mrs Hampton replied. 'I fear I have made a terrible mistake in sending her away. She pleases me and is willing, yet I'm stubborn, and I fear that my own silly pride has spoilt things.'

'Then why ever did you send her away?' Emily asked.

'Because she leads me so. Sometimes I wonder who is in control. She manipulates me, and always seems to have her way. I can refuse her nothing and so find myself having such spiteful thoughts. Tonight I decided to teach her a lesson by deliberately excluding her from my gathering.'

'You are just being silly,' Emily said firmly. 'You are a stubborn woman who doesn't know a good thing when she sees it.'

'I am starting to think you are right,' Mrs Hampton agreed. 'And can you not see that she is winning again? She makes me regret being away from her for even a short time. That girl possesses me.'

The guests needed little encouragement to begin the party. Mrs Hampton served the drinks herself while mixing with her friends. The girl who kept the door at The Cauldron was there, only tonight she wasn't in her feathers and skin-tight costume. Tonight she was looking like the respectable wife of a senior civil servant, which she was, dressed in a conservative style with her husband on her arm.

'Are you hungry?' Mrs Hampton called out twenty minutes into the soirée.

The guests broke off their conversations and turned around. There was muttered agreement.

'Then I'd better bring in the main course,' Mrs Hampton said, giving them her most wicked grin.

She swept out into the hallway, where a large trolley had been placed, and pulled it into the dining-room. The trolley bore a huge, lidded silver dish, as large as a small bath and standing on legs sculpted like the feet of a lion.

'Will someone help me lift it on the table, please?' she said. 'It's rather heavy.'

It took four men to lift it and put it on the table, and even then they had to heave and struggle.

'Ladies and gentlemen, please may I ask all of you to help yourselves. Take as much as you wish.'

She withdrew to one side of the room with a glass of wine in order to better observe their reactions. When it came to the matter of serving themselves, most of the guests had never been required to do much more than stir their own tea, so the invitation at first appeared to stun them. Finally one of the more practical of their number took hold of the lid and with the assistance of his lover lifted it up and put it beneath the table.

A communal gasp of delight was swiftly followed by applause.

The inside of the great dish was full of fruit and iced cream, which almost completely covered the centre-piece: a girl. She lay on her back with her knees bent and her hair hidden by a leather cap on to which wax fruit had been sewn. Her face was completely hidden by a mask edged with berries made of coloured glass and fruit leaves of silver.

'Don't be shy. There is plenty for everyone!' Mrs Hampton urged.

In the frenzy that followed, plates were quickly discarded, the guests preferring to use their hands to scoop up the mixture of fruit and iced cream and soon licking the food from each other's palms and fingers. The nakedness of the living female centre-piece was gradually uncovered.

Orange slices had been carefully placed in the glaze over her legs and belly and across her arms, and were quickly picked off and gobbled up. Glacé fruits were all the rage that year, and Mrs Hampton had spared no expense to create the delicacy. There were passion fruits, strawberries, lemons, mango, grapefruit and countless other fruits arranged artfully on the girl. On her breasts were two rings of coconut with cream inside, with a cheeky little cherry over each nipple.

Some of the guests couldn't contain themselves, and ducked their whole heads into the bowl. One pulled off a cherry and began to lick the cream up until his tongue found the girl's nipple, which he licked and sucked, the taste of coconut and cherry mingling with the delightful taste of a young woman's skin.

Between her legs different-coloured iced creams had been swirled to create a pattern, which in turn was covered by a layer of plums, each positioned to put the guests in mind of the even more delicious fruit beneath. The guests continued to gorge themselves, scooping the iced cream from her breasts and belly and then leaning over the dish to put their tongues on her bare skin. She had been told to stay still and keep quiet, but the girls who had prepared her in the brothel had not counted on the pleasure those tongues would provide.

Her nipples were sucked, pulled in different directions by two eager mouths, one belonging to a young cavalry officer and the other his young lady wife. They kissed her bare breasts, and the woman slipped her hand down to feel the girl's slender sides. Her husband watched this with delight, he too putting his hand down, and they slid their palms across her body to touch fingers with each other.

The girl was biting her lip, trying hard not to cry out as an ample lady with bared breasts grasped an ankle, lifted her foot and sucked the slices of fruit from between her toes. It tickled terribly, and the woman's grip on her ankle kept slipping because of the melting fruit and iced cream. The woman was not to be put off, though, bending the girl's leg and sucking her delicate little toes into her mouth as she stroked a hand down the girl's leg and reached for her pussy.

One of the guests found a banana floating in cream within the dish and scooped up a generous blob of vanilla iced cream on its end, which he offered to the girl. She obligingly opened her mouth and sucked it off. Seeing how well she did this some of the men could resist no longer, and started pulling down their trousers. Soon the girl was surrounded by a dozen rock-hard cocks of great variety.

The men began to lather themselves with the contents of the dish. Some of them plucked out pieces of fruit and stuck them to their members. The girl laughed at the line of pricks that surrounded her. The cavalry officer's wife helped her kneel upright, and a good deal of her covering fell away, running down her body in a slow avalanche. She held on to the rim of the dish and looked at each penis, turning first to one side and then the other. Eventually she made her mind up, and picked a long slender cock which was adorned with pineapple. She licked along the top of it first, sticking her tongue out of the slit in the mask and pulling the fruit from the head. She cleaned it efficiently, kissing and licking until the whole thing twitched, then let him come in her mouth, swallowing his spunk and pushing her backside in the air so that the guests on the other side could get a good look at her slit and bottom. No sooner had she swallowed one than she was putting her tongue out and licking the next.

* * *

Emily watched the orgy developing on the table with interest. She herself would wait until she was more drunk before indulging. Apart from anything else, she didn't want to have to compete with such an array of erections. Men, she reasoned, were soon spent, and when they were she would unmask the little slut and push her face down between her legs. If any of them had a hard cock left to play with they were welcome to jerk themselves off over the girl while she performed at Emily's sex. She also wondered about Mrs Hampton; her old friend never seemed at a loss, especially when she was the centre of attention. Tonight, though, she had withdrawn from the orgy before it had even begun, and that worried Emily. Poor Mrs Hampton, she thought – to lose someone is one thing, but to create a distance out of sullen pride and then regret it later is far worse.

Emily found her friend placing an empty glass on the tray and picking another up with the other hand.

'Trying to get drunk?' she asked.

'Perhaps,' Mrs Hampton said.

'You shouldn't worry,' Emily advised. 'She will be back. It would take more than a cold shoulder to disaffect that little minx. Now kiss me. It's bad enough us missing the pudding without you being miserable. It's your party, my dear, so why don't you start enjoying it?'

Mrs Hampton decided to try and put her misgivings aside, and grabbed her friend by the waist. She began to kiss Emily and her friend responded by leaning into her and putting her soft hands on Mrs Hampton's face. They clung together and their kisses became so passionate that Emily was eventually forced to pull away in order to breathe.

'I see you still have a taste for me also?' Mrs Hampton whispered.

'You know it. Were you not the first to plunge your fingers inside me? To push me up against the wall when I was a mere innocent?'

'Innocent?' Mrs Hampton said, laughing. 'You were never innocent.'

'Well, perhaps not, but whatever was left, you soon rid me of it.'

'You needed it. But was it all in vain, I wonder? It seems you prefer boys now,' Mrs Hampton teased.

'I like men, but only when they are crawling along the paddock with their things dangling in the muddy grass. For love, only a woman will do. You ruined me for men.'

'And to think our queen doesn't believe that kind of thing can happen,' Mrs Hampton remarked, and pointed at the table.

A woman with her hair in the latest fashion and a flowing blue-and-white dress had pulled the girl from the dish close to her. They were kissing, and the girl's bare breasts were leaving marks on the woman's expensive gown. The observers could clearly see the woman's hand working underneath her dress, and the way her hips were grinding as the girl kissed her.

'Thank goodness she's wrong,' Emily said.

'Do you really mean what you said?' Mrs Hampton asked.

'About preferring women? Good heavens, yes. But much as I love you, I tend to prefer a girl who is more in awe of me. You will never be like that. But then, are we not similar in this?'

Mrs Hampton's laughter seemed to be the only answer Emily required.

The dish fell from the table with a loud clatter, upset by the mass of naked and semi-naked bodies

235

pushing all around the girl. Cream and fruit sloshed out on to the floor, but the guests barely noticed. The orgy had reached an ecstatic peak. Several couples were sprawled fucking on the floor, some sharing their partners and others pulling strangers into passionate embraces. Mrs Hampton watched with interest as one of her guests, a young heiress of great beauty, was bent over the table and taken roughly from behind. Mrs Hampton smiled, reflecting that the pretty young thing would find plenty of takers for her charms tonight.

'Come, let's acquaint ourselves with your guests,' Emily urged.

'Oh, very well,' Mrs Hampton said.

They went to the table and Mrs Hampton put out her hand to the girl, who kissed it and pulled her closer. Mrs Hampton laughed and cupped the girl's breast, then paused and frowned. 'Don't I know you from somewhere?' she asked.

The girl said nothing, but rose up on the table, put her hands on Mrs Hampton's shoulders and kissed her deeply. Mrs Hampton returned the kiss, enjoying the zest of fruit on the girl's tongue and lips. Then she gave a start, the moment her hands roved over the girl's bottom. 'Eleanor?'

'Yes, Mistress,' Eleanor said, and pulled off her mask.

'But how on earth did you get in there? Did I not send you away?'

'Yes, you did, but I couldn't stay away from you. Please don't be angry with me.'

'Oh, Eleanor, how could you serve yourself up to all my guests like that? Have you no shame?'

'If I haven't, then it is you who must be thanked for it,' Eleanor replied. 'It was you who wanted to share me with everyone, and I didn't mind at all until I realised that you didn't care for me.'

'Care for you?' Mrs Hampton exclaimed. 'But my dear, of course I do. I have spent the whole night wishing you were here. Sending you away made me realise what a fool I had been. Amelia was a willing little serving girl – she would always open her legs on command and would lick me till I was fit to scream – but she didn't have your determination. At first I thought it was wrong, but now I have grown to love it. To crave it.'

'And me? Do you love me too?' Eleanor asked.

'Let me show you,' Mrs Hampton said.

She took Eleanor's hands and gently helped her off the table. Her heart was beating fast as she began to unbutton her dress and let it fall down her elegant body. She was wearing a slip of black silk underneath, and she let Eleanor raise it from her body to reveal her stockings, garter belt and heeled shoes. Her nipples were hard and she guided Eleanor's hand to the brush of hair between her legs.

'After this I'm not sharing you,' she promised.

'I don't want you to,' Eleanor said. 'I want to serve you and be your lover and be everything you need.'

'I need you to touch me,' Mrs Hampton said. 'Touch me, Eleanor, feel my need for you.'

Eleanor put her hand firmly against Mrs Hampton's crotch and began to work her fingers back and forth, tugging at her clitoris gently and letting her fingers run into her mistress's hot hole.

Soon they were kissing and sinking to the floor, holding each other tight and rubbing their crotches together. Mrs Hampton pinned Eleanor on her back and raised herself above her maid, her dark thatch of hair just above Eleanor's mouth.

'Suck me,' she said. 'Taste me. Fuck me with your tongue.'

Eleanor pushed her tongue inside her mistress,

237

eager to obey. She rubbed her tongue along Mrs Hampton's swollen slit, craning her neck to push her whole mouth against that delicious opening. Some of the other guests had paused to watch the two beautiful women tangled together on the floor.

Mrs Hampton's lips tightened and her hips twitched uncontrollably, and then in one glorious moment she was coming. Her pubic hair was slick with juice as she rubbed herself firmly against Eleanor's mouth, her lips splayed open and her breasts bouncing as she rode her maid. As soon as she had come she shoved herself down Eleanor's body and kissed her, their mouths smeared with cream and come.

'Eleanor, I want you to stay with me. Forever,' Mrs Hampton whispered.

'I will, Mistress,' Eleanor replied. 'It is all I want.'

'But not as my servant, not down in that draughty old room. I want you with me, in my bed every night. That's where you belong,' Mrs Hampton said.

'No, Mistress,' Eleanor said. 'You know how much I love to be with you, but that isn't my place. You are the lady of the house and I am just a serving girl, but I'm a loyal one and will always be at your beck and call. All I want to do is make you happy.'

'Then be my lover. Share my bed,' Mrs Hampton said.

'I can only be your maid. That is all I am, but I will love you forever. You know the world and what you want, and I am just a simple girl.'

'A simple, wilful and brave girl!' Mrs Hampton declared, and laughed.

'Then we are agreed? You won't send me away any more? Ever?' Eleanor asked.

'Never. You are mine, Eleanor. You belong to me.'

The two women kissed each other and sealed their pact by rolling about on the floor once more, touching and stroking each other's bodies without a care in the world, their arousal heightened by the knowledge that the other guests were watching.

**nexus**

The leading publisher of fetish and adult fiction

## TELL US WHAT YOU THINK!

Readers' ideas and opinions matter to us so please take a few minutes to fill in the questionnaire below.

**1. Sex:** Are you male ☐   female ☐   a couple ☐?

**2. Age:** Under 21 ☐   21–30 ☐   31–40 ☐   41–50 ☐   51–60 ☐   over 60 ☐

**3. Where do you buy your Nexus books from?**

☐ A chain book shop. If so, which one(s)?

_____

☐ An independent book shop. If so, which one(s)?

_____

☐ A used book shop/charity shop
☐ Online book store. If so, which one(s)?

_____

**4. How did you find out about Nexus books?**

☐ Browsing in a book shop
☐ A review in a magazine
☐ Online
☐ Recommendation
☐ Other _____

**5. In terms of settings, which do you prefer? (Tick as many as you like.)**

☐ Down to earth and as realistic as possible
☐ Historical settings. If so, which period do you prefer?

_____

☐ Fantasy settings – barbarian worlds
☐ Completely escapist/surreal fantasy
☐ Institutional or secret academy

☐ Futuristic/sci fi
☐ Escapist but still believable
☐ Any settings you dislike?

_____

☐ Where would you like to see an adult novel set?

_____

## 6. In terms of storylines, would you prefer:
☐ Simple stories that concentrate on adult interests?
☐ More plot and character-driven stories with less explicit adult activity?
☐ We value your ideas, so give us your opinion of this book:

_____

_____

_____

## 7. In terms of your adult interests, what do you like to read about? (Tick as many as you like.)
☐ Traditional corporal punishment (CP)
☐ Modern corporal punishment
☐ Spanking
☐ Restraint/bondage
☐ Rope bondage
☐ Latex/rubber
☐ Leather
☐ Female domination and male submission
☐ Female domination and female submission
☐ Male domination and female submission
☐ Willing captivity
☐ Uniforms
☐ Lingerie/underwear/hosiery/footwear (boots and high heels)
☐ Sex rituals
☐ Vanilla sex
☐ Swinging
☐ Cross-dressing/TV
☐ Enforced feminisation

☐ Others – tell us what you don't see enough of in adult fiction:

_____

_____

_____

8. Would you prefer books with a more specialised approach to your interests, i.e. a novel specifically about uniforms? If so, which subject(s) would you like to read a Nexus novel about?

_____

_____

_____

9. Would you like to read true stories in Nexus books? For instance, the true story of a submissive woman, or a male slave? Tell us which true revelations you would most like to read about:

_____

_____

_____

10. What do you like best about Nexus books?

_____

_____

11. What do you like least about Nexus books?

_____

_____

12. Which are your favourite titles?

_____

_____

13. Who are your favourite authors?

_____

_____

14. Which covers do you prefer? Those featuring:
(Tick as many as you like.)

- ☐ Fetish outfits
- ☐ More nudity
- ☐ Two models
- ☐ Unusual models or settings
- ☐ Classic erotic photography
- ☐ More contemporary images and poses
- ☐ A blank/non-erotic cover
- ☐ What would your ideal cover look like?

_____

15. Describe your ideal Nexus novel in the space provided:

_____

_____

_____

_____

16. Which celebrity would feature in one of your Nexus-style fantasies?
   We'll post the best suggestions on our website – anonymously!

_____

## THANKS FOR YOUR TIME

Now simply write the title of this book in the space below and cut out the
questionnaire pages. Post to: Nexus, Marketing Dept., Thames Wharf Studios,
Rainville Rd, London W6 9HA

Book title: _____

**NEXUS NEW BOOKS**

*To be published in April 2007*

### SINDI IN SILK
#### Yolanda Celbridge

After the destruction of most of the northern world in a long-forgotten war, Madagascar and French Polynesia survive as the most powerful places on Earth. And silk stockings have become the most precious currency. Only bare-breasted noble-women and vampire girl-slaves are permitted to wear such finery. Sindi, having been a whip-wielding slave-mistress, becomes enslaved and a smuggler of illicit stockings from Zanzibar. When the prince of Madagascar is victorious in the war against his twin brother, the prince of Zanzibar, both men fall in love with Sindi. And when it is time for the victor to choose a princess, only the girl whose legs fit the one pair of silk stockings surviving from the old times will do. And it will be her destiny to become Whip Mistress of the Islands, *Princesse du Fouet*, and *Dame des Bas Sacrés*, Lady of the Sacred Stockings.

£6.99   ISBN 978 0 352 34102 0

### THE GIRLFLESH INSTITUTE
#### Adriana Arden

Probing the lowest levels of the outwardly respectable London headquarters of Shiller plc, Vanessa Buckingham stumbles into a hidden world of twenty-first-century slavery. Turned into a living puppet by Shiller's enigmatic director, Vanessa is forced to record every detail of the slave-girls' lives, from intimate psychological testing at the mysterious Fellgrish Institute, through strict training and ultimate submission to the clients who hire them. In the process Vanessa must confront both her own true nature and a terrible dilemma: can there be such a thing as a willing slave? Should she expose Shiller's activities as immoral – or let herself become another commodity in its girlflesh trade?

£6.99   ISBN 978 0 352 34101 3

# NEXUS CONFESSIONS: VOLUME TWO
## Various

Swinging, dogging, group sex, cross-dressing, spanking, female domination, corporal punishment, and extreme fetishes . . . *Nexus Confessions* explores the length and breadth of erotic obsession, real experience and sexual fantasy. An encyclopaedic collection of the bizarre, the extreme, the utterly inappropriate, the daring and the shocking experiences of ordinary men and women driven by their extraordinary desires. Collected by the world's leading publisher of fetish fiction, this is the second in a series of six volumes of true stories and shameful confessions, never before told or published.

£6.99    ISBN 978 0 352 34103 7

If you would like more information about Nexus titles, please visit our website at www.nexus-books.co.uk, or send a large stamped addressed envelope to:
Nexus, Thames Wharf Studios,
Rainville Road, London W6 9HA